Mrs D'Silva and
The Lucknow Ransom

Glen Peters was brought up in an Anglo-Indian community in early post-independence India. His family was from Lucknow. After attending university in London he had a successful career with an international accounting firm. He lives in Pembrokeshire where he runs an arts charity and a renewables business.

Mrs D'Silva and The Lucknow Ransom

Glen Peters

Parthian, Cardigan SA43 1ED
www.parthianbooks.com
First published in 2013
This edition published 2016
© Glen Peters 2013
All Rights Reserved
ISBN 978-1910901229
Edited by Jessica Mordsley
Cover by Robert Harries
Typeset by Elaine Sharples
Printed in the EU by Pulsio SARL
Published with the financial support of the Welsh Books Council
British Library Cataloguing in Publication Data
A cataloguing record for this book is available from the British Library.

To my grandson Lennox

To my grandson Heath.

Contents

The third sex

Lakshmi was born in a section of concrete drainpipe on the same day that a thousand other babies came into the world in the sprawling district of Howrah, across the river Hooghly from Calcutta.

She was the twelfth child in a family that already struggled to feed their growing numbers and her mother's sunken eyes and emaciated frame showed the toll taken by a decade of continuous breeding. Worse still, Lakshmi was of indeterminate sex and seen to be unlucky for her impoverished mother, father and eleven other siblings. On the day she was born her eldest brother died of a fever that was never diagnosed, as her parents could not afford a doctor or the fees for the medicines that might be necessary.

The baby was given away to another woman just two days later in exchange for a few paisa that would barely have paid for a bowl of rice, and was then passed on to a *hijira* who was pleased to take the baby under her wing and call it her own as she had no children. She named the baby after the goddess of wealth.

Lakshmi grew up in Howrah without any formal education in the company of other *hijiras* who were themselves illiterate and therefore placed very little importance on schooling. In accordance with the age-old traditions of her community, she did however learn to dance, to sing and especially to impersonate. She developed considerable talents and by the age of ten she would entertain her adopted community in their brothel, together with the men-folk who came to experience darker pleasures.

The Mother Guru of a larger *hijira* community bought Lakshmi, seeing potential in the child's talents, and encouraged her to develop her skills in impersonation and role-playing. Lakshmi's favourite guise was that of a *fakir*. She could sit semi-naked for hours in the most uncomfortable lotus position without moving a muscle. She called it her deep meditation.

By the age of twelve she had become obsessed with cinema and she, in the company of her Mother, would take the cheapest seats in the front row of the *Janta Electric Picture House* and watch the latest runs of Bombay films over and over again. This auditorium became her dancing school, her theatre academy and her dream factory. She could play the dutiful, demure housewife, the film actress Hema, the romancing Shashi, but it was the dancer and seductress which she had perfected to such a degree that by the age of fourteen, the men who came to the brothel would offer the Mother untold wealth to take her for the night. Not one of them succeeded.

One evening they had a new visitor, a noted political figure from Gonda in northern Uttar Pradesh, who was referred to as the Gonda *Gunda*. He was widely known as an extortionist and criminal who had been charged four times by the local police and managed to buy them off each time. The Mother did not exclude anyone from her house irrespective of caste, status or criminal record and the politician was entertained with the same enthusiasm as her other guests.

'Mother, I have heard many good things about your house.'

'We have a very good reputation – or should I say a very bad one.'

'*Arey haan* give me "very bad" any day! Whiskey now. Johnnie Walker, the very best.'

He proceeded to get drunk while several other *hijiras* waited on him, flattered him and stroked him. But the Gonda *Gunda* had his mind set on a special prize.

'I'm very pleased to be here, Mother,' he announced loudly after he had consumed half the bottle. 'One of my friends was here a few months ago and described the best dancer he has seen in his life. Lakshmi was her name, a new young addition to your household, I believe.'

Lakshmi, who was playing the *sarangee* at the time in a corner of the room, looked at her Mother Guru. 'Gurumati, that's me he's talking about,' she said excitedly, flattered that her fame had spread far and wide.

'Oh no, not today. Our honoured guest has a lot to do tomorrow and he will be going soon.'

'But please Mother, don't let me go away unfulfilled. Your reputation, my happiness, so much depends on me seeing this Lakshmi dance.'

And so, much against the Mother's instincts, she allowed Lakshmi to go away and dress up for her dance to the film hit '*Mera dil pyar hai*'. They dimmed the lights, put on the record and Lakshmi emerged in her gold and vermillion finery to dance for the Gonda *Gunda*.

No dance teacher or acting school would have prepared her this well. Every part of her body moved in time to the rhythm of the music as she moved closer to him and whirled her arms in a mock embrace. The politician gaped in awe. He had never seen anything like this before from someone so young. In his drunken state he kept reaching out, trying to touch her or grab her, but Lakshmi skilfully evaded his hands, like a snake-catcher who dodges the poisonous fangs of the swaying cobra at the last moment.

The music came to an end and the man arose, stumbling on his feet. 'I want her, now.'

'She is not available, not to you, not to anyone.'

'Do you know who I am?'

'You could be Gandhiji for all I care.'

'I could have you shut down in less than an hour.'

'Don't even try. Bigger dicks than you have failed.'

He was a huge man, tall and well fed. He grabbed the whiskey bottle, by now nearly empty, smashed it on the end of a table and lunged forward towards the Mother who had been reclining on one of the cushions smoking her evening *hookah*. The bottle slashed her face and she cried out in pain. The force of his attack unbalanced him and he fell to the ground.

Lakshmi, who had seen the event unfold in slow motion, sprung to the Mother's defence. Years of dancing had made her nimble, muscular and very strong. The jagged bottle had fallen out of the Minister's hands as he tried to get up. Lakshmi saw her chance and took the bottle from the floor, driving it as hard as she could into the man's neck just as he was raising himself off the ground. She was quick, precise and lethal. He reeled, fell and immediately blood spurted out from the thick carotid artery on the side of his neck, soaking into the crimson Kashmiri carpet.

'Now he's going to die on our hands,' shouted the Mother as she got on her knees and clasped her hands on the

4

Minister's neck in an attempt to halt the rapid loss of blood. 'Lakshmi, pack your things and run, *jaldi*. The police will be looking for you. Someone run and get Doctor Tiwari.'

Lakshmi went on the run posing as a *fakir,* travelling by night on foot and collecting alms by day, evading the police that had been on the look out for her in every brothel and *Hijira* community in the district. And she kept on running for many years until she decided she must make her life elsewhere.

Joan's flight

Joan D'Silva was leaving Calcutta too. Fleeing the Maoist *Gundas* that had made her live in constant fear. Suspicious, untrusting eyes seemed to be everywhere at Howrah station. It was busy as usual, thousands of people were being disgorged from trains arriving from far-flung places such as Delhi and Amritsar and were being met and greeted by families and loved ones. There were lots of people touching the feet of elders, *namastes*, a few hugs amongst men and some handshakes. Red tunic *coolies* haggled with travellers over their payments for carrying oversized luggage, contributing to the noise that filled the dark coal-smoke air of the cavernous station.

Joan hired a *coolie* to carry her bags and they were soon part of the heaving throng heading towards the booking office. Most ordinary people queued for hours to get a ticket, weeks before their departure date. The rich merely sent their peons.

She wore one of the few dresses she had packed, navy blue and long-sleeved with a pleated skirt and white piping around the collars. She looked the height of sophistication and well suited to the best class of passenger on a BOAC flight; but together with her eleven-year-old son Errol in his grey short trousers and jacket they looked like actors who had wandered off a film set. This was definitely not what Joan had intended for a low-key getaway.

She saw in every person that stared at her a potential informant who would scurry away to report her whereabouts to a hit man, a torturer or abductor. She avoided eye contact and did not engage in conversation. And yet this is what she had chosen, to stay in India rather than flee to the safety of London. The stories of the cold unfriendly people in an alien land had got the better of her. Instead they would go to the railway colony at Lucknow, to stay with her late husband's brother and his wife.

A man in a striped shirt and dhoti wearing cheap plastic sunglasses and chewing a mouthful of betel nut came and spoke to her. 'Madam, where will you be wanting a ticket to?' he said.

Joan gave the man a blank stare and replied with a firm, 'No thank you.'

He persisted. 'All tickets booked many weeks madam. I can help you. Small *baksheesh* only. Where do you go?'

The queue hadn't moved an inch and showed no sign of doing so. She had begun to perspire in the morning sun. Her face was moist with sweat and her dark navy blue dress baked in the rays of the sun. She wiped her face with her handkerchief soaked in Eau-de-cologne but the relief was short lived.

'Ma, when are we going to get on the train, Ma? I'm getting tired,' groaned Errol.

'*Beta* take your blazer off, you'll feel much better.'

Joan mulled over the idea of using the ticket tout. Sensing that he was about to succeed with his offer, he asked for a third time, 'Please say where would you be going? I'm helping you.'

'Lucknow,' she murmured.

'Yes madam! Please be giving me two minutes,' said the betel nut chewer as he scuttled off into the crowd.

A few minutes passed. There were mutterings of discontent from the queue. One particularly vocal man was railing against the Congress government, saying that the state of the railways was entirely their fault. He seemed to be getting nods of approval from the fellow sufferers. Still nothing moved and they all gave up complaining when a boy came around selling peanuts in small open bags made of newspaper. Soon the queue was busying itself shelling peanuts. Errol longed to do the same but Joan felt it was unbecoming for a *memsahib*.

'But Ma I'm hungry, Ma,' pestered Errol.

Then the betel chewing man returned with a sense of urgency, looking like he might have some news for Joan. He cupped his hands around his mouth and said quietly to her, 'Two tickets available madam on Janta Express at one o'clock.'

Joan maintained her calm, blank expression as though she was unimpressed by the offer. She pulled out her handkerchief and wiped her brow. The crackling sound of the peanut-shelling brigade in front of her got louder and she could see the chances of getting out of Calcutta were receding fast.

'How much baksheesh?'

'Only fifty madam, total price rupees two hundred second class,' he said again softly and smoothly but enough for Joan to hear.

She hesitated, twisting her face as if displeased with the offer. The man held his ground.

'Only fifty, very good second class.'

Her instinct for escaping to safety told her to follow up the offer but her experience of dealing with touts held her back. This one looked and sounded like all the others she had been swindled by; she recalled when a man by the House Full sign at the Regal cinema sold her tickets at twice the price when the auditorium was nearly empty or the fellow that sold her fake tickets for Holiday on Ice.

'Madam, good price. Come with me and we get tickets now.'

She gestured to the *coolie* to follow her; his expression showed that he had seen it all before as he hoisted a bag on his head and carried another on his shoulder. The people in the queue began muttering again about corruption and the government but those behind Joan seemed pleased that they were at least able to move a step forward. Together they walked to a place around the back of the ticket hall where the betel nut chewing man knocked on a door and a *babu* answered, ushering Joan inside. Errol was none too pleased about being left outside and decided to put on his brave face, sitting on one of their bags.

A few minutes later Joan reappeared and instructed the *coolie* to follow her to platform twelve leading Errol by the hand, a practise that he had come to hate. Betel man hurried off to find his *babu,* no doubt to extract his commission for the transaction, and Joan was left doubting the wisdom of what she had just done with little more than a few hundred rupees left in her purse, barely enough for a couple of nights in a cheap hotel.

The 14.27 Janta Express to Lucknow arrived from the sidings ready to pick up its passengers, who by now were spilling over the sides of the platform. Joan stood in the vicinity of where the second-class coach was reputed to be. This was the time when those travelling without reserved seats would jump through the windows of the moving train in an effort to secure a seat or a bench for their family. Travelling by second class, Joan and Errol needed only to find their compartment as their seating was assured.

The platform had now erupted in pandemonium, with people shouting out instructions and crowds jostling to squeeze through the doors of the carriages and shove through their huge bags and tin boxes which seemed to be such an important part of railway travel. Errol thought a fight might break out but soon the chaos seemed to abate and an uneasy order returned to the platform with vendors resuming their sales of snacks, tea, newspapers and magazines.

'Ma, can I have a comic for the journey. I love those war comics!' Errol pleaded.

'No time now darling, there's the train.'

She'd seen their carriage, with the distinctive Ladies Only sign, and was soon pulling Errol by the hand through the crowd to ensure that he stayed with her. The *coolie* followed a few yards behind, Joan looking back to check her bag was safe on top of the man's head.

Joan used her elbows to carve out a path to their carriage, and they were soon established in compartment 21-24 with her bags packed under the seat and in the luggage racks. The shared carriage's green Rexine seats, which exuded the smell of disinfectant, doubled as four bunk beds by night.

There was a passenger in there already, stretched out occupying one side of the railway carriage. Errol knew immediately there was something suspicious about her. Her shoulders were too broad; she was too muscular. He looked again and again until his mother reminded him that it was rude to stare at people.

Joan's previous encounters with *hijiras* had been in the street or the market where they were invariably caught up in some argument with traders over money. She remembered one of their kind lifting up the skirts of her sari to expose her private parts to some shocked customers at a *chai* shop all because the shopkeeper wouldn't part with a few rupees in exchange for a song and dance routine. Once on the Number 54 bus on the way back home an irate traveller had given up his seat to a woman only to discover she was a *hijira* and demanded his seat back. The abusive exchange which followed had turned the air a darker shade of blue.

Joan had never had the opportunity of meeting or speaking to a *hijira* before so she smiled to acknowledge her travel companion and her greeting was returned with a faint smile and a shake of the head.

With about ten minutes to go before departure, two elderly women appeared with their *coolie* and attempted to stack their bags in the now crowded luggage racks. No one said a word as they tried to pack themselves in. Such was the tolerance of railway travellers that they put up with the most unspeakable overcrowding in compartments. One assumed that if the authorities allowed it then good luck to the person trying to break the rules.

They both wore 24-carat gold nose rings and a liberal display of jewellery indicating that they came from well-heeled families. 'These are our seats,' said the woman in a red sari, pointing to where Joan and Errol were seated and holding out a slip of paper.

'Oh!' is all Joan could say as she moved over to accommodate the two newcomers. And the crowded compartment fell silent again as the five passengers huddled together in the same compartment with their oversized luggage. Each one suspected that the other was occupying the seats illegally and by the look of disdain on their faces, the newcomers appeared to be not at all happy with the *hijira* in their compartment. They were socially regarded as bottom of the caste pile and these women wouldn't be seen dead sharing sleeping accommodation with these outcasts.

Perhaps, Joan thought, the betel man and the *babu* had conspired to take her two hundred rupees for a fake ticket, and she and Errol would be evicted when the ticket collector arrived to check that all was in order. She cursed herself for deciding to deal with the tout. Here she was seconds from being left abandoned on a Howrah platform at the mercy of the people she was trying to escape from.

Trying to lighten the atmosphere of brooding discontent, Joan reached into her handbag to pull out a bag of sugar-coated *jujups* which she had reserved for later in the journey. Under Errol's longing gaze, she offered the sweets to the *hijira*. She looked hesitantly at the bag, unsure if she should accept, then smiled and took two.

Joan turned around to the other women. The red sari woman shook her head. Having seen that a *hijira* had just dipped into the bag she was not tempted to accept. Then Joan took one for herself and Errol and said, 'Please take, they're very good for the train journey.' Maybe the temptation of the sweets overcame the woman's repugnance of the *hijira* but she looked at her companion and then they took one each. In seconds all five occupants were loudly chewing their *jujups* and Joan sat back, pleased with her attempts at social cohesion.

But peace and harmony were short-lived. An official dressed in a white starched shirt and trousers, a clipboard and a handheld ticket clipper looked inside the crowded compartment and in seconds knew he had some work to do.

'Tickets please!' he proclaimed in an officious tone. Joan handed him her tickets which he examined carefully, taking his time with running down the list of names, and she was surprised to see that he ticked her and Errol off his list. He did the same for the two women. 'But I have no reservations here for this person,' he said with some disgust, gesturing to the *hijira*.

'*Chullo*,' said the official to the *hijira*, indicating to her that she should leave the carriage. She didn't move a muscle. The collector called a *coolie* and instructed him to take the luggage off the train. The *hijira* yelled a curse which stopped the *coolie* momentarily. If he even touched her luggage his entire family would be struck with cholera. The curse of a *hijira* was regarded as a serious threat by many Indians and the *coolie* was not prepared to let his already miserable life get any worse. The locomotive blew its loud, deep throaty whistle as a warning that it was about to move and the official called out to another colleague, probably more immune to superstition, to help him with the eviction.

Most people's instincts for self-preservation would have kept them silent at this point. But Joan could not let an injustice be carried out without intervening. She knew that the *hijira* was no more a legitimate traveller than herself having bribed to get onto the passenger list. '*Inspectorjee*,' she shouted, 'please leave this person alone, I don't mind sharing my berth with her. Why should we risk the possibility of her curse derailing this train or something equally terrible? I'm sure you would not want an administrative error to make us all suffer, *hah?*'

The two other women in the compartment seemed to agree by signalling their acknowledgement with an upward shake of their heads. They too were well aware of the curse of the *hijira* and had all been told stories of people who had met some dreadful fate after being cursed.

The inspector looked at the *hijira* for one last time. The train was beginning to move and he would have to either stop the train or give up his crusade. He opted for the latter.

It had been a tiring day for Joan and Errol and when night came they both fell into a deep sleep. They didn't hear either of the women snore in unison or the constant squeal of a defective wheel-bearing beneath their compartment. Joan dreamt that she was at a huge feast where people had gathered to celebrate an event and the people there seemed vaguely familiar. Suddenly people began to collapse from the tables and appeared to be dying. Joan was one of the few people who watched in horror as people convulsed in pain and she stood by helpless. Someone shouted 'Poison, it was the poison.' She tried to pick up one old man who lay lifeless in her arms.

She found herself being shaken by her son and awoke in a deep sweat. 'Ma, you were making funny noises,' said Errol, who had been listening to his mother talk in her sleep.

'Oh, just a dream Errol. Now let's get back to sleep.'

Soon Errol was sound asleep again. But the fear and the reality of what she had just been through kept Joan awake, staring at the blue nightlight until dawn. Dreams meant a lot to Joan. She had dreamt of her husband the night he perished in the 1955 Pathankot train crash, and the day before her son's abductors had freed him she had dreamt of his release.

Joan knew this was no ordinary dream.

The smell of Lucknow

Calcutta smelled of caramelised sugar and boiling milk, Bombay smelled of rotting fish, but Lucknow's was the sweetest, most sophisticated, most alluring smell of sandalwood. It wafted around the rickshaw, the station and even the humblest *coolie* carrying her bags.

The perfume immediately made Joan feel safe, secure and pleased with herself that she had managed to fly the city of *Gundas*. Now, she felt safer in the city of the *Nawabs,* where she could sleep at night without fearing for her life.

A bank of cycle rickshaw *wallahs* greeted her at the steps of the station, keen to transport a *memsahib* to the railway colony. They rang their cycle bells; each one louder than the other to attract her attention and Errol was drawn to the one that had a battery-operated horn, which sounded like a duck. 'Look Ma, I had one of those on my bike.' The rickshaw man sensing that Errol had picked him out of the crowd shouted out to him that his was a new rickshaw, the most comfortable in Lucknow. 'Quack, quack,' he beeped again and again; Joan beckoned to him and they were soon on their way.

Lucknow's roads were wider, there was more space, there were trees and the pavements were cleaner. The *Nawabs* had indeed built themselves a garden city several hundred years earlier and you could still see the remnants of their lavish design on building facades and avenues of majestic banyan trees now being covered by crudely painted signs and hoardings. One, advertising Swami Naik and his *Ashram of Universal Light*, caught her attention. The Swami was at the centre, surrounded by light, with foreign faces gathered around him.

They left the busy station area behind them; here the road widened and there were freshly planted trees on the roadside, with brick surrounds to protect the fledging plants from the cows that had made the street their home.

Irene, Joan's sister-in-law, was sitting on her veranda reading the morning papers when the rickshaw arrived at the gates of her bungalow. She yelped at the sight of Joan and Errol.

'My God, is that you Joan?'

Errol was the first to jump off the rickshaw and give his aunt a hug.

'You were the last people I expected to see this morning. What happened to London?'

'I just couldn't do it in the end Renee. How could I leave you all behind and go so far away? Remember you told me once they didn't shower or bathe because it was so cold and that they used Max Factor to kill the smell.' They laughed out loud and Joan felt good to be with the only people she could call on as close family. Her brother-in-law Gerry embraced her warmly.

'Stay for as long as you like, Joanie,' said Irene. 'We need to get Errol back into a good school; I'll have a word with Dougie Kellor at The Martinere. He'll have Errol as a boarder I'm sure.'

'Oh but isn't that a Proddy school?'

'Yes, but by far the best, that's if you want Errol to do well.'

'Thank you for being so sweet, you don't know what a relief it is to be away, far from danger. I have to find myself some work to pay my way though. I don't wish to be seen as a sponger.'

'That's nonsense Joan, I don't want to hear such talk!' But Joan knew she had to find employment, as she had no savings to speak of. Errol would need new clothes and then there would be some fees to pay at his new school and she couldn't expect to live off the kindness of her sister-in-law for too long. Teaching was the only job she had done after her husband died. She'd left school at sixteen and learned to type and take shorthand but it was in the classroom where she came alive, those bright young hopeful eyes absorbing every word and she enjoying every second of them. But for now she was content to spend a few days contemplating her future.

Sunday Mass at the Cathedral was packed, with the faithful brimming out of every pew. Latecomers were not welcomed either by the congregation or the clergy and those who arrived after the first reading stood outside the church hoping not to be noticed by their ever-vigilant parish priest, Father Rosario. The Spanish priest had served them for ten years and would soon be departing for Bombay where he had been promised a bigger role in the church, or as he told Irene, 'I've been kicked upstairs to get closer to God.' Nothing pleased this pastor more than to see a packed church; divine reward he believed for all his prayers and hard work.

Anglo-Indians, who made up about half his congregation, had fallen on hard times after Independence and Father Rosario was forever helping them out financially with a few rupees here and there. His generosity also extended to passing them tins of American Aid buttermilk and bags of rice which arrived every month for the poor of the parish, donated by the Catholic charities in the United States and intended for the impoverished slums and famine-stricken villages of rural India. But Father Rosario believed in charity starting with his own fading flock and they had returned the favour by making sure the church was never empty at eight o'clock on a Sunday morning.

The priest looked after the wellbeing of his parishioners and rigorously applied the rules set out by the Vatican. While the newly elected Pope John was liberalising the previously strict interpretations of the liturgy, Father Rosario stuck fast to the old rules of conduct and behaviour and enforced them uncompromisingly. Oddly, this dose of tough love gained him respect and admiration and a steady trickle of converts took their baptismal vows every fortnight.

Joan's mother had brought her up as a Catholic, although her father never cared much about religion. When Joan's mother died, her father remarried within a year and the eight-year-old Joan was rejected by her new stepmother and sent to live with her aunt. Her aunt despatched the young Joan to board with the Loreto nuns in Lucknow. The convent where she was educated continued to keep her within the faith and she was once even tempted to become a 'bride of Christ' until she found out that the long hours in prayer as a teenager were not for her.

Father Rosario's sermon this Sunday was about people who made up their own religion as if they were God. 'The Holy Catholic Church has laid down a clear set of actions it expects you to follow. If we want to be members of God's chosen faith, the only true faith, then you must abide by its rules. You can't say I'll take a bit of that and that and not that; I'll divorce my wife but come to church every Sunday or I'll send my son to a Protestant school and take Holy Communion. You can't play God and that is that.'

The congregation sat listening attentively, each one with a prickly conscience for having at some stage broken the prescribed code, aggressively monitored and enforced by Father Rosario. The father of a family of six children in the third row moved in his seat nervously and looked at the tired, sunken eyes of his wife who could not bear the thought of more. The intermittent churchgoers looked at the floor and Father Rosario straight at them.

Joan listened and wished the priest would move on to his next position in Bombay speedily, allowing a more modernising successor to take his place. She was dressed in a white sleeveless dress and patent leather shoes, with a lace headscarf covering most of her face. Women of her generation were shedding the once-obligatory head covering while attending mass but Joan used it selectively depending upon whether she wished to draw a curtain around herself or dispense with the veil and let the world see her. Today she wanted to create a little mystery around Mrs Joan D'Silva, so when she sat in the front pew with her in-laws she kept the veil on.

After mass it was usual for the congregation to gather outside the church to catch up on the gossip before dispersing for their Sunday lunches. The talk these days was usually about how terrible things had become, how they just had to get out, and who was leaving for one of the English-speaking dominions of the old British Empire.

Mrs Braithwaite was saying, 'We're done in Lucknow now and in this country. We're getting our papers together any day.

We've heard from my sister who lives in a place called Brighton. She says it's very nice by the sea.'

'Oh, Mrs Braithwaite, we'll miss you. Won't you miss the sun and your friends at the club?' asked someone.

'My dear there're very few of us left now, and getting fewer every day. My hubby had a bit of a scare the other day with his ticker and that's been a message to me from the Almighty that it's time to get out now. There's nothing left for us anymore and I've got a few more years to live, so I'd rather spend it with my near and dear.'

Overhearing the conversation, Irene said to Joan, 'and you decided to stay on with us my dear and brave it out. Good for you. Now let me introduce you to Mr Ed Storey,' she said, pushing her way towards a man who was talking to Father Rosario with one eye on Joan. He stopped mid-sentence when he saw her coming towards him. Dressed in a white linen jacket and grey gabardine trousers, he looked by far the best-dressed man in the little gathering. Parishioners had once worn their best clothes for Sunday but now sadly had resorted to wearing the contents of their *dhobi's* basket. The noisy congregation still funnelled out of church into the bright hot morning sun.

'This is Ed Storey,' said Irene, 'manager of the local *Apna* factory. Ed, this is my sister-in-law Joan D'Silva.'

'Ed, good to meet you.' She shook his hand.

She categorised men's handshakes into two groups; those that were weak and effeminate, were uninterested in women and probably lacked libido and those that were firm, workman's hands which made a woman want to know them more. When Joan felt the strong hand that Storey extended, with the rough calluses on his upper palm and the way he looked directly into her eyes, she was intrigued.

'I don't believe I have had the pleasure, Mrs D'Silva. But then you don't live here in Lucknow do you? I'm sure I couldn't have forgotten you.'

'I've recently arrived from Calcutta. My sister is putting me up at the railway colony.'

'You must ask your sister to bring you over for a bit of *cha* to Gorabad, *hah*?'

'I will enjoy that,' said Joan. She looked at Irene who smiled shyly, delighted that the two had hit it off so well.

'Why don't you come and join us for a bit of *khana* now? There's only the four of us and you'd be most welcome,' said Irene.

'Oh, I couldn't barge into your family lunch just like that!'

'No please do,' insisted Gerry who had caught up with the group, having been cornered by someone who was looking for a job for their son on the railways.

'Oh very well, I'd be pleased to accept on one condition.' They paused. 'That we stop on the way for some *jalabees*. I can't come to lunch empty handed.'

'*Arey,* not *jalabees!* You know once I start eating them I can't stop.'

'The best in the U.P.'

Errol had wandered off to examine Storey's car, a white Ambassador, the only one parked by the church steps. Ed signalled to his chauffeur and soon the group were pouring into the roomy automobile. Superbly upholstered seats, smelling of ageing, cracked leather, sank to accommodate their weight. Two large continuous seats, front and back, meant that Errol didn't have to sit on Joan's lap to make space for the other adults. The car purred out of the church gates with its six occupants, provoking envy amongst those left behind to get home in their *tongas* or cycle rickshaws, and then kept them in a heavenly cushion of comfort as it traversed the potted roads of Alambagh.

The Sunday *khana* was always held at midday at the Shaw household. Fasting before communion was obligatory, leaving the churchgoers ravenous by the time they got back home at midday. The smell of *ball curry* and onions frying in ghee wafted through the gardens as they walked down the drive.

They walked on to the veranda to sit at a table under a whirring *punka,* which the *khansamin* had laid out for their Sunday feast. Irene hurried to the kitchen to taste the gravy and give it her approval, and to check the *pillau* rice to make sure it was free of sticky clumps, a common mistake which made Gerry very grumpy. They helped themselves to the rice and Irene dished out four meat balls for each of the diners with lashings of dark red curry to soak into the saffron *pillau*. The mix of red, yellow, green and the glistening gravy created a mouthwatering spectacle.

Talk was minimal in the first minutes of the meal with only the clatter of spoons and forks on the plates, punctuated by the screeching of parakeets in the trees outside.

'So how are things at the factory these days?' asked Gerry eventually, taking a sip of sweet watered-down lime juice.

'We're not having the best of times. I'm afraid law and order is going down the commode. No one is afraid of authority and they've all got their hands in the till. It's a good target, you know? A brand-new factory, built by foreigners.'

'I've heard that Gonda chappie is back in town trying to run as an MLA in the next election. Now tell me what is the country coming to when criminals get to be members of the legislature.'

'I really don't blame those of us who are getting their papers together and buggering off to Blighty or wherever.'

'Surely you're not thinking of leaving us?' asked Joan.

'Not yet but I've got these head office *wallahs* breathing down my neck once too often. Sometimes I do feel like sticking this factory in their faces and asking them to get on with it.'

Lunch and conversation then gave way to Canasta whilst the party sipped iced mango fool and licked generous dollops of pistachio *kulfi* from an ice pail. The rich creamy buffalo milk mixture, sweetened and flavoured with ground pistachio nuts, cardamom and rose water, was the perfect antidote to the pungency of the spices in the earlier course.

Lucknow had been hit by an unusually early heatwave and the *loo,* a cruelly hot wind, had begun to blow, defying anyone to wander out of the shade between midday and late afternoon. Joan, who was used to the more temperate climate of Bengal, hated the biting heat of the U.P. Gerry and Irene retired for their afternoon nap, leaving Joan and Ed Storey to keep each other company for the rest of the afternoon.

Meanwhile, the driver had become Errol's best friend as he showed him the inner workings of the car and took him for a drive around the railway colony, which thrilled the young boy. The driver explained how the gears were used in conjunction with the throttle to make the car go faster or slower. Errol was quickly becoming a convert from trains to automobiles.

Storey was less formal once he was alone with Joan and seemed keen to know more about her.

'So what brings you to Lucknow?' Ed asked. He was lighter in complexion than Joan, with a craggy face, handsome despite some wrinkles. He had an air of unfailing confidence which made Joan wonder if he had ever been a military man.

'It's a long story. I had to get away from Cal. There were some people I upset. Maoists. The Workers' Revolutionary Movement.'

'How does a teacher get caught up with Maoists?'

'It's a long story. You really wouldn't want to know. But just when I thought I'd got away from one set of problems I seem to have become saddled with another set.'

'Tell me more.'

'Ed, do you believe in dreams?'

'That we have them yes, but as anything more meaningful? No.'

'Oh well, you won't be interested in my dream then.'

'Go on. I didn't mean to sound negative.'

'I've just dreamt of people dying at a feast from some horrible poison. I've had dreams before which have come true. I feel I need to stop it but don't know how. It could be happening anywhere.'

'Look Joan, just think of the dreams you've had which never came true. Really honestly. If you were to follow up every dream you'd never get to sleep.'

'But this was just so real.'

'Get your mind off it. Tell you what, come shooting with me, that's one way of keeping trouble at bay,' suggested Storey.

'I wouldn't know one end of a gun from the other!'

'Oh, it's easy, just hold the wooden end, point with the other and squeeze the trigger. You'd be a fine shot. I'll be going to the *jheel* next week, why don't you come along with me?'

'But I've never...'

'Go on Joan, we could make fowl curry. It's beautiful there by the water at sunset with hundreds of gorgeous birds.'

'Oh, OK then. I'll give it a try. Thanks,' she said, knowing that it would make her in-laws very happy if she went out with Storey.

Joan tried to turn the conversation around to Storey, to extract a little more from his impervious exterior but he politely sidestepped her questions, giving little away. Gerry and Irene arose from their afternoon slumber and were pleased to see Storey and Joan still together. As dusk began its final hour of descent into darkness Ed called for his driver to take him back home, much to the disappointment of Errol who had begun to call the car his own.

'I think that man has an eye for you,' said Irene.

'Go on, don't talk rubbish, he's just very lonely,' said Joan.

'Joan, you don't mind me asking but is there any other man in your life?'

'No; nothing I'd call deep and meaningful. There was this guy, a teacher at Don Bosco's who I spent time with and he was very good to me, but it didn't lead to much; there was no *khutai* in him. You know us girls need a man with a bit of *khutai* to get us going.'

'Too damn right Joanie, that's what I'm going to tell my Gerry, he needs a bit more *khutai* even at his age.' She laughed loudly and Joan couldn't help but smile back at her.

'Well,' said Irene, 'We'll have to find you a man with a bit of that *khutai* while you're with us.'

Ransom note

Back in 1961, while Lucknow housewives kept up a constant supply of *parathas*, puris and samosas for their families, putting pounds around their middles, bestowing protruding bellies on their sedentary husbands and chubby cheeks on their children, the keystone of their culinary achievement was a dazzling yellow can. *Apna*.

At the factory managed by Ed Storey, thousands of cans rolled off the production line every day, feeding the rapacious appetites of India's burgeoning middle class. *Apna* was a cheap alternative to *ghee*. While *ghee* was made from butter and not within the reach of most ordinary people, Apna was a hydrogenated palm oil cooking fat that was far more affordable. Its characteristic yellow tins printed with palm trees were to be found everywhere, in grocers and in the kitchens of both rich and poor up and down the country. When empty, they were recycled and used to make all manner of cooking utensils, stoves or even tin toys. Apna was probably the biggest, most recognisable and trusted brand in India.

The Lucknow factory, built with foreign money, made an obvious target for the social jackals who believed that it was fair game to take a bite out of those who were extremely wealthy. But it was still a shock when a ransom note arrived at the factory one Monday morning, typed in crimson red on a page torn out from an exercise book:

Your company is the product of destructive capitalism. We the Workers' Revolutionary Movement aim to deduct a levelling tax for the poor of the sum of Rs 20 Lakhs. You have 10 days to find the money. Please await your deposit instructions. Ignore this and the consequences for your company will be disastrous.

Civic unrest was spreading through India. In a year's time the country would be caught in the grip of the third election in its short history as an independent democracy. Nehru would be taking his dominant Congress party to the polls, hoping that he would again win a landslide vote of confidence from citizens up and down the country. His message of a secularist long-term socialist agenda was beginning to gather opponents and as India, still reeling with the after-effects of partition, inched its way forward towards modernisation, longing to take its place on the world stage, a new generation were being fired with very different ideas. Maoists inspired by the Chinese revolution were firebombing and terrorising rural landowners. *Dacoits* too had been getting braver by the day, raiding rich landlords, relieving them of their money at gunpoint, then killing the entire family. Abductions for ransom were becoming commonplace in the rural hinterland and the wealthiest merchants were employing armed bodyguards to keep their abductors at bay. But never had anyone attempted corporate extortion on this scale.

'Sir this looks like a prank. Twenty Lakhs, a child's typewriter, I find it hard to take seriously,' said Mr Mathur, Storey's deputy, holding the piece of paper with a look of disdain.

'But can we afford to take any chances? We must report the threat either to our Head Office in Delhi or to the Police,' said Storey.

'Yes perhaps the police, sir. Shall I call them? But no, not Head Office. They might think us stupid *goonks*.'

An hour later Inspector Mallothra of Lucknow's police department pulled up in his jeep outside the factory. A *kurta* clad, paunchy, balding man in his mid-forties, sporting an intensely waxed set of whiskers, he looked most unlike a policeman. To be inconspicuous, a detective needed to look like any other citizen going about his business, yet Mallothra stood out as a man of some importance and distinction.

'Well I'm agreeing with the juvenile nature of this communication but we cannot take this lightly,' he announced after deliberating over the note for a long time.

'What would you suggest we do, Inspector?' asked Storey.

'Well, I would be ignoring it sir. These demands if they are genuine usually follow three stages; first a demand to judge the response of the victim, second demand, putting fear into the victim, and then third, some final act of violence to achieve a result,' said Mallothra.

'That's very precise, Inspector...'

'Yes sir. Mickey Spillane's Criminal Handbook.'

'The author has written a handbook?' asked Mathur.

'*Nahi, nahi,* I have distilled my operating philosophy from his books. He is the guru of crime in my mind.'

'But he is a fiction writer, Mallothra!'

'And an excellent criminal mind. Don't you think sir that good crime writers would make very good criminals?'

'I don't know,' said Storey. 'I'm not a student of the form.'

'Trust me,' chortled Mallothra. 'I'm a detective. In the meantime keep your eyes open, your ears tuned and be suspicious of everything and everyone.'

Housie

On the first Saturday of every month the community of Lucknow gathered at the Anglo-Indian Institute to participate in an evening of light gambling, nicknamed Housie. Some came determined to win rich pickings, by fair means or foul; others came just to meet friends and catch up with the gossip.

They loved Housie and there was a time when this Institute would have been a sell-out. But tonight it was only half full, many of the regulars recently departed for some more prosperous Commonwealth country.

At least half a dozen tables would once have been dominated by the large Dalhousie clan, an extended family of every hue and colour. Now they lay empty. Mr and Mrs Wallace, a stately couple who occupied a large house in the Cantonment and were Housie goers, were now long gone to Canada. The De'Salles, pillars of the church who only came to the events to hear the latest gossip, had established a Portuguese lineage and managed to emigrate to Lisbon. Some said Housie nights were never the same without Mr De'Salle's loud guffaws of laughter, sometimes at the most inappropriate points of a game, he having once roared all the way through ten minutes of one session for no clear reason.

Joan wore her favourite radiant blue dress from her very

small collection, managing to inject a bit of Hollywood glamour into an audience who had seen better days. She always took great care over what she wore and how she looked, and tonight she knew that everyone at Housie would want to know who she was, where she had come from, and why she was unattached.

'I say Joan, I hope Irene doesn't mind me saying this, but you look a real *putaka* in that dress. You could give that Jane Russell girl a few tips in the looks department.' Gerry adored the movie star and collected playing cards with her pictures on them.

Just as Joan had anticipated, the place was soon buzzing with stories about 'the teacher recently arrived from Calcutta'. Seeing a new face in their midst had aroused interest, particularly as she was attractive and single.

Errol too had been invited to come along and he sat near his uncle Gerry who explained the game.

'Now son you're going to help me aren't you? There's a strip of paper here with numbers in rows. That man's going to call out numbers picking them from the cage and if we have a number on your sheet we tick them off. As soon as you have a complete line, you shout "line" and we win five rupees. If we tick off all the numbers in this sheet we shout "House" and we win twenty rupees.'

'Twenty rupees!' said Errol, 'that's six months' pocket money.'

'Not all for you smarty pants, we have to share it fifty-fifty.'

As Joan was paying for her numbers, Doug Kellor, principal of the Martinere school, advanced on her with a sweaty palm outstretched.

'Hello, I'm Dougie,' he announced, his eyes drifting to her blouse with its top button undone.

'Nice to meet you. I'm Joan D'Silva from Calcutta.'

'And who are you with this evening?'

'My in-laws, Irene and Gerry Shaw.'

'Ah, you're the teacher they spoke about.'

Joan collected her numbers and walked back to the table to join Irene and Gerry. Kellor followed.

'Watch that *badmash* now Joan,' shouted Gerry as they approached and Kellor laughed. 'Where did you get that bum freezer from?' Gerry indicated Kellor's ill-fitting short linen jacket.

'It's the pot calling the kettle, *hah*. How are you, you old bugger?'

'Now then, I see you've met Joan. She's a very good teacher,' said Irene, 'what about offering her a job in that school of yours?'

'Oh really Renee, do you have to be so blunt?' said Joan, somewhat embarrassed by her sister-in-law's directness.

'But how could I refuse?' said Kellor. 'Come and see me soon and we'll talk about it.'

'Eyes down, eyes down in five minutes,' a voice yelled out, telling people to sit down.

'I must get myself a *chota*, would you like one Joan?'

'A rum and cola if you would, thanks, Mr Kellor.'

'We're going to get along very well, Joan and please, Dougie will do nicely, *hah*?'

The caller was Mr Braithwaite, who stood on a platform in the middle of the hall with slicked back hair and a bow tie. He began to rotate a large spherical cage and it rattled as its contents, a collection of numbered balls, whirled around in the enclosure. The piercing sound of the cage as it spun settled everyone down for the start of the game. Kellor quickly joined Joan's table with her drink in time for the call, 'Eyes down.' Then there was pin drop silence and Kellor's eyes were down, not on the game but on Joan's bosom.

'Kiss and run, number one,' called out Braithwaite as he picked up the first ball from the cage. Both Joan and Irene quickly ticked off the number on their strips. Joan took a sip of her rum and cola as a reward and Kellor slipped in another sideways glance at her.

'What two babies do?' called Braithwaite and Gerry quickly ticked off his list, nudging Errol in the ribs and he returned a bright gleeful smile.

'What on earth is that?'

'Twenty two, Joan. You got it.'

And so the cryptic calling out of numbers continued until Joan was one number short of a line and the caller announced, 'Legs.'

'That's eleven, isn't it? Line, line I've got a line,' shouted Joan, putting up her hand.

The game continued and someone else got another line. There were a few false calls until both Irene and Joan were waiting for just one number to fill out their sheet. The caller announced, 'the house with a bamboo door, fifty four.' There was a shout of 'house' from the back of the hall which was subsequently found to be in error.

Gerry nudged Errol in the ribs again.

'Just one more sonny boy and we're going to be rich.' Errol was far too excited to respond. 'Close your eyes tight and keep repeating the number thirteen.'

Braithwaite gave the cage another few turns and then called out, 'Unlucky for some.' Errol still had his eyes shut when Gerry jumped up in excitement and it was only then that Errol knew that he was to share the princely sum of twenty rupees with his uncle.

When they got home the *khansamin* had cooked potato cutlets served with tomato sauce. These were exceptional cutlets stuffed with *garam masala* spiced mince in the centre and covered with crumbed potato on the outside, accompanied by a hot coriander, chilli and tomato sauce.

Potato cutlets were the perfect fusion of the simplicity of a British dish with the complexity of Indian cooking. It was the perfect compromise for diners who wished to emphasise their European credentials but couldn't come to terms with bland food. Here in the Shaw household their cutlets looked on the outside like any dish on an English dinner table and yet the inside was hot, spicy and very Indian. Joan loved them so much that she accepted a second portion, probably disappointing the cook who usually fed on the leftovers at table.

At ten o'clock Gerry switched on the All India evening news which always made the events of the day sound grave. The news on radio generally relayed subjects of national importance: famine, floods, resignations of top government officials or big investment projects worth several *crores*. Foreign assassinations, military coups in far-off African regimes or the announcement of some hostile speech by India's enemies also got coverage. With the exception of the cricket results involving India, there was not much room for trivia or rejoicing.

'*This is news from All Indian Radio read by R K Subramanian*,' they heard through the crackling medium-wave static in the background. Gerry always stopped talking during the news as though a holy man had come down from a high mountain to deliver a sermon. He would sit respectfully right through the broadcast and raise his eyebrows occasionally when there was something that he wanted others to know was of some significance.

'The chief minister of U.P. has expressed regret at the abduction and murder of a prominent Lucknow businessman whose body was found discarded by the roadside on the Grand Trunk Road near the outskirts of the city. The notorious Workers' Revolutionary Movement is believed to be behind what was an attempt to extract a ransom from the family of the dead man. The chief minister said that that he would be working diligently with the civilian police force to bring them to justice.'

Educating Errol

Unlike an average boy of eleven, Errol had been through the experience of being abducted for five days, eating and sleeping with his captors on the run before escaping in the middle of a gun battle with the Indian Army. Even so, the prospect of boarding school, and tales of bullies and fags, was still intimidating. But soon he would be eleven, and the idea of being with a lot of other boys his own age was beginning to grow on him.

Now, mother and son were pulling up at The Martinere in a horse-drawn *tonga*, Errol's heavy tin trunk adding to the scrawny animal's burden as it made its weary way past the *maidan* through the gates of the boy's school. There was immediate help on hand from two khaki-clad *chaprasis* who helped heave the trunk off the *tonga* and carry it away, their two lean bodies curved in a mirror image of each other at either end of the tin box's carrying handles.

A plump grey-haired middle-aged woman came up to greet them.

'Hello, you must be Errol and Mrs D'Silva. The Principal would like to see you now, Mrs D'Silva. Errol, you can wait here and I'll show you round afterwards.'

'Joan, lovely to see you,' said Dougie Kellor, as she entered his dusty old study, piled with books and papers in every corner. Other than his desk, a chair and two stools, the only other piece of furniture in the room was a purple velvet-covered sofa in an embossed paisley pattern. On the walls were fading photographs of people in military ceremonial dress, and a dusty marble bust of the school's founder Claude Martin stood on a pedestal in one corner. Replicas of this bust could be seen everywhere, in the gardens, the crypt, the church and the infirmary.

Kellor rang a little hand bell which was answered by a peon who came to the door. He ordered tea for Joan.

'Now then Joan, come and sit on the sofa with me, it's a lot more comfortable than these hard stools. By the way, may I say, you look so fragrant today.'

Joan had never been called fragrant and was rather taken aback but smiled in acknowledgement. Perhaps what he meant was she looked like a flower, which was a nice compliment to receive. She had worn a white cream blouse and a matching flouncy skirt, which she smoothed over her knees as she sat down on the sinking sofa. An uncomfortable spring in the upholstery protruded somewhere into her left buttock. She remembered Kellor's obvious lechery at Housie and had ensured for this meeting that the buttons on her blouse were buttoned all the way up to her neck.

The peon arrived with two cups of tea, which had already been poured with milk and sugar added, offering her one of the cups and Kellor the other.

'I'll join you on the sofa Joan, if I may, where we can talk about your son.'

Kellor eased himself onto the sofa and began sipping the hot tea far too loudly; Joan felt that this man had not been brought up too well. He was too close on the sofa for her to feel at ease and she pulled her skirt tightly over her knees with both hands and eased away from him.

'Now, your boy! I have not been able to secure a full scholarship for him yet but I have a proposal to put to you which may be mutually advantageous.'

Joan looked up from her cup.

'Oh dear, Gerry led me to believe that you were able to support the poorer boys from our community. You know Doug, we have no income at the moment. I've had to resign my teaching post in Cal. If it wasn't for the generosity of my sister-in-law, I'd be out on the streets.'

'And that is how my proposal fits in so well. We are now short of a teacher in the junior school as I've been losing so many of my staff in the exodus to Australia and Canada. If you were to accept the position as a teacher, Errol would automatically qualify for free tuition. What do you say?' he asked, moving his head closer with a smile that didn't seem to come entirely from the heart.

He answered Joan's questions about the curriculum, the class she would be taking and her salary. Teaching was the only option of an income for Joan and Kellor was the only one offering her a job. But Joan's prospective new employer did not inspire her with the level of trust she expected of a Principal.

'It's a very kind offer Mr Kellor, but a bit sudden. Could I have a few days to think it over and talk to Gerry and Irene perhaps?'

'Oh please do call me Dougie. I tell you what my dear, I'll also throw in a nice bungalow for you in the teacher's compound. What about that?'

The offer of accommodation within the school grounds was unusually generous and she knew she was unlikely to find anything better. If Kellor's manner had seemed less licentious she would have flung her arms around him and kissed him in gratitude.

'Take your time my dear, but you won't get a better offer in a hurry, I can assure you. It's a beautiful little bungalow with a view of the Gomti river, covered in the most gorgeous pink bougainvillea.'

A job, a bungalow, financial security; Joan mulled over the image of a secure future. Maybe Lucknow would be a good place to live and work for a while until it was safe to get back to Calcutta. And it would be a relief not to live off her brother-in-law anymore. There was a moment's silence in the Principal's office. Each tick of the Longcase mahogany clock seemed to echo around the cavernous room. Joan looked down at her shoes, and Kellor looked directly at her for an answer.

'Well, I'd be very pleased to accept your offer as I have to earn an income quite soon. But tell me Mr Kellor, you have not taken up any references or checked my qualifications.'

'I can assure you my dear I am fully aware of your capabilities. When you've been in education for as long as me, you get a sixth sense.'

'And what does it tell you about me?'

'That you're intelligent, resilient and reliable; three key requisites in a teacher. Ah yes! And you have good deportment.'

'Excuse me?'

'You know, you present yourself very well.'

He reached out with one hand and patted Joan on the knee, which was securely covered by her skirt and held down securely with both hands. His predatory smile made her stomach churn. Joan decided that the interview had come to an end and arose.

'Well Mr Kellor, I'd better not be keeping you.'

'Now then, I'm pleased you have decided to pursue your teaching career here Joan. By the way, how are relations with the other side?'

'The other side?' asked Joan.

'You know. The Pope's mob?'

'Ah, Father Rosario! I don't know him very well and if you're suggesting that I go and consult him, I will make my own decisions thank you.'

'Oh yes of course. I was only thinking what he might say when he finds out that not only have you decided to teach in a Protestant school but you're sending your son to be educated there.'

'I can't see a problem with my conscience. That's what matters after all. You aren't going to try and convert me are you?'

'You know you will have to attend Anglican services here on Sunday mornings with the boys? All our teachers are expected to do so.'

'I see no problem with that.'

'Splendid. Start Monday? Better get right in as soon as you can to the start of term.'

Joan agreed. Kellor shook her hand holding on to it for a little longer than was comfortable; she pulled away from his damp clammy palm, half-smiling in a mark of polite farewell.

'Now what about the boy? Is he here?'

'Yes I did bring him with me. He is sitting outside.'

She ushered Errol into the office, holding on to his right shoulder.

'So young man,' he said puffing white smoke from his pipe upwards, 'what did they teach you in that school in Calcutta?'

The boy detected a sense of arrogance in his tone and he

stiffened a little in anticipation of this extra quick delivery at the wicket from the Principal's opening bowl. This was not a question that Errol thought he could answer directly because he felt he had learned so much. Where to start?

'To study hard sir, to respect my teachers and to love my country, sir.'

'*Hah, hah,* to love your country! And what about history and literature and arithmetic? Did they teach you any of that?'

'I like Algebra, sir,' said Errol. Joan glowed with pride. The reply was designed cleverly by the boy to impress Kellor as he noticed the Principal's shelves were littered with the English classics by Scott, Thackeray and Eliot but not a science or maths text in sight. Kellor would not be able to question Errol on his mathematical ability and the strategy worked.

'Algebra *hah?*'

'Yes sir, I had got to solving simultaneous equations before I left. I loved simultaneous equations because they were like a quiz game sir.'

'Simultaneous equations like a game? What games do you play?'

'Cricket sir. I'm a fast bowler. I want to be like Desai.'

'And what class would you wish the boy to be admitted to?' he asked Joan.

'He was in year six Mr Kellor.'

'Six then it will be. Be here next Monday and make sure you have ordered the uniforms and all the necessary inventory listed here. And now young man, perhaps we can look forward to your several years of diligent work here at The Martinere. Well Mrs D'Silva, that's all in order then. I think you should start as soon as you can. The boy can stay as a boarder as I'm not sure you'll want him in the bungalow with you. It's healthier if he is with the other boys, eh?'

On Monday Joan started her job at The Martinere Boys' School, replacing a teacher who had recently emigrated to join family in London. Her two-roomed bungalow sat in its own small plot with a view of the Gomti from her veranda, as Kellor had promised, and the bougainvillea was there in full bloom. It was bathed in sun in the mornings and cool in the shade soon after midday as the sun moved towards the back of the house. She asked the head *mali* to plant some geraniums in half a dozen terracotta pots which she kept inside the veranda to shield the delicate plants from the harsh direct sunlight, and in a few days they would begin to bring a splash of crimson red colour to the railings. The previous occupants had left some furniture and Irene lent her linen and cutlery to make the place liveable. Gerry had acquired some old railway furniture from the waiting room at Lucknow station, which had been easily repaired. In days Joan had been set up in her new home.

Errol had mixed feelings about his mother teaching at the school. But life as a boarder would give him the taste for independence and despite the odd bit of teasing, he soon settled into being away from the watchful eye of his mother. Joan promised him that she would not interfere with his independence but that he'd be welcome to come home for *tiffin* whenever he wanted to.

On her first Monday morning with Year Five, she faced a class of thirty boys all dressed smartly in their white shirts and khaki trousers.

'Morning Miss,' they said in unison as she entered the class.

'Good morning class, my name is Mrs D'Silva, it is originally a Portuguese name which I got from my late husband, who was from Goa,' she said, writing her name on the blackboard. 'I used to teach a class just like yours in Calcutta for five years and now I've come to live close to my sister in Lucknow. Your parents sent you here to learn and I'm paid to teach, so if we both do our job we'll get on very well. Now let me get to know your names by calling out the register.'

She began to read the names in alphabetical order as the boys all indicated their presence until she came to Mathur, Ashok Mathur. The boy, about five feet tall, stood up at the bottom of the class. Some of the boys nudged each other to share a joke about Ashok, which Joan picked up on.

'What was funny about that? Please tell me your name?'

'Amarnath Miss. Nothing funny Miss,' came back the reply.

'So are you always in the habit of grinning and laughing while teacher calls out the attendance register? Or is there something very funny about Ashok that you wish to tell me?'

'No Miss.'

'Good, well let's continue then.'

After a disastrous first year as a teacher, Joan had learned that firing the first shot in establishing respect with the class was essential early on in a teacher's relationship with her pupils. She'd never been trained as a teacher, but had acquired a great deal of knowledge through her experience over the last five years. Each year she got better and more satisfied with her achievement. Recognition came at the end of the summer term, as parents would line up to come and see her, bringing gifts of sweetmeats, flowers and trinkets. Her pupils would be sad and tearful and some would touch her feet as a mark of respect and gratitude. Each year the queues of parents waiting to see her increased and there were more tears, even from some of the tougher boys who were better known for their bullying ways. But Lucknow was a fresh start where she had to rebuild her reputation and this was her first class.

'Our first lesson today is history. Now let me see if I can test you on something. Who do you believe is the greatest Indian that ever lived?' asked Joan.

'Gandhiji Miss,' said one.

'Nehru,' said another.

'Shashi Kapoor,' said the film buff and so they reeled off names.

'Kapoor is definitely very popular today, but when he is old and not so handsome will he still be the greatest Indian that ever lived and our prime minister, Jawaharlal Nehru, may not be prime minister one day and then will he be your favourite? But with Mahatma Gandhi, the world and his country will remember him for many years to come, perhaps centuries. And why do we think that is?' said Joan looking at the class and at some boys who were looking very pleased with suggesting the Mahatma.

'He was a saint Miss.'

'Yes he certainly was a very good man, but what did he do for India?'

'Helped us get our independence.'

'*Haan*, he did and he did it through non-violent means. That means he didn't believe in fighting physically, like some of you boys do to get your own way. He will be known as the greatest Indian by the rest of the world for his peaceful protests of fasting and civil disobedience, which really brought the mighty British Empire to its knees and led to our independence. Today, we see others like Martin Luther King in America, using Gandhi's way to get equal rights for black people. So remember that when you think you can settle a disagreement with your fists. What else was he famous for?'

'Miss, he liked the *dalits*.'

'Quite right, he believed we're all equal and that the caste system which separates us is unfair. He loved the untouchables just as much as everyone else. There are no *dalits* here in this class for example and perhaps in the entire school; the only ones are those cleaning the rooms or doing the gardens. One day hopefully when you are famous leaders you will do what Gandhi did and give untouchables a better chance in life, *hah?*'

The silence in the class indicated that her lesson had got through to the pupils of Year Five. Treating each other as equals was a concept that sat most uncomfortably in Lucknow with its huge divisions along religious, ethnic and caste lines. Most of the boys would have been brought up in privileged homes, where less fortunate untouchables would only have been seen doing the most servile or dirty work.

It was Ashok Mathur who, absorbed through all this, put up his hand.

'Miss, my father says that we can't all be equal and that Hindu teaching tells us we are born into our life because it is our destiny.'

'Ashok that is a very good point, but you know Gandhi was a Brahmin and believed in destiny too, but still thought that we need to respect everyone else as members of the human race. The British thought that Indians were inferior to them and that we were destined to be ruled forever. Now we can prove otherwise; we have Nobel Prize winners in science, our engineers in Bombay have established the country's first nuclear reactor and we have the world's biggest democracy.

The white people in America think they are superior to the black people who come from Africa through slavery. History shows us that those in power think that they are better than the people below them but it doesn't last long.'

The idea that the boys in Year Five might be the same as everybody else on this planet would continue to be an anathema to most of the class, probably for the rest of their lives. They would continue to live in relative privilege and probably never get to speak to an untouchable except in a position of superiority, certainly never befriend one on equal terms. But it was these moments that gave Joan the greatest satisfaction, when she felt she had planted the smallest seed of humanity in their burgeoning minds.

The *Imambara*

The second note from the blackmailers arrived as mysteriously as the first, the day before the deadline. Yet again the message was delivered in its amateur form, typewritten in red on a sheet of paper torn from an exercise book.

Here are your deposit instructions. Ignore these and the consequences for your company will be disastrous.

Workers' Revolutionary Movement

But any idea that this was the work of inexperienced juveniles was soon dispensed with when they read the instructions. The blackmailers gave the most precise and detailed instructions with exact timings and they had chosen a drop site with great ingenuity. Even the sceptical Mathur, Storey's deputy, commented on its originality.

The blackmailers had chosen the *Imambara*, a monument built as a memory to the grandson of the prophet Mohammed during the eighteenth century reign of the Nawab of Oudh. The building enabled the Nawab to please his god, do good for his people, and build a monument for future generations to remember his name.

In the seventeenth century, the Mughal Empire was the biggest in the world and stretched the entire width of the subcontinent of India. But a hundred years later the Nawabs had taken control of significant kingdoms and Lucknow became the capital of Oudh, a magnificent territory. The Nawabs, bored with the primitive and crude architecture they found, brought in the finest painters, designers and architects from Persia to enrich their lives and leave a sumptuous legacy of buildings. Their use of stone, gems and metals, together with their sense of design, transformed the dull landscapes and towns into places of great beauty. Lucknow became a capital city thanks to these artisans and engineers.

At the *Imambara*, Indian, Persian and Mughal architecture fused together. At its core was a towering, cavernous hall, which amplified the smallest sound of footsteps reverberating around the arches, and pillars whitewashed in blue-tinged lime. Over the main hall, the intricate construction of tunnels was a deliberate attempt to deceive the mind. There were dozens of different tunnels and passages, some in complete darkness, and hundreds of identical doorways. There in the subterranean network various rulers had imprisoned people or merely deposited them as a test of their survival instincts.

The Nawab had a daughter who was reputed to be the most beautiful young woman in the entire kingdom of Oudh. He loved his daughter dearly and wanted to make sure she was married to the most suitable man he could find from one of the other princely states. She wasn't short of admirers and one by one they came to visit this vision of beauty. From the safety of her first floor *purdah* window she observed these potential husbands and turned them down every time as she was already in love with her teacher, the man who had been her mentor and guru since she was twelve years old.

Now she was twenty-two, they would come to the labyrinth to be on their own and, in the dark, in his role of teacher, he shared his knowledge in ways that eventually led to the young woman becoming pregnant. They tried to elope but were noticed by one of the guards and the Nawab, a normally tolerant man, became a deranged tyrant. He had the teacher flogged and then taken down to the maze together with his daughter. The couple were bricked up in one of the tunnels and left to die. It is said that their remains are still hidden somewhere within. People who got lost in the maze have reported a ghostly couple who helped them find their way back to the entrance.

And it was here that the Apna blackmailer had listed a complex set of left and right turns to earmark a specific location to deposit a large 20 kilogram can of Apna, sealed with the money inside. This was to be done by four o'clock in the afternoon on the fifth day, just before the *Imambara* closed its gates to the public.

When Mallothra read the note he twisted the ends of his whiskers with his fingers as if he was sharpening the ends of a lethal weapon.

'I'm beginning to see that these people are not amateurs, Mr Storey. I've often wondered how perfect the *Imambara* is for committing the perfect undetectable crime. The tunnels are dark as pitch, making the detection of any criminal activity almost impossible.'

'But you're not expecting me to take this seriously all of a sudden are you?' said Storey.

'*Nahi*, not for the moment, sir. I still believe in my three-stage ransom theory according to the philosophy of Mr Spillane. But I am beginning to think that we aren't playing with hoaxers. I will post a detective to monitor any suspicious activity in and out of the labyrinth tomorrow in case they come looking for their booty.'

By four o'clock on the day of the deadline the sun had lost its searing bite when Mallothra took up his position of surveillance in one of the towers overlooking the courtyard of the *Imambara*. From there he could see everyone who entered or left the labyrinth. All were with a guide, someone familiar with the layout. Occasionally courting couples might wander in seeking the dark cloistered anonymity of what locals referred to as the 'love tunnel'.

Mallothra was determined to identify anyone suspicious entering the tunnel, picking up loiterers and having them followed. By four fifteen the guards had cleared most of the visitors and the final bell announcing the closure of the palace had sounded three times. In five minutes the place was empty with the exception of a crow that hopped about the central courtyard looking for scraps of food. There was plenty of sustenance for the bird and he pecked and hopped from place to place, filling up for his supper.

When finally the detective was satisfied that there was no one left in the establishment, he came down from his place of hiding and drove back to the *thana* telephoning Storey when he got there.

'Just as I thought Sir, nothing this time but perhaps in a few days things may be a different matter.'

'Let's hope you are wrong Inspector,' said Storey, 'let's hope you are very wrong.'

The *jheal*

Despite the blackmail, Storey appeared to have other things on his mind this evening. He had invited Joan for a shoot to the *jheal* at dusk. The *jheal* was a lake surrounded by impenetrable jungle and host to thousands of birds, large and small: the favourite hunting ground for those lucky enough to possess a working shotgun and a knowledge of the surrounding jungle. Its underground springs provided a perfect refuge for wildlife, providing ample supplies of water even in the hottest months of the year. At dusk the amber rays of the sun were reflected in its still waters, rippling with the movement of birds as they paddled to and fro feeding on the insects and worms that thrived in the rich watery environs.

The several square miles of densely wooded forest also played host to the non-aquatic birds that hid high in the trees away from the eyes of most predators. In amongst the hunting grounds were dangerous swamps ready to consume those who decided to tread the deadly terrain without the necessary knowledge of how to navigate the territory. Storey had been here many times with a local hunter and had got to know the area well, enough to feel confident of taking Joan D'Silva there on their first date.

In a handwritten note, Storey promised Joan that she would have the time of her life and that she should dress sensibly for the occasion. She consulted Gerry and Irene and concluded that sensible clothing entailed khaki long slacks and a shirt to match. Not having either of these garments in her possession she borrowed a pair of Irene's slacks and spent most of the previous evening taking in the waist, as her sister-in-law was a few sizes larger than her. With it she wore a bottle-green blouse. Gerry commented that she looked very '*havva havva*' for a shoot and that Storey should be very pleased with her appearance.

'Ah Joan! You're the best dressed shooting companion I've had,' said Storey as he greeted Joan on his veranda, kissing her on the left cheek. 'Ready for some adventure then?'

'I've come all prepared and I can't wait.'

'Let me tell you a few things about what we'll be doing. Firstly let me introduce you to my old friend,' he said, stroking a polished mahogany wooden gun box that sat on the dining room table. He clicked a latch and opened the lid displaying a leather-lined interior, which immediately gave off the fruity distinctive aroma of *3-in-1* that had kept the weapon in a state of readiness for many years.

'This is a Holland and Holland shotgun given to my father by the Nawab of Kutch in 1939,' he said, lifting out the barrel and fixing it to the butt with three simple easy motions. The smooth lines of the gun and the intricate engraving of its metal reminded Joan of a piece of fine jewellery.

'That is beautiful, can I touch it?' she asked. The dark steel barrel was surprisingly cold compared to the warm protective glow of the wooden butt.

'Look through the bore of the barrel,' said Ed Storey as he held it up to the light. The inner bore amplified the rays of the afternoon sun, creating a kaleidoscopic explosion of patterned light.

'Today we're going to be shooting teal, mallard, peacock, pheasant and wild cock, plus anything else that might make a good *vindaloo*. The *Khansamin* has a knack for a good bird curry and they all look forward to me going out on one of my jaunts.'

Joan expected the driver to have the Ambassador on standby for the couple to step into and carry them off to their jungle expedition, but instead she saw the sparkling chrome of a green Royal Enfield motorcycle with attached sidecar. These machines had for the last five years been made in India under license from the British-owned company and this model, a 330cc Bullet, was no more than a couple of years old. It was a bang-up-to-date accessory for a sporting man.

Storey kicked the starter and the engine coughed into life with a throaty rumble that built to a loud roar when he revved the engine. The *malis* mowing the lawn stopped to marvel at the *sahib* showing off his toy. Joan had never ridden in a sidecar and was excited as she climbed into the seat with some help from Storey, pulling on a leather helmet.

They rode out in the late afternoon sun, which was beginning to lose its heat. The engine progressed to a smooth purr as they built up speed on the long straight road out past the outskirts of the town, breezing past the traffic of bullock carts and Mercedes trucks. Heads turned, people stared at this gleaming miracle of engineering. Joan soon became used to turning with the bends in tandem with Storey as he swerved every now and then to avoid a cow sat in the road chewing the regurgitated contents of its day's foraging.

When they arrived near the *jheal*, Storey parked his bike at the end of a rough rutted road and Joan extracted herself from the sidecar in the most ladylike fashion she could manage. She took off her helmet, shook her thick black hair free and Storey stared. Joan caught his gaze for just a split second – the slightly dropped jaw, the widened eyes – and he mumbled an incoherent comment about the discomfort of sidecars. He took the gun out of its box in the sidecar, assembled it and popped a few dozen cartridges into the large pockets of his khaki shooting jacket.

'Are you ready for this?' he asked Joan, and she nodded. 'See that hole in the jungle? We're going through that. Hold on to me, you'll be okay. It's dark and there are prickly things all over the place, but nothing you should be scared of.'

Storey crouched down to half his height and Joan followed. The tunnel got darker the further they stepped into it. Pinpricks of sunlight barely managed to reach them as she edged forward holding Storey's right hand. In the semi-darkness the sound of screeching birds was deafening. There was a squelching sound as she stepped through puddles of muddy water. She could feel the water seeping into her shoes.

'You okay?'

'I'm fine.'

As the light at the end of the tunnel grew, Joan was relieved to see the lake come into view. The still, dark water was covered with green vegetation and lotus flowers near the banks. Aquatic birds of every colour darted to and fro in groups.

Taking his gun from her he broke the barrel and inserted a couple of cartridges, giving Joan a few to hand him for the next round. And then they waited.

'What happens now?' said Joan softly.

'We wait for them to get airborne. Can't shoot them when they're feeding, it would be far too bloodthirsty.'

Some minutes later a tussle broke out amongst a flock of mallard on the *jheal* and a few birds took off, flying away from the water towards the dry land. Storey aimed in front of the birds and fired one cartridge; two birds fell from the sky but now the entire *jheal* erupted, the sky filling with birds. Storey fired the second cartridge. Joan wasn't sure how many birds came down with the second cartridge but immediately Ed was reloading and fired again, and again, until the sky had cleared.

'That was the easy bit,' he said. 'Now we have to pick them up. You took the dog's seat.'

Joan's ears were still ringing and she was sure she had a mild dose of shell shock caused by the loud bangs, the smell of the cordite and the screeching of the birds. It took her a while to hear what he was saying.

'Where did they all fall? I only saw the first two.'

'Oh well, if I'm a guessing man I'd say that they were all pretty much in the same area. Watch the kites begin to circle in the sky and there'll be a dead bird just there. Shall we go and pick them up?'

'You play the *shikari* and I play the dog, *hah?* Nice way to treat a girl on her first date.'

'Very well, if you put it that way I'm not being very gallant.'

'I'm only teasing. Here, give me one of those gunny sacks.'

They walked holding hands, with Storey leading Joan zigzagging through the swampy shores of the lake over to where the dead birds had fallen. She put her feet carefully in his footsteps.

'I'm glad you know your way around here.'

'Plenty of experience. And I've walked through minefields in my time.'

'Where?'

'In Egypt. But that was another life.' He paused. 'Look at

our handiwork,' he said, pointing to the carcasses of dead birds strewn on the ground. She held the gunnysack while Ed bent down and picked up the fallen birds, examining each one and announcing its breed, sex and age.

'Oh look Ed,' Joan said as he picked up a Mallard, which she recognised by its distinctive shiny green and black colouring, 'wasn't she beautiful?'

'It's a he actually. The males are the good-looking ones because they need to attract females, unlike us, where the women are the attractive ones and the men are fat and ugly.'

'There are some exceptions.'

They were almost through picking up the birds when they came across a hen that was not quite dead. It fluttered every now and then. Ed quickly grabbed it between his legs and wrung its neck. Joan winced.

'I read once that many of these birds are monogamous. I wonder if that one's husband will miss her tonight when she doesn't come home,' said Joan as they walked back to the bike.

Ed stayed silent for a few moments and her comment hung in the thick evening air. Then he said, 'It must have been a sad day when you realised your husband wouldn't be coming back.'

'It was. It's taken me years to get over it.'

'And have you?'

'Yes, I believe so, in the strangest of ways. Perhaps I'll tell you about it when I know you better.'

Storey helped Joan out of the sidecar when they arrived at the factory gates. It was getting dark and the single fluorescent strip light at the entrance had begun to flicker into life. The *chaprasi* was already opening the heavy iron gates having heard the thundering exhaust of the Royal Enfield a mile away. Storey offered his hand to help Joan out of the sidecar but she extracted herself without his assistance with complete poise and grace.

'I feel such a mess, and I smell just like one of those birds.'

'Not at all, you look like you've been to a shooting party,' said Ed.

They walked into the large front room and were met by a myriad of little oil lights that had been lit and scattered over shelves, tabletops and corners, making the place look like a temple at *divali*. The warm orange lamps twinkled, washing the cushioned sofas with soothing light, while sandalwood incense sticks, to keep away mosquitos, gently glowed and burned.

'Joan, will you stay for a bit of *khanna*?' asked Ed.

'But Ed, I'm such a mess and I surely should be getting back before it's too late tonight. Gerry and Irene are expecting me.'

'You're not their child! Why don't you go and wash off the dirt from the journey, I'll get a bath run up for you right away. Please stay.'

Ed left the room. The *khansamin* moved silently to collecting the day's game from the sack, taking the birds away to feather and clean them before preparing Ed's favourite dish, duck *vindaloo*. The smell of frying turmeric and coriander was soon wafting its way into the large living room.

Ed reappeared with a scarlet red gown.

'Look, you can get into this after your bath, it's a present given to me when I was in Egypt.'

The garment was covered in golden embroidery of Egyptian symbols of animals and other hieroglyphics. Joan picked it up, passing her hands over it, and whispered, 'It's just beautiful!'

The *chaprasi* showed her to the visitor's bedroom where a pair of slippers, a fresh set of white towels and some iced drinking water had already been set out.

The bedroom walls were hung with framed pictures of pyramids, sand dunes and riders on camel trains. There was a picture of a pouting, voluptuous belly–dancer, festooned with jewellery which just about kept her decent. There were no pictures of Ed.

Storey was topping up his glass of beer when Joan returned to the living room. She was barefooted and stepped silently. Suddenly she was there beside him. As he caught sight of her in the Egyptian gown he tipped his glass, spilling liquid over his linen trousers.

'How do I look?' she said with a twirl.

'You look the image of the Queen Cleopatra. I thought I was seeing her ghost appear right here in my own house.'

Joan laughed. 'Flattery will get you everywhere. Are you a devotee of Cleo?'

'Absolutely, you see her everywhere in Egypt. She was a woman of exceptional beauty, highly manipulative of course, and very headstrong. I'm sure only the former applies to you, the beauty bit.' He took her left hand and gave it a lingering kiss.

'Oh thank you,' she smiled. 'Perhaps a little headstrong too. Do you mind strong women?'

'Oh no, I've always been attracted to strong women rather than the demure types. But you don't wish to hear about that do you? Right now I feel very rude not offering you a drink.'

'You know my favourite drink is rum and cola. Do you have it in the house? If not, I'll join you in a small glass of Eagle beer.'

'I'm not a Coke sort of person but I must remember that for future reference. Here I'll get you a beer.'

Storey poured Joan a glass of beer; she noticed his hand quivering a little. The *khansamin* came out to announce that dinner was now ready, and came forth holding a steaming hot dish of duck *vindaloo* served up in a gold-rimmed bowl of Stoke pottery. Chunks of the dark meat swam in a reddish brown tamarind sauce which had been sprinkled with chopped green coriander. The characteristic smell of wine vinegar in the sauce, mixed with the spices, titillated Joan's senses. Her stomach rumbled in anticipation. And to heighten the evening's gastronomic delight, as an accompaniment, the cook had made pea *pillau* rice.

'Right, let's tuck in,' Ed said. 'I'm starving.'

'Your *khansamin* is a treasure arranging his lovely meal in just over an hour,' said Joan as she helped herself to a plateful of rice.

They ate in silence for a short while, then Ed broke the pause by asking, 'Had any bad dreams lately?'

'Thank God no, but it's still very much in the back of my mind.'

'You should try to forget about it.'

'And what about you, Ed? How are things at the factory?'

'It's not the best time,' said Ed. 'That factory is my baby you see, and so the idea that someone is trying to sabotage it gets right through to me.'

'Sabotage it? What do you mean?'

'We're being blackmailed,' Ed said. 'By the Maoists. But I won't give in. Once I give in there will be more demands and the factory will become the subject of a protection racket.'

'How awful. Do the police know?' asked Joan.

'Yes. But don't worry about that now,' Ed smiled at her. 'I hope you enjoyed your first shoot?'

'I've had a lovely day Ed.'

'So have I.'

'I'd just like you to know that I'm not ready for anything

serious. There are too many things going on in my life, and I need a little more stability and reassurance about my future before I...'

'Before we go to bed together?'

'Ed, is that a joke?'

'Joan, I'm not going to take advantage of you. Don't worry.'

'Well... as long as you know where I stand.'

'Look, you're a beautiful woman. You must have plenty of men lusting after you, men who don't care about you being married or a widow or whatever, who are only after one thing. I'm not one of them.'

'That's not what I've heard.'

'Don't believe all you hear. Now look let's put that to one side. Would you like to dance with me?'

'What, here?'

'Yes right here, I have a gramophone.'

'We're halfway through our dinner!'

Ed lifted up the mahogany lid on the turntable and placed a 45 RPM record of James Moody's saxophone solo 'I'm in the Mood for Love'.

'Come on Joan, I won't bite. Trust me,' he held out his hands and Joan hesitantly joined him in the middle of the room.

They danced a slow waltz at a comfortable distance as the smoky, moaning saxophone played, lingering each note into another. Ed looked at Joan and smiled and she smiled back. The music continued as they moved through a wider circle of the room and the distance between them gradually decreased into the third minute of the tune. Storey was touching her cheek with his by this time and Joan was lost in her thoughts, her mind drifting back to the warm bath as his right arm was wrapped around her now. The music ended.

'Did you know that in eighteenth century Europe, it was known as the "naughty ladies" dance,' said Ed.

'I can see why.'

'Can I kiss you?' asked Ed and she allowed him to make contact with her lips but held back before he could take his request any further.

'You're a good dancer Ed, I was quite carried away.'

'So was I. Shall we dance another?'

'You know Ed, I hope you don't mind but it's been such a long day and I'm dying on my feet.'

'Oh, just another dance, that was so divine.'

'I'm sorry Ed, this little girl has reached her bedtime.'

'Well okay, you retire to your bedroom and I'll see you in the morning. You don't want me to tuck you up, do you?'

'Oh no I've learned to do that on my own.'

'Sweet dreams little girl.' He blew her a kiss and Joan retired to her bedroom.

The test

An invitation to look around the Apna factory may not have seemed the most obvious sequel to Storey's initial courtship of Joan but knowing how much it meant to him, she was pleased to accept. It was a Saturday morning and Joan was free of teaching duties as her class took to the school fields to participate in their formal physical exercise period followed by sports of their choice. Errol had been asked to play in the junior cricket challenge so Joan trundled off in a *tonga* down the road to Gorabad, where the factory had been built to accommodate this modern new technological wonder of modern manufacturing.

A turbaned bearer greeted her on the veranda. '*Memsahib, salaam. Sahib* says I should make *chai* for you before visiting the factory.' She sat in a cushioned cane chair on the veranda sipping on her cup of *chai* served in Storey's best bone china, until she felt rested from the bone rattling ten-mile *tonga* ride.

Ed was at his office, a single storey red-brick building, the inside of which smelled of *Brasso* metal polish. The building was just inside the factory gates and Joan was ushered in by the bearer. Storey wore a white coat making him look more like a doctor than a factory manager and there were several white-coated men, but what marked out Storey was his dark blue tie, worn with a stiff-collared white shirt. He extended a firm handshake with a, 'Hello Joan'.

Joan had made a special effort to impress Storey on this visit, knowing that he thought he was a bit of a *burra sahib* and that she would be on show to the rest of the staff. So far, Storey had behaved like most of the men she had known, using his status to impress her. But Joan believed there was a deeper side to him that she didn't know and so far he had not revealed much of it.

Her mother had once counselled her that finding the right man required great dexterity and the subtlest of techniques to divert him from his boyish pursuits. Being overly keen in one's approaches would make the man suspect that he was about to be trapped and like a suspicious animal wary of being held in human captivity, he would scurry away. On the other hand, a little mystery and intrigue always helped to make a man want to find out more and keep coming back until he felt he had the full measure of a woman. Of course the secret in finding the right man was never to allow him to find out everything about you. And it was that early piece of advice that unconsciously informed Joan's demeanour and her dress sense that day.

She'd put on a sleeveless polka dotted dress and wore a headscarf to match for the *tonga* journey. The American hit 'Polka Dot Bikini' had inspired a range of fashions in popular magazines from Europe to as far afield as Singapore. The door to door trader Hong Kong John, as he was known, had brought Joan the very latest of these textiles in cotton prints and she was the first to get a dress made up of the yellow polka-dotted fabric. The brightness of the dress on an attractive woman stood out vividly against the grey neon-lit interior of the factory.

'It's so nice to see you. You look so, what should I say...'
He appeared lost for words.

'Windswept, shook up, sweaty, all from that dreadful *tonga*
I'm afraid,' she said.

'Oh no, radiant and lovely!' Storey smiled. They sat down
in his office on two wooden armchairs with cane backs and
sunflower yellow seat cushions. He proceeded to give her an
introduction to the finer points of the manufacture of cooking
fats and of the innovative technology being deployed here in
India for the first time, thanks to the collaboration of east and
west. She listened attentively.

Joan sat back in the chair with her legs crossed, the skirt of
her polka dotted dress rising above her knees exposing her
exquisite walnut-coloured legs.

'How many people work here Ed?'

'Oh, sixty-five on the permanent payroll and another thirty
or forty casual workers doing unskilled jobs. We're under
pressure from government to increase the permanent payroll.'

'Are you suffering from any adverse publicity since the
blackmail?' asked Joan.

'Shhh,' he said putting his finger to his lips. 'It's very hush
hush. We're keeping it quiet so as not to cause a panic. Don't
mention it outside, especially not to friends here in Lucknow.
You know what the gossipers are like.'

'I understand,' she nodded. Storey announced that it was
time to walk around the factory.

Inside the factory building, the hum of the conveyor belt
drowned out any reasonable conversation. Empty tins of Apna
moved down the conveyor belt until they were filled by a
nozzle that oozed the liquid oil, the next in line capped the
top with a lid and a third extracted whatever air was left in

the top of the can with a vacuum hose, finally sealing it off with a sucking noise.

There were several production lines for different sizes of tin and the large factory shed was populated by dozens of workers in brilliant white spotless outfits, all going about their work in a planned and ordered way that quite impressed Joan. At a time when most things got done by a form of ordered chaos this seemed to be most modern and streamlined.

All the operators seemed to be well practiced in their role on the production line and some of them smiled at Joan and acknowledged Storey as they passed. Men at the far end of the conveyor belt kept up a continuous flow of bringing in empty tins and placing them on the conveyor and Joan was intrigued by the use of this very traditional manual method in the midst of the most advanced automation.

Ed continued to explain the process to Joan as if she were a visiting dignitary and she continued to nod sagely as he explained how the process had been developed in America and brought to India under license. Joan noticed the gleaming floors which were cleaner than her own home, the concrete slab base having been painted over a battleship grey. Ed saw her looking at the floor and explained how important it was to have complete cleanliness to avoid any risk of bacteria infecting the batches of Apna.

'And this is Mr Mathur my deputy who ensures that every can that leaves this factory is pure and free from any agents that might do harm,' announced Storey, dragging the middle-aged man in a white laboratory coat closer in to meet her.

'*Namaste*,' said Mathur with his hands together. 'I try to do my best.'

'You have a striking resemblance to a boy in my class at The Martinere, Mr Mathur,' said Joan.

'*Accha*, now you are Mrs D'Silva. My son Ashok speaks so much about you.'

'He is my favourite pupil. I know I'm not supposed to say that but he is a lovely boy.'

Mathur smiled as a proud father would and Storey seemed pleased that there was already a connection between Joan and his factory.

'Do you have just the boy?'

'No Madam, I have a daughter who I hope will be married very soon.'

'Ah yes the lovely Alpana and what a *tamasha* that will be eh Mathur?'

Mathur shook his head in agreement and beamed. In fact the wedding had become his main preoccupation helped by the constant reminders by his wife about the daily tasks that he needed to complete. Work at the factory had been relegated very much to second place.

'Mr Mathur have you prepared the test for Mrs D'Silva?' asked Storey.

'Yes sir, all ready to go.'

'Test, what test? I wasn't aware I had to sit an exam?' asked Joan.

'My dear, you probably insist that you cook with the best *ghee* and quite right you are to do so. But if everybody in this country were to cook with *ghee* there would not be enough cows left in the entire world to produce the milk necessary to feed everyone's appetite. So here we are able to use modern biotechnology and create a fat that tastes like and smells like the real thing.'

'Not the same as *ghee* though,' said Joan.

'Believe me, in blind tests with housewives, not one of them has been able to reliably differentiate between Apna and the real *ghee*.'

'I'm sure I could, and I'm not a housewife,' insisted Joan.

'Very well then, we'll conduct a little trial which Mr Mathur here has prepared.'

'Mr Mathur, are you ready to conduct the Apna versus *ghee* trial?' asked Storey.

'Yes Mr Storey. I have just asked your *khansama* to make two *chapattis*. They will be here in two minutes. Please come with me into the laboratory area.'

The *chapattis* were delivered and Mathur spooned a portion of Apna into one *chapatti* and one portion of *ghee* into the other. The warm bread quickly melted the fats and they were rolled to form a filling. Joan had to turn her back to Mathur while he performed this operation.

'*Accha* now please turn around and take a bite of each *chapatti*.'

'Isn't this going a bit far when we could have just tasted a small spoonful?' asked Joan.

'Madam, we have to replicate the exact culinary conditions under which these fats are consumed,' said Mathur politely.

She obediently took a bite out of the sample. Joan was absolutely sure she could taste the one *chapatti* that had the authentic *ghee* filling but was conscious of Storey's bruised pride if she told the truth. So she switched her selection and pointed to the one she thought had the Apna filling. Mathur asked her if she was sure and when she nodded that it definitely was *ghee*, his face lit up with delight that his boss had been proved right and that technology had triumphed again.

'Yes you have picked the authentic product and that is our Apna, not *ghee* as you thought. Mr Storey it proves your guest has good taste.'

'Yes, well you see we do have a very good product.' Storey looked proud. 'Shall we go back to the house and have some *chai* and a delicious almond cake that the *khansama* has made with our very own Apna?'

'I couldn't be keeping you from your duties, Ed?' said Joan.

'Not at all, its nice to have such grace in our midst today. Let's walk back to the house for some *khanna*,' he said looking at her and she feigned a shy smile.

The massage

They walked over to Ed Storey's bungalow down a gravel path, their shoes crunching the stones as they went. Storey's feet dragged from time to time as he sauntered beside Joan. At a full six inches taller than Joan, she had to keep looking up at him into the sunlight as he described the various species he had grown from seeds imported from Sutton's Nurseries in England. 'I've got three excellent *malis* working for me and they do a splendid job of both the lawns and the flower beds.'

'Do you cut any of them for the house?' asked Joan.

'No, can't say I know much about flower arranging myself so I just admire them here in their natural setting.'

They walked up onto the veranda and into the sitting room with its large slatted French windows opening out onto the garden. Joan sat down on the veranda again while Storey went to get her a glass of lemonade.

'Penny for your thoughts my dear,' said Storey returning with a glass of lemonade and a beer.

'Oh, you get the beer and I get baby's lemonade.'

'I'm sorry, I had just assumed...'

'Don't worry Ed, lemonade's fine. Tell me,' she said holding one of his hands and putting it on her lap, 'is all this blackmail business worrying you? I've been through it myself. I know how bad it can be.'

'Yes, it's quite a stressful time as I don't think I can screw this up.'

'Sometimes it helps to unload a bit.'

'And how can I be sure that you're not secretly working for the Movement? It's okay, that's only a joke!'

'Oh yes, I'm the honey trap, come right in and tell me all.'

'You know even if you were telling the truth, you couldn't stop me. I've been here before in a funny sort of way. I joined the Indian Army in 1941 in Lucknow after leaving school at the age of seventeen when other Anglo-Indian boys of my age were getting jobs on the railways. Eighteen months later I found myself attached to the British Army in Egypt hunting for mines, helping to win the war against Rommel. I had a close friendship with a fellow Punjabi soldier and together we took on the treacherous task of finding and diffusing the thousands of bombs and land mines that the Germans had cleverly lain down in the desert sand. So you see by twenty I was in one of the most dangerous jobs a young man could have chosen.

'One day towards the end of a long shift of mine clearing we came across an unusual device none of us had seen before. Most of the German mines were from the same factories in Germany and once discovered were easy to disarm. This contraption looked like a home made device and we had to try to understand how it had been put together before attempting to defuse the detonator.

'We were both getting very thirsty in the one hundred and ten degrees of heat and my canteen was empty so I stepped away to get it filled, when I suddenly heard this loud bang and Kuldeep was history.'

Joan held her hands to her face. '*Arey,* Ed, how terrible! Right there in front of you! How ever does one get over something so tragic?'

'Well that's the point of me telling you this story; if I seem a bit blasé about this blackmail it's because nothing can compare to that day. At first I just wanted to get back to work and continue in the memory of my dead companion, the war was still going on, remember. But gradually depression overcame me and I couldn't concentrate, or eat or sleep. The army doc said I was suffering from trauma and that I should be sent to Cairo for a period of convalescence. And that's where I found Latif, who was a belly dancer entertaining the army officers in the city. It is to her that I owe my recovery to sanity. It wasn't a sexual sort of thing.'

'It doesn't seem wholly platonic the way you describe her.'

'Oh, she was outrageously sexy with the way she could move her body. But I was just a boy and she was twice my age. I would go and see her at the end of an evening when she had finished her professional duties dancing for private events in the city. She would read me poetry by the great Omar Khayyam and I would sing her pop songs I had learned as a teenager. She loved me singing "When I'm Cleaning Windows", the George Formby song, and she would go hysterical when I made his funny face. I might have been the son she never had. Then she showed me how to smoke the hookah which got me hooked for life. It blotted out the images that haunted me. After a month with Latif I was back in action and then the war ended, thank God. I went back to Cairo but never found her again. Perhaps she married some wealthy client and is now living in a comfortable cottage in Kent.'

'I've never smoked a *hookah*, strictly a man's thing.'

'Nonsense, the women behind *purdah* in the Nawab's palaces of Northern India and Rajasthan all smoked the *hookah*. Can I introduce you to its wonders?'

'I'm really not sure.'

'Go on, if you want to help me unburden. It's something you have to do together. I'll light one up for myself and you can try it if you like.'

They had finished their beer and the bearer was now clearing away the glasses. Ed told him that he should light his *hookah* after which he was discharged for the rest of the day, and soon they were left on their own in the bungalow. Ed disappeared for his *hookah* and returned a few minutes later with the contraption. The sun was now setting, a golden red ball descending quickly below the brick walls of the garden. Storey sat back on a cane chair getting closer to Joan. Their bodies touched.

'You see the water in the glass bowl down here,' he pointed to the bottom of the hookah, 'it filters out all the nasties you get in pipes and cigarettes.' He sucked on the end of the long pipe and the water bubbled away. He then exhaled a plume of sweet, pleasant-smelling smoke. 'Now try yourself.'

Joan took in a small intake of the smoke from the *hookah*, coughed a little and then took another puff.

'*Hah,* not as bad as I thought.'

Over the next half an hour Ed told Joan more of his stories as a young sapper in Egypt while they took it in turns to draw on the *hookah* and the room began to fill with a herbal-smelling bluish smoke. It was dark outside and the crackling crickets had raised the call frequency of their evening mating ritual to a loud crescendo.

'I'm not sure if I'm helping you much Ed but I'm beginning to feel like I'm floating on a cloud. What was in that *hookah*?'

'Let's say that it's a herb that helps promote a sense of well being. That's what cured me, I believe, of my sadness and my fear. It's all natural healing. I just wanted you to experience something of my healing.'

'This feels wonderful Ed; I'm feeling so good,' said Joan, lying back and sinking into the soft sofa, swivelling her head around to loosen her muscles.

'Look if you've got a stiff neck from riding that *tonga*, let me massage your shoulders. I've got very good healing hands.'

'Something else you learned from Latif *hah*?' said Joan. The smoke she had inhaled had begun to make her less inhibited and she now wanted Ed to touch her. '*Accha,* let's see what you can do for me then, I want all the medicine you have doc.'

Storey closed the blinds to darken the room from the last of the late evening twilight, sat beside Joan on the sofa and began to give her a deep massage across the top of her shoulders. Joan instinctively murmured with pleasure. Unzipping the back of her dress, he ran the pressure of his thumbs right down to the small of her back. She mumbled into the cushion on the sofa, 'Ed, I've never had a massage as nice as this before.'

'I've only just started Joan. Why don't you turn over? You'll be like new when I finish with you.'

Feeling ever-more relaxed, she turned over and Ed began to massage her legs and thighs. She stretched out her arms and stroked his head, drawing it closer towards her, closing her eyes. The idea of throwing off all inhibitions and allowing desire to take its course seemed dangerously tempting.

But at that moment the black Bakelite phone in the living room intervened, its jangling ring piercing their cocoon.

'You'd better answer that Ed,' said Joan eventually, coming to terms with the futility of ignoring the call from the outside world.

He picked up the receiver and barked into the mouthpiece, 'Storey!'

His forehead furrowed into a frown.

'Something I have to tend to at the factory; won't be more that a quarter of an hour. Do make yourself at home and pour yourself another beer,' he said, his tone suddenly more abrupt.

Joan showered and dressed, combing out her hair as she went back into the living room where she sat on a sofa under a *punka* that blew lukewarm air over her face. Her head still felt heavy from whatever she had smoked in the *hookah* and there were traces of the herbal smell of smoke in the room where she sat. Had the phone not rung would she now be full of guilt? What did she feel she needed to know about Storey before she could be intimate with him?

A few minutes passed and Joan looked around the room to see if there were any telltale signs of Storey's past, possibly pictures of him with other women or close family. Instead all she could see were photos of groups of men with hunting rifles posing with their game at their feet and Storey somewhere in the picture. There was a picture of him looking fresh-faced with Blackfriars Bridge and Millbank in the background, but not much else to give Joan a clue as to his past life.

A peon came by to see if she was okay by herself in the gathering darkness. She asked him if he had a vase and a sharp knife and the man returned with both objects. Joan walked out into the garden where one of the gardeners was watering the plants in the remaining minutes of darkness. She attacked a small group of mauve dahlias with her knife taking long stalks of the freshest blooms she could find. The onset of summer had begun to affect the delicate plants and no matter how much the *mali* watered them, the unrelenting scorching heat of the sun had taken its toll on the flower beds. Only the youngest and most healthy survived. Minutes later she returned to the house with an armful of the flowers which she trimmed and arranged in the crystal glass vase, placing it in the centre of the mahogany dining table. She switched on the electric lamp which hung over the table and the mauve flowers instantly made a colourful statement set against the dark wooden interior and the framed faded sepia photographs of unsmiling people with dead animals. The peon, who had been fiddling with papers on Storey's desk, signalled his approval and said that the sahib would be delighted to see his flowers back in the house.

Having completed her short interlude in housewifery, Joan went back onto the veranda to wait for Ed. Her head was now throbbing with a dull pain, and she was slightly nauseous. The realisation that she had come close to being seduced with the help of some herbal drug was beginning to disturb her. Then the stillness of the evening was broken by the sharp piercing sound of someone yelling out in pain. The sound appeared to be coming from behind the factory wall. Each screech of anguish was preceded by a curse or abuse.

She asked the peon if he knew what was happening, but he shrugged and continued reorganising every scrap of paper on the desk. Joan decided to investigate the source of the commotion and walked towards the sound. Every shout made her flinch at the thought of the victim's pain.

The gate connecting the grounds of the bungalow to the factory premises was open and she walked in unnoticed to see a crowd of workers gathered around the source of the excruciating sound, as though they were watching a game of wrestling. Someone saw her and the crowd parted to allow her through.

In the centre of the circle of onlookers, someone was crouched on the ground and had been entirely stripped of his clothes and his head had been shaved: long clumps of what appeared to be his hair lay on the ground. One of the moustachioed policeman was hitting him with his *lathi*, on his back, the buttocks, wherever he could inflict the most pain and the fugitive yelped in agony at each strike, curling himself up into a foetal ball to minimise the impact of each blow.

With each stroke Joan felt as if a cattle prod was being stuck in her back. In an instinctive movement she rushed up to the policeman and shrieked at the top of her voice, grabbing his *lathi* at the same time.

'*Bus, bus*, you can't do this. This is illegal and wrong,' she shouted at the police sergeant, 'stop your men immediately.' The red-bereted policeman pulled back from the beating he was giving the person, who was now a bloody, dusty mass.

'*Memsahib* he is not saying who he is,' complained the police sergeant.

'Has it not occurred to you he may be frightened?' shouted Joan still with a fury in her voice. By the way the man groaned, Joan knew he was in extreme pain.

Suddenly Joan caught sight of Storey standing by with his arms folded as if he were supervising the beating.

'Ed, my God what are you doing?'

'My foreman has apprehended this intruder in the factory who has no right to be there and won't talk to the police. So we're trying to help him remember. God knows how our security failed but we need to get down to the bottom of this.'

'This is inhuman. *Nahi, nahi*.' She addressed the policeman in an effort to get between him and the victim. 'Ed, maybe he is desperate for a job, you know how much everybody wants to work here. He may have nothing to do with your damned blackmail. He may be deaf and dumb.'

'I don't think so. He looks too well fed to be desperate for a job.'

'Ed, take a look at him! Do you want this blood on your hands if he is innocent?'

'Joan, this might be distressing for you but the police know what they're doing and we have a full-blown emergency on our hands.'

'Now look you don't have to lecture me just because I'm a woman, you know. I've had a life too.'

Just then Mallothra arrived and signalled to the policeman doing the beating to step aside. He spoke to the curled up ball on the ground to answer his question but got no response. Police had received early training from their commanders that beating a suspect apprehended at the scene of the crime was the perfect opportunity for the police to extract a confession. The crime was still fresh in the mind of the guilty party and they were more likely to own up to their actions at the crime scene, than later after they had been apprehended. It was also a show of public strength that the law meant business and here were citizens seeing physical evidence that civic society was exacting its crude justice on wrongdoers. The police in their eyes improved their record of apprehending criminals when members of the public helped to catch them and Mallothra's hero Spillane would have definitely approved.

The fugitive had by now begun to bleed from the head and one of his eyes was swollen and closed. Naked, his body revealed a distinct lack of male genitals. Mallothra had him handcuffed and someone fetched a loincloth to cover his nakedness. He looked back at Joan with his one open eye; the other bruised shut.

'What will become of him now?' asked Joan. 'He could be just some innocent guy who happened to wander into the factory!'

'I don't think he is as innocent as that. Our *chowkidar* is highly vigilant and knows all the workers by sight and name. Singh, who deals with payroll, noticed that he was one pay-packet short when he doled out the weekly salaries. When he investigated, this chap was nowhere on the payroll and had fiddled his factory pass which was a forgery. I just wish I knew why he was there. Who would work for nothing? Mallothra, you'd better make sure you hold onto him in the *thana*.'

'Sir, I'm seeing a new development to your ransom issue now.'

'And that is?'

'The person you apprehended was one of the *hijiras* that live by the *chowk*. They are part of the low life of this city engaging in prostitution and extortion. Many of the biggest *Gundas* go to their brothel for sex and cheap whiskey. They have the idea that they are God's chosen people and I'm making them my number one suspects. It is possible the intruder you found was sent for reconnaissance purposes.'

'I thought these were illiterates.'

'Correct, but who knows times change *hah*?'

'Well, I hope you're right inspector. If you are, then we've nipped this blackmail in the bud.'

The police van drove away, Storey told his workers to disperse and Mathur began to close down the factory for the evening. Joan's disapproval of the beatings was evident by her silence as Ed accompanied her back to his bungalow.

'I think I'll go back to my place now Ed. I've got plenty to think about.'

'I'm sorry if you were distressed Joan but this is the harsh reality of the way justice is done.'

'Ed, there is never an excuse to behave like an animal. I thought you were such a nice sensitive, thoughtful person until just now. But you're really just like any other brute out there.'

'Please, Joan!'

'No Ed, how can I lie and be intimate with a man like you who condones harming innocent people? What if that was me? Your mother? Your father?'

'Look I can't change the system of justice around here.'

'Well maybe you should. We all need to play a part in standing up for what is right.'

'Okay, I'm sorry. Does that make you feel any better?'

'Ed, I don't want to feel any better or be placated. I want you to genuinely understand what you just did or condoned.'

'Okay, I won't let that happen again. Okay? You don't know the stress I've been under with the ransom thing. I lost my mind a little thinking that we may have caught the culprit. Now can we kiss and make up?'

He opened his arms and moved towards Joan who remained where she was and wrapped them around her and hugged her. 'Let me get the driver to take you back home.'

A visitation

When Joan returned to her bungalow that evening she found a note torn out from an exercise book weighted down by a stone. It was from Errol, written in neat handwriting, saying that he had taken three wickets and had been chosen for the next game. He hoped that she had had an enjoyable day out too. She'd never received a message in writing from her son and she held it to her breast with pride.

Later she slipped on the latch of her front door. It was not of the sturdiest construction and a child could have easily forced it open. But Joan had placed total trust in her safety with the night *chowkidar* and the reassurance he provided that someone was watching over her.

The *chowkidar* had come to check on her earlier with his kerosene lamp in one hand and a *lathi* in the other and a small following of pariah dogs from the school compound. He was an elderly man employed by Kellor and had worked at the school for many years. Like most other *chowkidars* he had two jobs, one by day and the other by night when he expected to get his rest while at work. Kellor had instituted a regime he picked up from the railway police, where sentries on duty had to blow a whistle every hour to signal that they were on guard and to ensure that they kept awake. However most of

79

these seasoned night watchmen had perfected the art of blowing their whistles in their sleep and thereby continued to get their much needed nightly slumber.

It was not that any of the residents in the school had ever experienced any acts of violence or serious crime and armed with a three-foot *lathi* and a lamp, he was unlikely to be a deterrent to anyone with serious intentions of robbery or harm. But his presence provided a symbolic reassurance to all who slept in the school compound.

Joan showered in cold water, dried and rubbed herself in talcum powder to relieve the heat of the humidity of the night, lay down on her springy bed, covering over her nakedness with a fine cotton sheet. The linen had been gently starched and its characteristic fragrance of freshly boiled rice reminded her of the hours the *dhobi* would have spent washing, starching, drying and ironing the sheets. Through one of the large open windows she had a view of the stars in the midnight sky, which brought tranquillity to what had been a disturbing day. The cruelty of the beating of the *hijira* and Storey seemingly complicit in the punishment kept haunting her as she tried to get off to sleep.

She heard a whistle blow and felt pleased that the watchman was still awake on duty and that she was in her bed looking forward to a good night's rest if only she could get comfortable. The incessant noise of the barking pariah dog outside annoyed her far less than the oppressive heat indoors. Pariah dogs were tolerated and even kept as pets by some of the servants because they acted as excellent intruder alarms, their warning bark at strangers being a first level of defence when trespassers encroached on their territory. They proliferated rapidly in the early spring with vast litters of pups only to be rounded up and poisoned to death in the winter by the railway colony's pest controllers.

The noise of the barking seemed to abate after a while and Joan heard the second of the watchman's whistles from the front gate, this one a short sharp blow probably because he was half asleep and could only manage a small puff of breath. Tiredness had overtaken her somehow and now she moved from side to side in an effort to settle comfortably. The breeze coming through the open window was warm. She began to perspire and decided to take off the sheet that covered her. Joan fell in and out of sleep for the next hour and it was sometime after she had counted her tenth shooting star that she fell into a deeper sleep.

It was an uncomfortable sleep. She dreamt of dancing *hijiras,* headless horsemen and the night watchman blowing his whistle, all in the same dream. Storey danced closer to her than before and she tried to move apart but his strong arms pulled her closer to him the more she resisted. She had finally pulled herself away by stepping on his toes and escaping into a room, which she had double locked. In her restless sleep she dreamt an intruder had forced himself into her room and she awoke with a startle at the sound of the latch being broken; her pulse pounded.

In a half-awake instinctive gesture she opened her eyes to pull up the sheet she had abandoned earlier and in the blurry gloom saw a very dark half-naked person with long matted hair, hands on hips, dressed in a *loonghi* loincloth, staring down at her from the bottom of her bed. She opened her mouth to shout the loudest, shrillest scream that she could manage but before she could, the person had held her down, clasped their hand over Joan's mouth and used their knees to pin down her legs and prevent her moving her lower body.

Joan's strength rapidly returned from her slumber and she forced every muscle in her body to move and wriggle free but she was held down firmly and her mouth clamped shut. She tried again with all the force she could gather together to get free but it was as if every muscle of her body had been frozen.

'*Sssh choop!*' the person commanded whispering into her left ear. They smelled strangely of sandalwood and not of sweat. The *chowkidar* whistled and the intruder, distracted, relaxed for a split second in which Joan's persistent efforts to free herself were briefly rewarded. She managed a half-sound that was quickly silenced.

'Do you want to talk about the blackmail at the Apna factory?' the stranger said and waited for a reaction from Joan. She half nodded.

'Well then. Keep quiet. These hands are strong enough to kill. I'm Lakshmi, the guru of *hijiras* and I'm stronger than most men.'

'*Nahi, nahi*, I don't want to have anything to do with your blackmail,' said Joan shaking her head.

'Just keep quiet and listen will you?'

'I can yell and have the *chowkidar* here in a second.'

'I wouldn't do that, for his sake and for yours. Now listen, your lover boy the *sahib* needs to release one of my sisters who is being held in the *thana*. If not we will get our revenge in a most unpleasant way. We've nothing to do with whatever is going on in that factory, you tell him.'

Just then the *chowkidar* called out, '*Memsahib*, is that you? Are you talking to someone? Are you alright?'

The *hijira* clasped her hand over Joan's mouth again but the watchman's lamp was now sweeping the dark. Lakshmi let go of Joan; she jumped off the bed wrapping the sheet around her and the *hijira* was gone, disappearing into the night.

The only noise now was Joan's heartbeat, throb after throb, accelerating by the second and she took deep breaths to calm herself. Like a slow dissolving scene in a film, frame by frame she felt herself emerge from a state of semiconsciousness into the awakening reality of the early morning. The latch on the door was still intact. A little tremble went through her and suddenly she felt cold.

'*Memsahib* was someone here a moment ago?' said a voice shining the torch through the window in Joan's face to see her dazed vacant look.

'There was this man, or woman, who said she was a *hijira*, standing just there,' is all she could get out. 'I was asking her what she wanted.'

The watchman blew his whistle loudly in rapid short bursts to raise the alarm. The shrill noise penetrated the still night and soon lights were coming on in the neighbouring dwellings and the second slumbering *chowkidar*, who had long since fallen asleep, came to enquire if he could help and was joined by Kellor and Matron who came to investigate the disturbance in their pyjamas and both wearing the most irate expressions.

'*Hijira sahib*...'

'I don't bloody bloody believe it! Here on my patch! *Chullo!*'

The bleary-eyed watchmen went looking for a *hijira* lurking in the grounds, thankful that Kellor led the way sweeping the solid darkness with his torch, its beam reaching out as far as the perimeter of the boundary which was surrounded by a ten-foot high wall. There was a strong possibility the intruder would still be in the grounds. The search proceeded in between the rows of cannas, the *chowkidar* using his *lathi* to prod the plants here and there, then in the plots heavily laden with marigolds and then finally in one of the empty outhouses. By the time they had combed every corner of the garden, the first hint of dawn began to clear the blackness and Kellor was able to carefully survey the grounds in the dim early morning light. He squinted to focus his eyes over the vegetation looking for the slightest sign of movement, the odd twitch of a stem, or anything not in keeping with the gentle swaying in the morning light breeze. He shook his head, finally concluding that wherever the *hijira* was, she was not in these grounds, and that it was time to call off the search.

'Can't find a thing Joan,' said Kellor, 'not even any tracks or signs of a break-in or any disturbance. Sure it wasn't a bad dream from a *vindaloo*?'

The noise had awoken the *khansamin* who lived in the servants' quarters and she was pouring steaming cups of tea to soothe and reassure all that the morning had arrived and that wherever the *hijira* might be, he was not hiding in the compound. Joan sipped her cup of sweetened Orange Pekoe.

'It was not my imagination, I swear to God. She was right there.'

'It's okay Joan we believe you. It's okay,' Matron kept saying. 'There have been a number of sightings of some very odd spirits and ghosts in these grounds.'

'I just couldn't see her face, it was dark, her matted hair fell on my face and she seemed to smell of sandalwood,' said Joan, attempting an identification of the man.

'A sandalwood-smelling *hijira?* What did they do Joan? What did she say?'

'I really can't remember, it took a while for me to recover and shout for help.'

'There was a *fakir*, *sahib*, who died after being run over by the express train at the level crossing. The *memsahib's* description sounds like him,' said the *chowkidar*. Hundreds of people died everyday on the railways either falling off trains, walking in front of them as they sped through a railway crossing or having fallen asleep on a section of the track that was being used for shunting carriages. The railway police had a few nights earlier recovered the body of a *fakir* from the crossing, presumed to have been run over in the night.

'This was not a ghost, I can assure you,' said Joan getting indignant and Kellor thought it wise to dismiss the *chowkidar* for the rest of the day who went off to find his dog.

The incident would have been put down to the sighting of a ghost in the school compound, had it not been for the discovery of the *chowkidar's* pariah dog. The dog lay stiff in the bed of long cannas; its mouth foaming, its eyes wide open. It seemed to have met its death that night without a whimper.

In fifteen minutes a couple of policemen had arrived at the bungalow and were scouring the gardens and deep foliage that could have concealed a dozen men bent on doing harm. Detective Inspector Mallothra was dressed in a crumpled black *kurta* and a *dhoti* and looked as though he may have come directly from his bed. His usually well-oiled flattened hair stuck up in the air in parts and his normally waxed moustache resembled a bottlebrush.

Kellor had got to know Mallothra as he had unsuccessfully tried several times to get his son admitted to the school. But the headmaster had turned him down on the basis that he considered the boy far too dim to keep up with the rest of his class. Mallothra continued to bear a small grudge against Kellor which he did a bad job of disguising.

He recognised Joan from the factory.

'More trouble with the *hijiras, hah*?'

'This one was the guru, she said. Are you still holding the one who was beaten?'

'No, not right now, some anonymous person gave bail in the night.'

As Mallothra's constable tied a rope around the dog's head and dragged the dead animal to the van, slinging it somewhere in the back, he turned to Kellor as he left.

'*Achha* we'll see what killed the dog but it looks like a common rat poison the exterminators use. The intruder may have evaded us this time but every interaction is an opportunity for us to piece together a little more evidence. The *hijiras* are making a consistent pattern of causing trouble.'

Joan stood in the shower for several minutes to wash off the lingering traces of sandalwood from her early morning visitor. That was no ghost. Was Lakshmi trying to clear her name or was she one of the criminal gang? What was the *hijira* doing at the factory? If the *hijiras* weren't the blackmailers, who were? And why pick her? Joan resolved to go and find Lakshmi in the *hijira* house.

The *chowk*

No one left the *chowk* bazaar empty-handed. In the noisy, busy, bustling Lucknow market you could find almost anything you needed and so much that you didn't know you needed. The brand spanking new pans sat side by side with dented, broken-handled utensils of dubious value. There seemed very little logic to the goods on sale. Bicycle chains, ammunition and car horns might all be tossed in together on one stall, whereas another might have several odd pairs of boots with shoelaces stuffed with boxes of tablets of unlabelled drugs, mixed in with used clothing and old acetate records. In this senseless accumulation of junk, people would come and pick and prod, ask the price and then move on.

The person looking to pick up a bargain must not make the mistake of showing even the slightest interest in an item. The haggling over prospective purchases was all part of the theatrical experience of the *chowk* which began with an expression of outright horror or disgust at the original asking price and culminating in some amicable arrangement. The place was a treasure trove for some, a place to beg or steal for others and somewhere to get rid of things that had been acquired by questionable means.

Alongside the bazaar were jewellery shops, crammed with

gold and silver gleaming under incandescent lights. Mothers of brides-to-be came here to choose the best they could afford, to pass on an inheritance so they would be remembered forever.

Some just came to sip tea or eat *chat* from the vendors that had set up their stalls by the smelly open drain that ran through the market. In the monsoon the bare earth floor became a treacherous place to walk as the cascading rain from shop awnings joined with water from the overstretched drain and spilled over into the market. But this did little to deter the persistent visitor to the *chowk* and merchants conducted their business unabated.

It was in the slums that bordered this market that Joan searched for the *hijira* that had come to visit her a few days earlier. Despite the discovery of the dog, no one had believed her story, and she knew that Kellor held the view that the so-called visitation was her sexual fantasy and the sooner they found her a man in her life, all would be well again.

Matron's servant woman, who kept the infirmary spotlessly clean, was at first perplexed as to why Joan might wish to wear one of her saris. Joan explained that she wanted to get used to wearing the garment so she could get a better bargain for goods when she visited the *chowk*. Dressing up as a *memsahib* commanded a premium when shopping. So the woman had helped her put it on. She was an irregular sari wearer and the woman servant had wrapped the several yards of plain cotton fabric around her waist and fixed it with a safety pin. Joan did not feel altogether comfortable in the garment and she moved with caution fearful that the garment might slip and fall. The sari, of simple white cotton with a brown striped edging, had been worn by the servant woman for years and, with a head covering, seemed to Joan the perfect disguise in which to enter the *chowk*.

Joan was putting herself at considerable risk making this trip. The *khansamin* had warned her not to venture out on her own to the market, unaccompanied. But a new energy had entered Joan and fear was the furthest from her concerns. Someone had intruded into the school compound in the middle of the night at some risk to bring her a message and Joan had to find out more. She also had to disprove Kellor's theory about ghosts and apparitions as well as the doubting Inspector Mallothra who continued to be fixated by his belief that the *hijiras* were behind all the trouble at the factory.

As soon as she stepped off the rickshaw at the edge of the *chowk*, she immediately became aware of how the servant's old sari transformed the way she felt and how people observed her, or more accurately, did not see her. The sense of having this newly acquired invisibility was like wearing a magical skin and it reminded her of her favourite story *The Invisible Man*. As a child she had always dreamed of being invisible and seeking justice for wrongdoings with the power of invisibility; starting a fight between two rogues by stealing their possessions or taking money from very rich people and giving it to the very poor.

Today's invisibility was different, for she could do none of those things, but yet, as she walked through the *chowk* without people even giving her a passing glance, she was just another woman running an errand for her rich employer or looking for a member of her family who happened to be scraping out a living in the market.

The heaving mass of people moved about in some unfathomable sense of chaotic order with yells of offers and counter offers being made by buyers and sellers at every stall or pitch.

There was a hoarding nailed to the wooden door of a shop that bore a photograph of the smiling Swami Naik extolling his virtues of Godliness and trust. The elections were several months away but the Swami's supporters reminded the shoppers and stall holders at the *chowk* that they would be very wise to vote for him. The Swami's promise of a better life included taking his people closer to God and ridding the city of the scourge of corruption. Another hoarding of his photograph had a garland of marigolds draped around it as though he had already achieved the distinction of some deity.

Then she passed through a roped section where everything on sale appeared to be new, many of the goods still wrapped in their original packaging. There was a pile of cardboard boxes containing Bush radios with the new innovation, a Magic Eye which allowed the listener to tune in accurately to a short wave radio station. She stopped for a quick look at the place where stacks of brand new Raleigh bicycles sat, still in their protective wrapping. One day she might come here to buy Errol a bicycle, when she had some disposable income.

There was a downpour and huge droplets of water pelted her as she ran for cover under an awning belonging to a sweet shop. But the shopkeeper shooed her away and told her to move along, swearing at her audacity in using his shelter. The ground had become slippery and Joan slid over the surface. She noticed other women had hitched their saris up between their legs to avoid soiling the lower half of their garments. The rain eased and she stopped to look around again.

She had been told that the *hijiras* lived at the far end of the bazaar and as she had reached the last two rows of stalls she began to wonder if she would find them. She daren't ask anyone, for her accent, her hair style and looks, would reveal her true identity as an impostor, or even worse, perhaps a police informer. She would risk being beaten or stoned if discovered, so Joan carried on walking, her head covered to obscure her identity.

Just when she was beginning to lose hope, she spotted a row of wooden dwellings at the end of the bazaar. Each was painted in the brightest hues of pink, mauve, and yellow, yelling out to passers by that something different and exciting resided within. There was a long-fronted two-storey house in the middle, washed in a bright lime green colour with an upper balcony, low banisters and small windows along it. Women in very bright saris leant out of each window, some reclining on cushions on the balcony. Some were old, others young and some didn't quite look like women at all. There must have been a couple of dozen there exhibiting themselves.

Men strolled in the street opposite the house looking at the women as though they were observing a tableau at a fair or a rare circus attraction. Some of the inhabitants of the house seemed to be having a conversation from the balcony with the men on the street. Joan maintained her slow walk, head covered, only just able to observe the people around her.

This was by far the busiest and most crowded brothel she had seen before. While in Calcutta most of the sex trade was conducted behind closed doors; here the women appeared to be conducting their negotiations out in the open, some acting as intermediaries for others. This was undoubtedly the *hijira* community she was looking for.

The wet ground was still treacherous to walk on and Joan watched her step as she trod carefully, negotiating the puddles in the floor. She missed the man with a push cart piled high with round aluminium cans that shone in the sunshine, as he came down the street, sliding and struggling to contain his heavy load which rose high above the ground. He tried to dig his heels into the ground to avoid the cart running away with itself down the slushy slopping street.

Joan didn't see him through her head covering, as she was more intent on looking at the women up on the balcony to see if she could spot Lakshmi. She lost her footing, slid into the cart puller, and broke his control of the heavy load. The aluminium cans began to cascade with the highest ones falling off first and bouncing down the street like noisy beach balls. Soon, over a dozen had followed a similar trajectory before the lightened load allowed the man to bring his cart under control.

All transactions between the women in the house and the men in the street stopped, as every eye focused on Joan and the cart puller with his cans now strewn all over the puddle area and some floating away in the open drain. Joan was too stunned at first to run, which in retrospect would have been the best thing she could have done. Instead she stopped to apologise to the man who was in no mood to be consoled, for not only would his entire day's earnings have been wiped out by the damage inflicted on his cans, but it was most unlikely that he would be allowed to use his cart again.

In his fury he reached out for Joan and pulled off her sari head covering, grabbing her by the throat as if to strangle her and exact his revenge. His shouting increased in intensity as did his rage and as the full effects of the financial ruin continued to sink in by the second. This servant woman would pay the full cost of his disaster with her life and damn the consequences.

Joan was herself in a state of shock having suddenly gone from a slow cautious walk undercover to being on the brink of strangulation. At first she was more concerned about her sari bottom being pulled away, knowing that its folds were only secured by a safety pin.

Then her instincts for survival kicked in and she swung her fist as hard as she could into the man's face and kicked him somewhere in the area of the groin, but the cart puller's hard and sinewy frame, obtained from years of hard toil, coped easily with Joan's punches as they bounced off him like a drum. A crowd of men, and what looked like women, was beginning to gather, but no one had as yet intervened. The intense pain of her windpipe increased from the constricting grip of her attacker. She felt her chest begin to burn with the lack of air in her lungs. The sky turned darker and finally black and then she was lifeless, being shaken like a rag doll.

A tall *hijira* ran out of the house. The cart puller didn't see the hefty punch land on his face and in shock he dropped Joan to the floor. Just as he was reeling from the first one he received a second to ram home the point that his time for histrionics was over.

The darkness persisted for a while and then Joan began to become aware of the smell of sandalwood and the hazy outline of a *hijira* leaning over her in a stuffy room, pouring cold water over her forehead. The *hijira* wore a woman's *choli* and a sari that had been folded between her legs. She had put a damp towel over Joan's forehead and was dripping a steady trickle of water into her mouth. Joan tried to swallow but her throat stung with raw pain.

Gradually she became more aware of her surroundings and realised she was now in the green wooden building, with the commotion still going on outside. She tried to talk but couldn't as the pain in her throat prevented her from doing so. The *hijira* gestured to her to keep quiet as she held a spoon with water to her mouth. She wore makeup, a thick heavy dark crimson lipstick clumsily applied to her lips. Only one earring hung from her left earlobe and her wig of henna-coloured hair had slipped to the right.

'You're lucky to be alive,' she said.

Joan was just able to lift up her head. It throbbed with pain caused by the temporary restriction of oxygen to the brain. The *fakir* put a cushion under her head and she felt more in control in that position. The room was strewn with other cushions and muscular, sari-clad *hijiras*, sitting around, fanning themselves. A couple of portly men were reclining amongst them, puffing out rings of blue cigarette smoke and drinking from a bottle of Johnnie Walker. One empty bottle lay on its side. The smell of sandalwood mixed with the smoke of Capstan cigarettes and whiskey filled the stuffy atmosphere.

'*Accha* so you found us, *haan?*'

'I couldn't stay away. You made me curious. Why me?'

'We had important information for your lover boy *sahib.*'

'You frightened me and killed that poor dog. Where am I?'

'This is my home, this is our community and you've me to thank for saving your life from that cart puller. Don't be fooled by these saris, we're as strong as *pahailwans.*'

'So you can be a man or woman if you please?'

'Yes, I was a full man out there when I punched the stupid fellow. Now I'm back to being a nice woman to bring you back to life. Bit like your Dr Jekyll and Mr Hyde *hah?* I saw the film. One person, two different characters. My destiny is to be a woman but I have a man's body. Here, we use our three sexual appearances to survive the challenging life we have been given and today we have saved your life.'

'We?' said Joan still finding it hard on her throat when she spoke.

'The *hijiras,* that's all of us here in this house.'

Joan looked around her to observe the other women in the room; some were tall and muscular with scarred faces and yet others small, refined and quite feminine. Lakshmi, the *fakir,* looked the tallest and the most masculine of them.

'Unfortunately most of this part of the *chowk* is owned by that Swami fellow and his *Gundas*. They are trying to throw us all out and seize control of this house. He says he wants to clean up the area but really it's to make him richer. His *Gundas* have tried to fire bomb and beat some of us up but he'd need an army to win. We're tough people. Remember it's the small mongoose that kills the cobra.'

'Lakshmi, it was you by my bedside?' asked Joan.

'Yes, we need to clear our name with that Storey *sahib* and we want you to convince him. One of my sisters came to work in the factory to make a few rupees to gain her freedom but all she got was a terrible beating and a buggering by one of the *behanchod* policemen.'

'Someone bailed her out.'

'Yes, I don't know who but she is still recovering from her injuries.'

'Mallothra says that you're behind the blackmail and the poisoning?'

'That Inspector son of a bitch just hates us like most of the religious bigots.'

'You're not exactly maidens of virtue,' Joan said, looking around her at the erotic imagery in the room; ample-breasted women in ranging states of nakedness in fond embrace with bare-chested warriors, many replicas from the temples of Khujarao.

'Maybe not, but I just saved your life.'

Joan held her throat; it was still very sore and it reminded her of how close she had come to dying. Just then there was a noise of more scuffles and shouting coming up the stairs. One of the *hijira* women shouted a warning '*Chullo, chullo!*' to Lakshmi and she slipped into one of the rooms in seconds. It was detective inspector Mallothra who came into the large room, followed by the cart puller and one of the *hijiras* who was ranting after him in her gruff loud voice, which the policeman ignored.

Joan was probably the last person he expected to see in the room.

'Mrs D'Silva?' is all he could manage initially as he stared at Joan sitting, half lying, on one of the cushions.

'Inspector! We meet again!'

'You've been causing quite a lot of *garbar* in this part of the world, I see.'

The cart puller with a swollen eye launched into another angry rant but sheltered his face behind the Inspector, knowing Lakshmi was in the room.

'I was nearly killed just now by that man behind you. Look at the marks here on my throat. A clear case of attempted murder,' she said struggling to get the words out despite the pain in her vocal chords.

Mallothra surveyed the room thoroughly, peering from just below his eyelids. He approached Joan to look at her more closely. His face was contorted in a show of distaste for what he saw around him. A room full of transvestites triggered the same emotions as the discovery of a macabre murder victim and he proceeded cautiously. The two male clients began to look uncomfortable and stood up to leave. They were ordered abruptly to stay where they were.

The detective's eyesight had begun to fail him in recent years so he had to get quite close to Joan and observe the marks on her throat.

'Did you do this?' he asked the cart puller who peeped out of his shelter somewhere behind the inspector's left shoulder.

'*Haan, Inspectorjee* but she destroyed half my load and this *hijira* punched me in the face,' he tried to explain.

'But you tried to kill her!'

'*Arey haan*, I was just teaching her a lesson *Inspectorjee*.'

'Do you know who you tried to kill? The sister of the *burra sahib* in Railway Colony.'

'*Arey Inspectorjee!* I didn't know. How could she be here walking around in a place like this?'

'Mrs D'Silva did you hit this man in the face?'

'Look Inspector, tell him I'll compensate him for the tins that were damaged if he comes to see me. How much does he want?' said Joan, who did not want the incident getting out of hand. The mention of fifty rupees turned a key in the cart puller's desperate mind. It was more than a month's wages. He immediately became silent and began to shake his head to one side in acceptance of the deal on offer, his attitude immediately changing to the subservient cart puller he had been before the incident with Joan.

'I have a jeep outside Mrs D'Silva,' said Mallothra. 'This is not a place where you should be staying too long. I feel if I stay here too long I shall find more criminality and have to embarrass your hosts. *Chullo*, let's go.'

Joan stood up for the first time since she had regained consciousness and wobbled a little. The inspector reached out to steady her but she declined to take his hand. Lakshmi came to her assistance and helped her down the stairs. Mallothra's driver seemed confused as to why his sergeant was about to give a ride to a woman out of a brothel, but nevertheless saluted and opened the door for him ignoring Joan. When Mallothra insisted that Joan sit in the front with the driver he was even more confused and sat up erect and alert as though he was about to be attacked.

A big crowd had gathered to see what a Police jeep was doing in the *bazaar* by the *hijiras* house, as if they might expect some important government minister, film star or *Gunda* figure to emerge. But when Joan came out with Mallothra they were disappointed and began to drift away. The driver beeped a number of times to clear the path ahead, and they drove inching their way through the crowded bazaar. Lakshmi gave Joan a little wave as they drove away.

'May I ask Mrs D'Silva, what were you doing visiting the *hijiras*?' asked Mallothra leaning over from the back seat to ensure Joan could hear him. 'You must have expected something bad to happen in a place like that.'

'I was actually looking for a present for my brother-in-law, Mr Shaw. He smokes a pipe from time to time and I wanted to find a black ebony one. The *chowk* seemed to be the only place in Lucknow to go and find one. I had to put on an old sari and not look too conspicuous. I didn't see where I was going with my head covered.'

'Yes I see. That is now clear to me,' said the detective inspector unconvincingly. 'These are very strange people these *hijiras*. They are not normal like you and me Mrs D'Silva. They were born with sexual defects you see and now they are always engaging in criminal activity, prostitution, extortion and things like that. The British outlawed them but we restored their rights soon after independence.'

'But *hijiras* are part of thousands of years of Hindu tradition are they not? Recognised as the third sex in sacred text isn't that so?'

'Yes, but what they do is so unnatural madam. My constable tells me that the Mother Guru of the house actually performs the sex change operations herself without anaesthetic and that they blow a bugle or horn to drown out the cries of pain. How barbaric and unnatural is that?'

'It's their own culture and tradition.'

'Sometimes old teaching has to be modified in the light of current day realities Mrs D'Silva.'

'But it's current day realities that you are trying to confront Inspector, aren't you? The realities of crime, the *Gundas* etc. You don't say that the current day reality of crime means that we must modify our ancient attitudes to stealing and taking one's life do you?'

Two cows sat sprawled on the road and the driver had to swerve to avoid them nearly going into the ditch by the side of the road, beeping as he went and the animals just sat there unperturbed chewing whatever they had eaten earlier. 'The cow is sacred in Hindu teaching, see Inspector. The current day reality of having roads doesn't make people move them on or eliminate them does it?'

'Yes our sacred cows, that's what's slowing down our progress Mrs D'Silva, too many sacred cows going unchallenged,' said Mallothra knowing that this was not an argument that he was going to win.

'Are you one of those who suspect that the *hijiras* are behind the blackmail of the Apna factory?'

'There are no other suspects Mrs D'Silva and you would be best advised to keep away from their snake pit of criminal deception.'

'That Lakshmi, the Guru of the household says she knows who is behind the blackmail.'

'I'm sure she does. Anything to put the blame on someone else.'

'Do you have any evidence, to prove your theory?'

'Not yet... But I will.'

Mallothra sat back in his *morah* on Storey's veranda later that evening sipping piping hot sweet *chai*. His slurps drowned out the familiar ebb and flow of the crickets' evening chorus. He was dressed in a black *kurta* with one leg crossed on the other knee, his foot oscillating in time to some imaginary rhythm going on in his head.

'Have a whiskey Inspector? It aids contemplation,' asked Storey.

'I have no vices Sir. As a policeman I have to be incorruptible and alcohol is not helping me achieve my goal.'

'Social drinking Mallothra, that's what the British taught us. You don't just drink to get drunk and do nasty things. It's okay to have a *chota* and put yourself in a convivial mood. Your hero Mickey Spillane couldn't think without bending an elbow with a bourbon.'

'Thanks but no Sir, it's better I stay this way. You see I have an uncomfortable idea to impart to you.'

'Oh?'

'You see, I'm increasingly coming to the opinion that the blackmailers are using the Workers' Revolutionary Movement as a screen to mask their true identity.'

'And your reasons?'

'Three reasons Sir. Firstly, terrorists don't send typewritten messages, they phone or use newspaper cuttings with circled words. Secondly, they are almost exclusively focusing on railways and government infrastructure. And thirdly sir...'

'Go on Inspector, let's have it.'

'This is very difficult but I think it is my job to be honest with you. You see I found Miss Joan in the *hijira* house today. I've been making more enquiries about her and find that she was intimately involved in an attempt in collusion with the Maoists to assassinate a judge in Calcutta.'

'Yes, she did tell me about it. But that was to save her son who they'd abducted and she didn't go through with it in the end.'

'*Hah, hah* but Sir, you see how convenient it would be for her to use them as a foil. That *hijira* we found in your factory and the way she defended him and then she is being your lady friend to get more information direct from your mind. What if she is in some pact with them? Here she arrives innocently from Calcutta just about the time you receive this ransom. Then she is making a bee line for your affection being a lonely bachelor as you are. I'm sorry to think loudly on this theory sir, I hope you don't mind.'

'No, no Inspector, speak you mind. I must say I haven't seen it that way.'

'Just be on your guard sir, that's all I can say.'

'I can see the Mickey Spillane in you Mallothra. That's exactly how he'd see a "devious dame", up to no good. Let's hope you're wrong but thanks for the tip off, I'll keep my eyes and my mind wide open.'

Storey downed his whiskey and asked his bearer to bring him another. Mallothra excused himself and left for home thoroughly pleased with himself for having got Joan's likely involvement in the blackmail off his chest. Now he hoped Storey would tread carefully in his dealings with her.

English class

The sight of *hijiras* on Joan's veranda the next morning, with the school's *chowkidar* demanding they leave, made her wince.

'It's okay, I'll deal with them,' she said and the man seemed relieved that he didn't have to face a string of curses that would have struck him down with a mysterious fever.

'So what is it you want now? You're making a habit of coming here.'

'We need some *buksheesh*.'

'Oh do you? Well I have nothing to give you. I'm a poor working woman, just like you. Who is this with you?'

'This is Pooja, my friend. We live together in the same house you visited.'

Pooja was little, her head mostly covered by her sari, unlike Lakshmi who stood tall, proud and uncovered, with the air of someone who would not take no for an answer.

'You'd better come into the house. I can't be seen with you; it will get me into a lot of trouble.'

They followed her into the front room, their ankles jingling as they went, and sat on the floor. Joan pulled up a cane chair and looked down on the pair.

'What can I do for you?'

'We would like to learn *Angrezee*.'

'But that's impossible. You don't even read or write Hindi. You've never been to school.'

'It's never held me back,' said Lakshmi, 'I'm just as good as all those good for nothing people in the *chowk* who shout and scream all day.'

'But why? I really don't understand why. And it would take years and I just don't have the time. I work all day here in the school.'

'It is the language of rich educated people, of foreign white people. We want to be respected by all those who think of us as dirt. That police inspector for example who thinks we are criminals.'

'But you're not children, you'll find studying hard and where will I teach you?'

'Right here. We'll come to you every week on the day your boys have the afternoon off for cricket.'

'So you've decided *hah*?'

'*Hah*! Don't you think its what you owe us for saving your life?'

Joan could have had them escorted off the premises by Mallothra in minutes but a sense of gratitude for having been rescued from the cart puller lingered at the back of her mind. The challenge of teaching a couple of uneducated *hijiras* how to speak English, helping to correct the cruelty of their lowly social position, also held a strange fascination for her.

So Joan decided to take on the arduous task of teaching the *hijiras* to develop a basic vocabulary, pass greetings and answer questions about themselves. She was astonished to find that within a couple of lessons they had not only begun to sing the entire alphabet but could hold a reasonable conversation of simple short sentences about themselves and enquire as to Joan's health and well being. Lakshmi had an astonishingly strong memory and had no trouble memorising words, even being able to replicate Joan's Anglo-Indian accent. Pooja was slower but followed in her friend's wake.

But Joan was speechless at Lakshmi's request after one lesson.

'Mrs D'Silva, you teach us to talk Shakespeare?'

'But that is impossible, you are miles away from that!'

'Who is this man that I hear about? Some say he was an *Angrezee hijira,* like us.'

'Shakespeare a *hijira?*'

'*Hah, hah.* A professor from Delhi came to our house last week for entertainment and I spoke to him in English and he was most impressed. He told us about the excellent speeches of Mr Shakespeare who is the number one *Angrezee* poet. He said that he made men dress up as women in his plays and that he was almost certainly one of us. So we would like to say some of Mr Shakespeare's words.'

The language of Shakespeare was not an obvious part of the syllabus for a lesson in English conversation with *hijiras* and most people for whom it was their native tongue would be unfamiliar with the bard's turn of phrase. Had it not been for a performance of *Hamlet* by a touring English company called Shakespeareana at The Martinere, Joan would have declined their request. But the play had been the first time she had seen Shakespeare performed in a theatre and the striking Englishman who had played Hamlet had left quite an impression on her.

'Well perhaps then the most famous of Shakespeare's opening lines is "To be or not to be". You can easily remember it and it is laden with meaning.'

'What does it mean?'

'Very simply, in this play the King is asking himself if it is better to live a hard life, or to die and risk the unknown after death.'

'Like me,' said Pooja, who never usually had much to say. 'We suffer a hard life now but God may give us a better life if we die.'

'Yes Pooja, but our life is not for anyone to take away, not even our own. That must be in the hands of God.'

'I like these words of Mr Shakespeare, "to be or not to be",' said Lakshmi repeating it over and over again.

Fear of love

Dear Mrs D'Silva,

I am writing on a matter of grave concern to us here in the parish of St Francis. We are aware that you have recently admitted your son, a Catholic, to The Martinere, a Church of England school. Perhaps you have done so out of ignorance or defiance of the rules by which Christ's representative here on earth, Pope John has demanded that we conduct our lives. Now to add insult to our Holy Mother the Church, you have taken up a teaching post at the self same school.

Just for the sake of clarity, let me point out that to send your son to a non-Catholic school is a sin in the eyes of God and one that is punishable by the severest penalty of excommunication.

If you are unable to withdraw your son from The Martinere before the end of this term then I will be forced to exclude you from our church forthwith. This is non-negotiable.

Your servant in Christ
Father Rosario
The Cathedral Church
Lucknow

Joan read the letter at breakfast and felt like someone had driven a skewer through her heart. Excommunication was the

world of pariahs and sinners and not one that she ever dreamt of being a part of. All she wanted was to get her son educated in the best school she could find and at the least cost to her given her desperate financial circumstances.

But unbeknownst to Joan, the rift between the Catholic St Francis school and the Protestant The Martinere went back a hundred and fifty years. Claude Martin, the rich French philanthropist and benefactor, had been the founder of The Martinere in the nineteenth century, and as a way of getting his revenge on the Catholic Church that had excommunicated him for his lavish lifestyle, he had bequeathed it to the Protestant denomination.

At the time of his death the full extent of his legacy became known and it riled the Church of St Francis that vast sums of money evaded them and had been left to The Martinere. For generations after, lawyers contested the will but the money remained safe in the hands of the trustees of the Protestant school. Now Joan had unwittingly stepped into an area infected with the bad blood of the past.

But the threatening letter was the last thing that would have made her change her mind. It had quite the reverse effect.

'I'm damned if I'm going to take my *beta* out of a good school because it upsets that Father Rosario,' she said to her sister-in-law Irene who was equally shocked by the tone of the letter and the ultimatum.

'We could go and talk to him and explain Joan,' she suggested.

'I'm sorry Irene but I'm not compromising my principles with that priest. You know I've always been suspicious of these Jesuits with their drinking and smoking habits and who knows what else, *hah*?'

Irene knew that she was not going to convince her sister-in-law to change her mind. Joan would take this attack as an all-out sign of warfare pitting the Church against her.

It may have been Father Rosario's ultimatum still annoying her like a wasp that had left its sting buried deep under her skin which made Joan pause outside the lime green and white Aum sign welcoming devotees to The Ashram of Universal Light. She slowed her bicycle and hesitated for a second, then turned down the track towards the Ashram. None of her family would have approved of experimenting with another religion but the priest's letter had made Joan deeply angry and the Swami had aroused her curiosity in more ways than one.

The Ashram lay a few hundred yards away from the busy road out of Lucknow, occupying an area of ten acres by the banks of the river Gomti. It was this crucible of tranquillity and reflection that attracted those who sought calmness and peace from the perceived chaos of the modern world. An assortment of brick bungalows were strewn amongst tall palm trees bending upwards to the blue sky overhead. Heavily laden with fruit, they symbolised the promise of what lay in heaven for the devotees who visited the ashram to pay homage to Swami Naik.

The site was dominated by a large hexagonal building with a coloured glass roof and a sphere at its apex. A large red banner hung from the entrance to this building with the words 'Fear is the absence of love'.

Joan was greeted by a shaven-headed white American man dressed in a cotton *kurta*.

'Morning sister, *namaste*,' he greeted her, 'welcome to the Ashram of Universal Light. Is this your first visit?'

'Well, I was actually just passing by and was curious to see what you do here. I'm new in the area you see.'

'Sister, your timing is perfect. The Swami himself is here in ten minutes to give his morning *darshan*, it would be an excellent opportunity to find out more about us.'

'Oh, I hadn't intended to stay, but,' she hesitated, 'okay I'll come for a little while.'

'Excellent. My name is Bahadur, which means brave. The Swami gave me my name because he said I was being really courageous to give up my life back home in Boston and come and live here to confront my fear.'

'My name is Joan. I'm not sure if I'd be happy about changing my name...'

'There was never any pressure Ma'am. There is never any pressure here with the Swami. The Swami's unique teaching combines the best of Western thought with the ancient excellence of the East. And now, just one small thing,' said Bahadur, 'could you fill out the questionnaire?'

The questionnaire was more a registration form and asked for a recommended donation of 20 rupees.

'The donation is purely voluntary sister,' said the American, and Joan dug into her purse for some money which she put into a box by the counter, whereupon the man put a garland of yellow marigolds around her neck.

'Welcome to our community of Universal Light and may you be at peace. Please follow the path to the hall of Universal Light and someone will show you to your place. *Darshan* begins in a short period.'

As Joan walked down the path towards the hall she gradually became aware of being drawn towards it as though she were swimming in a warm tide being pulled towards some sunny coral shore. She was happy to swim with the tide and allow her curiosity in the Swami to carry her along.

There were more people beginning to converge on the hall

and when she got to the entrance, a blonde woman with ice-blue eyes and a white sari gave her a *namaste*. She took Joan by the hand and led her to a space by the main dais on the painted concrete floor of the hall.

'I'm Jai and I will be your guide for this morning,' she said as they both sat down cross-legged on the cool stone floor. There were at least a couple of other women in the front row who, like Joan, wore garlands of marigolds, perhaps also visiting the Ashram for the first time.

Joan looked up and saw that the hexagonal roof structure was constructed of coloured glass in bright hues of turquoise, amber, blue and red. The bright morning sunlight created a colourful display of filtered light on the dais. The background hum of human activity slowly increased as people gathered in the hall, filling Joan with a sense of anticipation.

'Jai, do you live here?'

'Yes, I do. I'm honoured to be one of the Swami's inner circle.'

'Oh! And how long have you had this favoured position?'

'For at least a year now.'

'And what do you do?'

'Mainly I'm the Swami's personal assistant and devotee. I also help with fundraising.'

The hall had now filled and an electronic gong sounded from the speaker system. About halfway through the reverberating chimes, there was a collective sigh of adulation from the audience as a statuesque-looking man, around fifty years of age, walked through the crowd towards the dais touching people on the head. He had a goatee beard and flowing grey hair down past his shoulders. As he walked, the people around him touched his feet. He was accompanied by a short portly man whose head seemed to be joined to the rest of his body without a neck in between; a heavy scar from the back of his ear to his ample double chin left a telltale mark of some past injury. Finally on reaching the dais, the chiming stopped and the Swami took to the stage. Jai gave Joan a smile and a nod, which seemed to imply that they were in the company of someone quite special.

The coloured sunlight now created a luminescent halo around the Swami as he put his hands together in a greeting. The hum from the hall ceased to absolute silence and he spoke for the first time.

'Greetings and unconditional love to you all, my friends.' A frisson of exhilaration ran through the devotees. 'Today is another day packed with the goodness of life. See that beautiful light shine down on us from above.' He extended his hands to the source of coloured sunlight streaming down on the dais from above.

'Last night in my meditation, a beautiful maiden of God came to me and led me through an astral journey of the world today. A world where there is much negative energy. A world where we're living in hate of our fellow human beings. I saw black men hanging from trees in Alabama, women and children in the death camps of Siberia, peasants here in our land being firebombed by *Gundas* and greedy landlords. The maiden cried and I wept in her arms. And then when I looked into the eyes of the perpetrators of all these terrible misdeeds from the Klansmen to the Stalinists to the thuggish *bunyas*, I saw fear. Yes, fear in their eyes. These were people without love of anyone, including themselves. Friends, as we now know, fear is the absence of love.'

The audience began to recite the mantra with the Swami leading them, at first softly and then gradually intensifying until the words 'fear is the absence of love' reverberated around the hall.

After nearly five minutes of chanting he signalled for it to come to an end.

'Now,' he continued. 'I have vowed to spend the rest of my life getting these poor fearful people who do so much harm to their fellow countrymen, to themselves and even to this world, to see how love can transform their lives. *Kama* or love is the most important aim as conveyed in ancient Hindu teaching. Without love we are nothing. I hope that many of you in this hall this morning will devote your lives to joining me on this unstoppable journey.'

He looked around the hall into the eyes of the many devotees gathered around him. Jai-ice-blue-eyes, next to Joan, stared in wide-eyed adulation with her head slightly to one side; others had their mouths hanging open.

'But before I can ask you to join me in this mammoth crusade, you need to be sure that you have no fear and that all you can offer is unconditional love. Unleash the fear in you. So let's go on a meditational journey. Please close your eyes.'

He paused, and one hundred and fifty pairs of eyes closed shut.

'Let me take you to a wonderful garden where each fruit you see is ripe and juicy and right for the plucking. Feel each fruit with your hands and enjoy the sensuous shape of those ripe fruit, the fulsome mango, luscious and brimming with yellow nectar. Feel the bananas, sleek and firm in bunches hanging low, taste the bunches of grapes as they burst in your mouth with sweet juices.'

Jai was beginning to move her hands over her arms, caressing her body and rotating her head in a figure of eight motion. Many of the other devotees had begun to get into a trance enhanced by the sound of a sarangee played over the speaker system. Soon Joan too had tuned into a long swirling wavelength shared by the rest of the audience in the hall.

But in the garden in Joan's imagination, the garden was not full of luscious fruit but prickly cacti. The sharp spikes hurt her; she tried to clutch each one but the pain held her back. She continued to soldier on through the garden grasping at each plant and recoiling at the pain until the cacti gave way to thick tropical vegetation with screeching parrots high in the tall trees around her. Now she could hold these fruit which felt soft and velvety and she thought she might like to eat one or two. Deep in the greenery she saw a *fakir* trying to hide at the end of the garden. Joan beckoned to the *fakir* and he slowly moved towards her. She was not afraid of him anymore as she sunk deeper into the meditation. Slowly the *fakir* approached her and she put out her arms to welcome him, finally throwing them around him and kissing him deeply. She could feel the heat of his body permeate through hers; he had been perspiring, and his wet half-naked body was covered in droplets of sweat. For the first time since the loss of her husband she sensed an intense sexual arousal making her breathe more heavily; she quivered a little, her spine tingled and the weight of her body on the floor appeared to have suddenly left her.

Joan saw her dead husband sat on one of the trees looking down on her and he smiled, making her bite hard into the back of the man's neck. The people she had feared back in Calcutta who might do her harm were now leaving the forest garden and the *fakir* transformed into a likeness of Ed Storey.

Jai, her minder, sensing Joan's deep meditation put her arms around her and they both held on to each other in a close embrace until the sarangee music faded and Joan's breathing returned to normal. Minutes later Joan opened her eyes, her clothes now wet with perspiration, her face warm and her companion fanning it with the end of her sari.

Swami Naik, who had been sat with his eyes closed all through the meditation, arose.

'My dear friends, I felt many of you had a good meditation and have begun to let go of your fears and to bring kama back in your life. Some will be continuing their journey towards perfecting the sense of unconditional love, others may prefer to stay as they are. Meditation comes out of a Hindu practice, the most ancient religion of the earth. We have taken it and adapted it for our own use in this Ashram of Universal Light which is my gift to you.

'Today we were joined by some novitiates who conquered their fear by coming through those gates into the Ashram. That was their first step towards unconditional love. Could I ask them to stand up so you can greet them in the traditional way?'

Jai motioned to Joan that she should stand and she arose, still feeling light-headed after the experience in her dream garden. There were a few others in the hall wearing garlands of marigold and the people immediately in their vicinity surrounded them, giving them hugs and embraces. Soon Joan was in a close intimate embrace with people she had never seen before. She had never hugged strangers before and would have once considered the idea repulsive. Now it seemed quite pleasurable; men hugging each other and women holding on to other women.

'Please come and join us again here at the Ashram if you choose to continue. May love be with you my friends in all you do. *Namaste* and goodbye for now.'

With a flourish the Swami walked off the stage through the crowd who were now standing up, clapping him out to a standing ovation. The neckless man walked by his side. The Swami stopped at Joan, who was at the front with the garland of marigolds around her neck, looking more radiant than any of the other novitiates.

'I hope some of the universal light shone on you this morning. I see from the deep green aura around you that you had a good meditation,' he said, holding both her hands. Joan, still in a semi-altered state somewhere between the garden and the hall, could only respond with a nod and a smile. But the Swami's minder brusquely moved him on but not before the guru looked at Jai and said, 'Hope we meet again, *haan*?'

And he was off through the throng that continued to clap until he was out of sight.

'I think the Swami likes you and would like to see you again,' beamed Jai. 'What an accolade from him on your first visit! How do you feel?'

'I feel fantastic, definitely not what I was expecting. How long did you say you have been here, Jai?'

'Oh I came last summer and just stayed. Before that I was living with a man on a trailer park, but it was a bad scene. I borrowed a few hundred bucks from my mom and ran away, all the way to India.'

They were still sat on the floor in the Hall of Universal Light and people were drifting out gradually into the hot summer sun. They glided more than walked across the surface as if they were fixed to wheels being pulled along like a deity being taken off in procession for some *puja* by the river Ganges.

'How many are there like you Jai, people who live here as the Swami's disciples?'

'Oh I don't know, maybe a hundred. Some come and go. But I've pledged my life to the Swami. I'm in his inner circle with disciples like Bahadur and we run the novitiate programme. Gee, I couldn't think of anywhere else in the world I'd rather be.'

'So you've given your life to the Swami, like a nun?'

'Well yes in a way, but he gives me so much back in return. And don't most women give their lives away to their husbands and family.'

'Or to their employers like me.'

'To be treated like slaves.'

'And what do you get back?'

'You've just seen it Sister; love, being rid of fear. I could never go back to those days in the US of A. I'm from Montana, grew up on a two thousand acre ranch, but I couldn't stay there. I went to LA after graduation day to become a film star, but soon discovered that every other country girl was trying to do the same. There was nothing for me there.'

'We're all social beings, afraid of being alone,' said Joan. 'If the Swami helps there then he must be doing you good. But me I couldn't sit around all day just waiting for this guy to turn up and shower his charisma on me.'

'Oh no Sister, there's so much to do. Swami wants us all to join and support his sponsor, Sri Shivaji who has come from Gonda to live with us and who wants to stand for MLA and change things in this corrupt world and we are helping him in his campaign. Just imagine once Shivaji gets to the State Legislature, how good that would be for all of us?'

'Is that the portly looking guy by the Swami's side?'

'Yes.'

'Oh, I'm not sure I like the look of him.'

'He's not everyone's favourite, in fact his nickname is the Gonda *Gunda*. I think he did some bad things in the past but the Swami has given him his blessing now and only sees good in him.'

Joan was about to say that it was a very Christian thing to do but stopped herself.

'What do you do to help? As a foreigner?'

'We're his conduit to a bigger world. We help raise funds from people in America who want to make this world a better place; wealthy individuals and some corporations.'

The neckless man beckoned to Jai.

'Oh, I have to go and get on with my tasks. Please come back,' said Jai as she hugged her again and glided across the floor like the others, her sari flowing in the wake of her movement. The ease and grace with which she moved and the sense of harmony that exuded from the faces of the novitiates made Joan feel there was something special that the Swami invoked in these people. The rest of the world, including Father Rosario, would make the world a much better place if everybody took *darshan* from the Swami.

That evening she sat down for dinner with Gerry and Irene indoors where a large ceiling fan swished cooling air down on the table, its blades a white quivering blur. The *khansama* had made crumbed mutton chops, which was always a favourite with Gerry. The smell of the turmeric-infused meat accelerated Joan's hunger pangs for she had not eaten since breakfast.

'I went to the Ashram today,' she declared.

'Oh, whatever for, Joanie?' said Irene.

'To see the Swami.'

'That fraud! Now what would you want from him?' Gerry exclaimed. 'Mallothra tells me that the Police have a dossier of complaints and unsubstantiated crime reports about him.'

'Oh, people just want to run down men of peace, especially those who feel threatened by the love they bring us on this planet.'

'Do you know the money that badmash rakes in from those gullible Americans that come to live in the Ashram shaving their heads off and singing "Hari Krishna" around the Gunj? And where does it all go? Switzerland, I'm told. That's where he goes every year to count his money.'

'And where may I ask do the hundreds of rupees collected every Sunday from the parishioners go? To keep your overfed parish priest in his beer and cigars,' said Joan knowing that she would not be offending her brother-in-law who didn't have much time for the church.

'This is on a completely different scale. These American have lakhs to give away, selling their Californian homes and coming to live at the Ashram. That Swami takes everything from them.'

'They value Indian learning and teaching from thousands of years unlike the British who thought anything Indian was inferior. So much in the current understanding of science, from maths to astronomy originated in the great civilisations of the Indus valley. Look at Mohenjo-daro! Well before the moguls invaded. But the Europeans claimed they invented everything. The Swami is just taking Indian learning and interpreting it for westerners. There is nothing fraudulent about that.'

'But these orgies of sex and drug taking that go on. That is not Indian.'

'Modern civilisation has made sex bad, but go back to ancient times and see the erotic art and the teachings of the Kama Sutra. Sex was celebrated and to be enjoyed,' said Joan, beginning to liberally interpret the teachings of the swami. 'Making love rather than war is now being adopted as the anti-war slogan in the west, but Hindu teaching was advocating this thousands of years ago.'

'Joanie you're not advocating open promiscuity, are you? That's what animals do,' said Irene, looking shocked.

'No, I'm just putting another point of view.'

The mutton chops had arrived on a large platter and the bearer was serving up two pieces for each of the three diners. Joan cut through the mutton with her knife and exclaimed,' 'Good heavens, this is tender!' as she took the first bite of the yellow crust.

Gerry remained silent and ceased his tirade against the Swami as he got on with the serious business of consuming his favourite dish. Then mumbled, 'You must be pulling my leg! Gullible bloody yanks; more money than brains.'

Testing times

Just as Mallothra had predicted, a third communication arrived from the blackmailers. Typed in red ink on the same paper, it read:

We note your disregard of our last demand. Regretfully we will now take action. We have infiltrated your factory and will contaminate one of your batches with a lethal poison if you have not complied with our instructions by one week from today.

The WRM

Storey called Mallothra and Mathur, his deputy, to his office to plan their response.

'*Achha* now you see Sir, I have hit the hammer on the nail. The blackmailers are performing to textbook Mickey Spillane,' said the inspector sitting back in his chair sipping a cup of sweet *chai*. The tips of his black whiskers curled up over the rim of the cup as he gulped the hot cardamom flavoured beverage.

'Mathur, we need to take this seriously now,' said Storey. 'Begin a thorough review of all our full and part time employees. Find out more about who they are and where they came from, their references, family histories etc, etc. Get Security at the gate to step up random searches and ID checks. I don't want any unauthorised access. Also get our chief chemist to initiate more stringent assay procedures for all production batches. I want to see all our test reports. How up to date is our testing?'

'And what do we tell the managers and supervisors?' asked Mathur.

'Nothing,' cut in Mallothra. 'My advice is to avoid any unnecessary panic. It also restricts the information to the blackmailers if they have infiltrated the factory.'

'Very well then, it's just between us. But I do believe we should let our head office know and check that they agree with our action.'

'*Hah hah*, that's fine. In the meantime let's keep in touch in case you see anything suspicious.'

Mathur left with his orders. Mallothra lingered, rising slowly from his seat and stretching his body as if to direct a supercharged supply of oxygen to his brain to help him think more clearly. 'What's on your mind Inspector?'

'I'm wondering sir if you have any suspicions at this stage amongst the staff.'

'If it's Mathur you're implying then he is as clean as they come, a devout Hindu and a long term employee. The others I don't know. Remember more than fifty percent of the staff have been with us for less than a year.'

'Mr Storey, Spillane would suspect everyone at this stage. It's my job you know; I am always looking for motives. Mathur's daughter is getting married and he needs a lot of money. Could he be working for someone as a stooge? This blackmailer seems to know a lot about the factory.'

'Who else is on your list, Inspector?'

'Pardon me but I cannot rule out Madam at this stage, you know the school teacher or as Mr Spillane would say "the Dame", I believe.'

'Joan? And where is her motive?'

'She could be an agent of those Maoists, wouldn't they see this as clearing her debt with them? We know she double crossed them. Remember they don't forget. Suddenly she appears here in Lucknow and a few days later I hear she spent the night with you?'

'You're having her watched?'

'Be careful Mr Storey, is all I can say at this stage.'

The Apna factory had been extended and upgraded in the past year to take advantage of the latest technology in the manufacture of hydrogenated cooking fats in a joint venture with Indian and European owners. There were few multinationals with interests in India and the Congress government had been careful to ensure that foreign interests did not retake India through the back door, having just parted company with one set of foreign rulers. But the company was known to have deep pockets and to be keen to keep its business in good order. Their pay and conditions and employee relationships were exemplary and the Delhi Head Office would not have wanted this incident to leak out to the public in general for fear of spreading contagion of copycat demands in other parts of the country. Storey called his boss Mr Ramaswamy later that morning with the news.

'I'm sorry I didn't alert you on the last attempt but we were assuming it was a hoax, or so we were advised by the Police. Now they believe the incident is serious and I thought you should know sir and how we're dealing with it,' said Storey.

'Very well, but let me say from the start that we have a policy of nil tolerance on fraud or corruption,' said Ramaswamy. 'Any hint of yielding to these people will signal to every corrupt government official that they can tap us up for a bribe the next time we open a factory somewhere. In fact Storey, I wouldn't be surprised if the Maoist label is the real hoax and that someone somewhere isn't using them as a cover for their embezzlement.'

'I hadn't thought of that. But the WRM have been active. The police are taking it seriously.'

'Very amateur stuff Storey, trying to derail trains, attacks on rural police stations. We're dealing with sophistication here from the sound of things, so think broadly, look widely beyond the end of your nose. With a bit of luck the real blackmailers will reveal themselves enough for the Police to catch them. Keep me in touch.'

Mallothra asked for all of the recent production batches to be tested. There was no sign of any contamination in the batches of Apna collected from the last week's production. Mallothra stood with Storey and Mathur in the factory's assay laboratory, its distinctive odour of hydrochloric acid mixed with acetone, in amongst the flickering blue flames of the Bunsen burners and the sea of test tubes, flasks, Liebig Condensers, chromatographs and other paraphernalia.

'We've run every one of our test procedures three times on each batch and so far nothing's come up. I'm beginning to think this might be an elaborate hoax *Inspectorjee*,' said Mathur.

'The blackmailers are putting us in a typical state of confusion. They want us to be in a panic and be frightened. We need to either identify the poisoned batches or catch the criminals and so far we have done neither,' said the inspector, grimacing at the smell of his surroundings.

'It's much against my principles but I'm beginning to think that we may be forced to pay the ransom and use that as a trap to catch the blackmailers,' said Storey. 'I can't think of any other way.'

'Against company policy sir.'

'Mathur, when you have worked so hard to make a success of this operation it's just so hard to have some rigid corporate policy see all our lives destroyed.'

'There could be no guarantee that we catch the culprits Mr Storey, in those tunnels. I'd need an army of policemen.'

Outside, there were chants being made against the company. Storey had shut down all production and laid off the workers until his laboratory had completed the testing. The workers, displeased by the sudden suspension of their income without any reason being given, had taken to protest. Sri Shivaji, in a bid to gain political capital, had come to lend his support to the protesting workers.

'*Dekho*, hear those angry voices? How do we appease them? And now we have that *behanchod* Gonda fellow stirring up the masses. I wouldn't mind betting that he is one of the perpetrators of this sordid ransom,' Storey scowled. 'Mallothra, looks like we might need your policemen now to quell a riot rather than solve a crime of blackmail. Mathur, run one last series of tests before we give the all-clear and resume production. I will go out and speak to the workers without giving too much away.'

Storey went out to the factory gates to talk to the workers who stopped their chanting when they saw him approach. The Gonda *Gunda* himself, Sri Shivaji, stood by the front, clad in the pure white colours of the Mahatma. He appeared to have appointed himself as their spokesperson.

'Mr Storey, these people need their jobs back. You or the company have given them no reason as to why they have been locked out. I demand on their behalf that they be compensated or allowed to resume their work.'

'Look, I don't know who you are or how you come here to speak for my workers,' said Storey from behind his safe side of the gates. And then in Hindi he addressed the crowd over the head of Shivaji.

'I hope that in the next two to three days we can resume work. But now we have an emergency, that's all I can say. If we went back into production we would be risking your futures and the future of this plant forever. Please understand and trust me.'

As if to solicit extra support he put his hand on Mathur who had come to stand by his side.

'I, my deputy and the Head Office of this company are doing all we can to resolve the matter.'

'It is okay for you in your posh bungalow and your comfortable ways not to understand how these people can live without pay,' continued Shivaji.

'Don't you lecture me about my ways you swindling son of a *shaitan*. What about all that money you have embezzled? The people you have seen off. And now you hide in that Ashram, *hah?* Give some of that wealth from those foreigners to these people you claim to represent. Go on, go on. *Jao, jao!* Go fuck some foreigners.'

Storey turned away and spat on the ground. Mathur looked at the ground in embarrassment at his boss's outburst.

'Look out, Mr Storey. We've got our eye on you. Just hope I don't get elected.'

'God help us all, that's all I say.'

He and Mathur walked back to Mallothra who had decided to keep out of sight during the interchange.

'You know Mathur, I'll change my mind now. Tell Head Office that we're starting production tomorrow and that we've given the all-clear.'

Conflict at The Martinere

The Teachers' Common Room was thick with the blue smoke of Capstan Cigarettes as Joan entered for her morning tea break. She detested the smell of cigarettes. This was not a place of relaxation but provided an enclave free from the noise of boys craving her attention. It was where teachers could smoke or indulge in the latest tittle-tattle, but strangers to this group were not welcome and even Kellor entered with caution. Joan had not yet established any close friendships with her peers and her entry to the room did result in a momentary pause to the conversation when her 'hello' was returned with a cursory nod of a few heads in acknowledgement.

She could feel the group's suspicion of her and resentment of newcomers. Who was she to break in on this elite group of Anglo-Indians? Was her appointment a return for a favour? And, throwing in a bungalow and a place for her son! That seemed hugely extravagant even for the lecherous old Kellor.

'Joan, how was your trip to the *chowk*?' crowed one middle aged woman, hoarse from a combination of her forty-a-day habit and several years of yelling at her pupils.

'Oh! News travels.'

'Yes my *ayah* dear, you borrowed her sister's sari. She couldn't stop talking about it.'

'What was it like dressing up as a servant, dear? How brave!'

'I was trying to see if the sari would get me a bargain,' said Joan.

'Heard you had a bit of an accident,' said someone else. Clearly they knew a lot more than she had assumed.

'Yes, I'm afraid it all went a bit topsy turvy.'

'You were quite the talk at the servants' quarters dear; you, the *hijiras*, that inspector fellow with the handle bars. You'd better be careful, fat Kellor will be pulling you aside for a bit of a chat before you know. Maybe he has already.'

'I'm sorry, I didn't know that my whereabouts had sparked so much interest.'

'You're being a bit naïve now my dear. I don't know what they did where you came from but here we *AIs* like to keep a bit of self respect for the community.'

'Where I came from people were a lot more welcoming and neighbourly. I see a lot of stuck-up self-opinionated people in this room that could do with a breath of fresh air now and then,' said Joan rising, picking up her unmarked exercise books and the day's copy of the *Hindustan Times* and storming out into the bright morning sunshine.

She sat on a brick wall, out of sight of the main playground, and glanced at the newspaper. On page two there was a picture of Jackie Kennedy with a headline announcing the planned visit to India of the United States' First Lady. It reported that opposition groups had made it known that they would make every effort to disrupt the visit to embarrass the government. The paper noted the security risk to the First

Lady from militant groups like the Workers' Revolutionary Party.

The annual summer dance at The Martinere was always preceded by a hockey match on the *maidan* next door and the winning team were ensured free booze for the entire evening which created a considerable edge to the so called 'friendly' game. The team this year, as always, would be the Alambagh Railwaymen who were having problems getting up a full team of their own.

The 1928 Olympics had been a triumph for Indian hockey. The national team had won the gold medal thanks to eight of the eleven players who happened to be Anglo-Indians drawn from every corner of the country. The crucible of the sport was the railway colony where every young man was encouraged to join a team and do his best to uphold their sporting tradition.

Young men who succeeded at the game were the heartthrob of every young woman in the communities that inhabited the enclaves from Bombay and Madras in the south to the colonies of Lucknow, Allahabad and Kanpur in the north. It was said that the men who were good with their hockey sticks made incredible lovers, and so the myth ensured that that every virile young player was amply rewarded for his efforts on the field by the attentions of female fans when he was off it.

But now the dwindling numbers of Anglo-Indians made it harder to get a full side and when Ed Storey revealed that he had been a keen hockey player in his youth, continuing in the army, he could hardly refuse the captain's request to join the team. This was his first game with the Lucknow Veteran's eleven that played friendly games with other Railway sides in the vicinity of Lucknow.

The Principal of The Martinere, Dougie Kellor, was corralled into playing for the opposition. The Principal claimed to be still as good an attacker as he had been at twenty, and was pleased to be playing on the opposite side to Storey who he regarded as a bit of a snob. In the end both teams had to play with seven men.

The boys from the school had been enlisted to provide crowd participation and seeing their Principal with the opposition they were divided as to whether they should be supporting his side or the opposition. Principals are not generally the most popular beings with the pupils of any school and Kellor was not an exception here at The Martinere. For once the boys felt they could legitimately jeer at their head without fear of reprisals.

The two referees supervised the toss and the game was underway. At first things picked up a pace as the players charged about the ground kicking up clouds of dust from the parched surface that hadn't seen any rain for six months. But both the heat and the lack of youthful stamina soon slowed down the game to a more manageable pace and Storey was the first to score from 20 yards into the opposition half. The crowd erupted at the sight of first blood and Kellor sneered.

There followed another couple of goals until half time and Lucknow were 2:1 in the lead. Errol, accompanied by three other boys, brought on lemonade and plain water to cool down the drenched players and Errol nudged one of his colleagues to point out Kellor lying on the ground as if he was about to pass out.

'Come here boys,' he shouted. 'Give us a swig of that stuff.'

Errol hurried over with a glass of lemonade which the Principal downed in one gulp asking for a refill. The boy then spotted Storey, another lonesome figure sat on the grass wiping his brow. He went over with his jug of lemonade.

'Uncle, some lemonade?'

'Ah, I'd prefer some water. Got any water?'

Errol scurried away to get a jug and glass of water and returned triumphantly. Storey drank silently.

'Enjoyed the game Uncle,' he said to make conversation while Storey downed the glass.

'*Hah*, your mother here?'

'No, not at the moment, I don't think she likes hockey. But she might be here later.'

'Do you play?'

'Just a little. I like cricket really.'

'Oh cricket, that's a *chukkah's* game. Play hockey, a real man's game. Here let me have another glass.'

Storey emptied the contents of the glass over his head and then shook himself dry like a dog that had just been for a swim, showering Errol in the process.

'That feels better. Now let's see if we can knock the stuffing out of those Alambagh *chokras*.'

The referee was blowing his whistle for the second half to commence and minutes later the battle was back in full flow. The Alambagh Railwaymen got a lucky corner shot to deflect off one of the Lucknow players into their goal and equalised with just five minutes to go.

The pace intensified now for the final push to decide the winners and the players found a new lease of life buoyed by the promise of free *grog* for the winning side. It was Kellor who charged into the attack with a vengeance which made the boys laugh and cheer at the same time. Storey was determined to stop him in his path when he was just 10 yards from the goal, with at least ten other players following behind.

It was then that Storey pushed his stick in a feigned attempt to get possession but aimed directly for Kellor's feet which brought the hefty fifteen stoner down. With Kellor down, Storey was then able to shoot the ball into the opposition's goal. Neither referee had seen the foul. A whistle blew, declaring a goal in favour of the Veterans, and the crowd went berserk. 'Foul, foul, foul,' they shouted. Kellor protested directly to the referees as did the goalkeeper but the Veterans had already declared victory and were dancing something that resembled a Highland Fling in celebration. The Alambagh team refused to play the remaining three or four minutes. It was Kellor who had to call them to order and finish the game which ended with seven very unhappy players and an ecstatic Veterans side.

'Hey Errol, that chap Storey. You were talking to him, weren't you?'

'Do you know him? You were calling him Uncle.'

'Well sort of. My mum is kind of friends with him. He runs the Apna factory and has a posh car.'

'Oh your mum's a bit desperate then?'

'My dad says your mum's a bit of a *putaka*.'

'Look, can you stop talking about my mother.'

But Errol's protests just exacerbated the goading he received from his friends and he wished he hadn't been anywhere near Storey.

'Well done sir!' said one or two of the boys as Kellor walked past and he nodded but missed the giggling and sniggering behind him as he walked back to his quarters. Storey did not stay behind afterwards. His driver drove him back home after he had spoken to his fellow team members.

'Things at the factory I have to attend to, gentlemen,' he said excusing himself.

Summer dance

The two biggest social events in Lucknow's Anglo-Indian Institute calendar were the New Year's Eve fancy dress party and the Summer Dance. Both events were occasions for highly indulgent fun. Men and women, the young and the elderly, were all excused for stepping a little outside of the boundaries of good manners and behaviour.

Drink played a big part in the exuberance of the revellers and the dance floor was the main arena where they played out in public their fantasies to be another Chubby Checker or Fred Astaire. The rear gardens and veranda of the Institute provided more private and secluded spaces for passionate exuberance and many a relationship bloomed from an original liaison at the Summer Dance. And indeed many ended, often abruptly.

Joan had come to the dance in the hope that she might see Storey; it seemed a very long time since they had spoken. She didn't know if she had forgiven him for his approval of the *hijira* being beaten but she knew she wanted to see him.

No summer dance was ever contemplated without the consumption of 'Fowl Curry', a tradition that dated back to well before the inception of the Institute. Its preparation began the evening before, with the 'shoot' at the *jheel* where a group of men from the community would convene to bag enough birds to feed a couple of hundred people. That required shooting a lot of birds and the expedition was planned by Braithwaite, a longtime stalwart and recently appointed steward of the Cantonment club.

Game was always harder to cook than domestic chickens but was infinitely more tasty and Zafar Ali knew how to tenderise the meat by marinating it for a day in strong curds, especially good at breaking down the tough sinews of the flesh. He would then fry it in the garlic and fresh spices and boil the mixture for hours until the flesh fell away effortlessly from the bones.

The curry would be served with steaming dishes of *mutter pillau* with its distinctive aroma of *basmati* peppered with green peas and whole cloves. All this had to be ready promptly at eight o'clock, two hours after the revellers had arrived and settled down to their first whiskies and beers.

Joan had dressed especially for one man whom she hoped would be at the dance. Her sleeveless red blouse and black satin pencil skirt appeared to attract every male eye at the Institute as she sat at a table chaperoned by Gerry and Irene. Gerry said that she looked like Ava Gardner, the American actress who had starred in *Bhowani Junction* as Victoria, the independent-minded Anglo Indian woman.

The time had come to serve the fowl curry, and Ed was still nowhere to be seen.

'I'm sure you'll have a perfectly good time my dear,' said Irene. 'I see the young men can't keep their eyes off you.'

'It's their fathers I'm worried about,' laughed Joan.

At the sound of the dinner gong, a dozen bearers emerged from the kitchens holding aloft the steaming pea *pillau*. They came forward to each table doling out large spoonfuls of rice piled high on each plate like small white snowy mountains with spots of pea green showing through. Behind them came a second swathe of men in white tunics who dished out the dark red curry.

An Anglican padre stood up to say grace, heightening the anticipation of the first morsel, and then a couple of hundred pairs of forks and spoons clattered on the porcelain plates, conversation falling silent as the gorging began.

Appetites having been satiated, whiskies and beer began to flow freely again and Sonny Lobo's band could now be heard more clearly. The saxophone languorously wafted to the tune of the latest hit 'Besame Mucho' accompanied by Sasha, their singer, in a tinsel dress who was Sonny's star attraction.

'He isn't here is he?' said Irene in Joan's ear above the slightly abating din.

Joan looked around the room theatrically and said, 'Apparently not, but it's not going to spoil my fun.'

'That's my girl,' said Irene, a glass of whiskey, her first for the evening, in her hand. 'There's lots of fish in the sea my dear. No need to pine on a man who wants to be a recluse. Now how could he possibly resist someone as *hava hava* as you?'

Joan smiled in acknowledgement at her sister-in-law.

'The fish in this sea may all have had a little too much to drink too soon. But it's nice to be out anyway with family.'

'That's it my dear, we're always here for each other. Don't let any man get you down.'

Just then Kellor came up to their table and asked her to dance.

'Oh!' is all she said, not completely bowled over by the invitation. 'I'm not very good with this Latin stuff.'

'Come on, I'll show you. It's just an easy quick step,' and

he was soon leading her away to the floor where there was already quite a crowd shuffling their way through the song. Kellor was a passable dancer and Joan enjoyed being put through her paces like an athlete that has lain dormant for some time and has just discovered an appreciative trainer. There followed the Fox Trot and the Cha Cha and Joan was getting into her stride, remembering the days when she and her husband George used to go to dances every week. They were nicknamed Fred and Ginger. Sometimes they would travel as far afield as Kanpur, Bareilly, Agra and beyond to attend a dance.

But Kellor wasn't George and when they slowed down the pace to a very slow waltz and the singer whispered the words to 'I'll be loving you always', Joan stiffened as Kellor tried to pull her close to him. His breath smelled of cheap whiskey, his belly protruded well ahead of the rest of his body. Joan was dying for the song to end.

'I'm not very good with these slow numbers,' she said.

'You're doing fine to me. I just love the way you move Joan.'

He moved his body even closer and Joan felt a retch rise up from her stomach as she sensed his arousal. She just had to get out of his iron embrace.

'I really must go now Doug, you're beginning to hurt me.'

'Joan, I just want to tell you how lovely you look,' and Kellor burped before he could finish his sentence.

Just then she saw a man, with sweptback hair in a white shirt, tap Kellor on the shoulder in an attempt to cut himself in on the dance. It was Ed Storey. Joan thought she might be dreaming. He tapped Kellor again, who replied with a 'Bugger off, *jao*!'

Joan looked at Storey with pleading eyes over Kellor's

shoulder. The principal was tapped once more and this time he swung round and flung a right fist aimed at Storey's left jaw. The latter merely stepped out of the way and as Kellor lost his balance it didn't take much of a knock across the face to knock him over onto the ground where he crashed with a loud thud.

Lobo's band continued to play on as if nothing had happened. The bandleader maintained that music was the best peacemaker in times of strife on the dance floor and most couples carried on dancing despite the skirmish between the two men. Joan returned to the cover of her table.

Ed Storey looked with contempt at his opponent dazed on the floor and turned round to walk away. He had not moved more than a few steps when Kellor leapt up and in one complete move jumped on Storey's back to bring him down. The two then exchanged clumsy blows on the floor until the younger fitter Ed Storey pinned down the principal with his knees and left hand and pummelled him with his right fist.

A braying crowd had now gathered around. A couple of the Railwaymen from the Alambagh team were being held back by their colleagues from piling in. Gerry had been sitting at his table with Irene, happy to let the crowd of dancers indulge in their regular Saturday evening rowdy behaviour, but when he caught a glimpse through the crowd of Storey about to pulverise Kellor, he knew the damage that the ex-soldier could do.

'*Bus bus,* enough. Stop it immediately,' he shouted, running in to pull the men apart and stop the fracas. The combatants were both bloodied, groggy and gnashing their teeth.

Joan felt that it was time for her to leave the Institute in case there was a repetition of the skirmish once the two men had regained their strength.

'You'd better come back and stay with us tonight,' said Irene,' I'll never sleep knowing you're on your own in that bungalow.'

'I really will be fine Irene, believe me,' said Joan picking up her bag and heading for the exit. She heard a woman sat on one of the tables murmur to her friend 'bloody *chutney Mary*' as she passed. Joan turned round and glared at her as she left.

Joan found Storey sat on the steps of the Institute smoking a cigarette, waiting for his driver to pick him up. With his head hung low, Joan could barely resist the temptation of hugging him but she held back, suspecting that sympathy was the last thing he wanted.

'It was a wonderful thing you did back there Ed for me,' she said as she sat on the step next to him. She wanted to touch him.

Ed was silent for a few moments. He puffed out a deeply inhaled plume of smoke and looked around to the woman by his side.

'I lost it a bit in there. Should have knocked his headlights out real and proper.'

'Ed, I've never been rescued in that way ever before. I don't know what I would have done otherwise. He is my Principal and he was taking advantage of me. Perhaps I should have kicked him in the *goolies* to save you the embarrassment.'

'He's totally unprincipled that man,' said Ed. 'How you could work for him defies me!'

'When your livelihood and your child's future depend on it, you'll be surprised how much abuse a woman can put up with from a man.'

'You're right, I was forgetting,' he said and for the first time that evening he reached out to hold her hand giving Joan a little shiver. They looked at each other and then she could no longer resist the urge to hug him. They embraced silently for what seemed like forever.

When Ed's driver arrived he found them still locked in an embrace. He came round to open the car door.

'*Chullo*,' said Ed to his driver without even asking Joan if she wanted to go with him. They kept holding on to each other all the way back to Ed's place, running their hands over each other's faces and bodies.

They stayed in bed at Storey's bungalow the whole of Sunday morning, making love, telling each other stories of their life, eating, drinking and making more love.

'You have a rapacious appetite,' said Ed, halfway through the afternoon.

'I haven't eaten since last night.'

'I wasn't referring to food.'

'Ed, we've got lots of catching up to do. You aren't complaining are you?'

'Good God no,' said Ed, kissing her. 'I just can't keep my hands off you.'

'How are your bruises?' said Joan. Ed's swollen right eye looked worse in daylight.

'Oh it'll be fine. I bet Kellor will be nursing a few bruises this morning.'

'And a bad head. I'm wondering,' continued Joan, 'about my position at the school with the way things worked out last night. Everybody seems to blame the woman. I know it. I could see it in their eyes. As if it was my fault that two men ended up nearly killing themselves.'

'Oh Joan, you're strong enough not to let those narrow-minded people get you down. Why should you get the blame when it was that drunken principal who made a fool of himself? You're just getting to enjoy your teaching and that Mathur boy thinks you walk on water. And I'm here to look after you if that fellow ever tries his funny tricks with you again. Isn't that something to feel cheerful about?'

'Thank you,' Joan said, kissing him and wrapping her arms around him again.

The governors

'Big *garbar* at the Institute last night,' was the general gist of the conversations over breakfast and at church that morning. The padre at the Church of England's St John's preached a sermon calling for moderation in drinking, touching on the sin of gluttony and the need for peace and tolerance in the troubled times ahead. Often with clear references to the incident at the Institute, he pointed to those in positions of power and influence who needed to take a strong moral stand, not indulge in heathen ways of the law of the jungle.

Gerry had received a string of calls praising him for intervening when he did and stopping Kellor getting killed. He breakfasted with Irene while the calls kept coming in, some from people who were at the dance and many more from those who weren't.

'Just nosey people who want to know what went on,' said Gerry after the umpteenth call.

There were no rules of discipline covering staff in The Martinere handbook for the school's governance. So when Brian Braithwaite, the chairman of the governors, found it necessary the next morning to convene a meeting to agree what action must be taken against the behaviour of their principal, he drew on his experience of standing military orders governing court marshals and other such disciplinary hearings, not quite appropriate for use in civilian life.

Edna McFarlane, one of the governors, who had witnessed the Kellor and Storey altercation, called Braithwaite early on Sunday morning after the dance. She described it as 'A terrible smear on our reputation!' and demanded that he do something about it immediately. Gerry too had called Braithwaite and complained about the principal's behaviour which he would not have even expected from one of his trolley men let alone the head of India's most prestigious Anglo-Indian school.

Braithwaite dispatched his *chaprasi* with a handwritten note, which he copied out six times on his club's stationery.

Fellow governors,
I write in the most extraordinary circumstances. The Principal of our school has been alleged to have engaged in unsavoury drunken behaviour towards another respected member of our community. The incident took place in front of hundreds of people so we have to be seen to act quickly and decisively, lest the reputation of this school suffers irreparably.
I'm therefore calling an emergency meeting of governors today at 6.00pm at the Cantonment Club. Please indicate to the bearer of this letter whether you will be attending.
Sincerely yours,
Braithwaite

He was surprised when all six of the members of the governing board had informed the *chaprasi* that they would be there and had actually turned up at his club by six o'clock on Sunday. Most of the governors had already heard a version of events of the previous night.

The Cantonment Club meeting room's usual smell of

Termite Killer, used to suppress the wood ant population, was drowned out by the fragrance of Mrs McFarlane's 4711 Eau de Cologne. She was fond of literally washing herself in the stuff before leaving the house and, to the immense benefit of the other governors, relieved the chemical odour of the stuffy meeting room.

'Good morning,' boomed Braithwaite as he entered to greet his fellow governors, smiling at Edna McFarlane, for whom he had a 'soft spot'. She was the representative for the Association of Anglo-Indian schools and was a consummate school governor serving on several boards in the U.P.

'Hello Brian, terrible *tamasha* this, *hah*?' said a shiny-headed man of about Braithwaite's age. Sidney Carter had been in the Indian Army with him, in the medical corps and had walked with thousands of retreating inhabitants from Rangoon fleeing the invading Japanese army into India some fifteen years earlier. Braithwaite had brought him onto the board a year earlier to balance what he referred to as the need for some more *pucker sahibs* on the governing body.

'Yes well, let's reserve comments about it for the appropriate time Sid,' said Braithwaite. 'As I said in my note to you this morning, we have to decide on how we respond to the incident last night involving our principal. We cannot allow classes to begin tomorrow morning with teachers gossiping in corridors about their leader, nor can we tolerate parents wondering what our position is regarding the discipline of the staff we employ.'

'Hear, hear,' said Sidney Carter.

'There isn't time for a long drawn-out enquiry. We have Edna's account and we have a damaged reputation. Now let's go from there. Let us start with a factual report on the events of the evening,' requested Braithwaite.

'I'll give my version of what I saw, as I was the only one there,' said Edna McFarlane and Carter scowled at her. 'Kellor had been drinking since he arrived. Joan D'Silva was with her sister and brother-in-law until Kellor asked her for a dance. Everybody had one eye on them as Joan is a very attractive woman and single, so when Dougie picked her up, you can imagine how all the gossiping started immediately. Everyone saw how Kellor and Ed Storey nearly came to blows at the hockey match.

'She is obviously a good dancer but I could see from where I was that she was not comfortable with this older man clinging on to her. I mean who would be? Kellor is hardly the dashing blade a good-looking woman would deserve. It was about that time Storey arrived from nowhere and tried to cut in.'

'Have Storey and Mrs D'Silva been conducting an affair?' asked Braithwaite.

'That is the rumour yes, amongst the servants, I believe,' said Edna

'Quite a philanderer, that Storey,' said Carter.

'The next thing we saw was Kellor and Storey exchanging blows. When the latter walked away satisfied that he had dealt with Kellor, our principal rose up and jumped on him from behind with much shouting and encouragement from some Railway men from outstation. They were a drunken lot. I really think we've got to make an example here.'

'Would never have happened in my day, such behaviour! The lowest of the low!' said Braithwaite.

'Are we referring to the jousters or the goading men?' asked Carter. 'And of course, let's not forget Joan D'Silva, the teacher around whom all this is founded.'

'And what do you mean by that?' asked Edna McFarlane.

'Well, from what I understand she turned up looking like a bit of a *Chutney Mary* on a man hunt; so do we find it odd that two men end up fighting for her?'

'Nothing of the sort; I was there remember. Yes she did look an attractive woman out for a good evening, but then I wouldn't have expected her to have come to a dance dressed in the *dhobi's* dirty washing. How did I look, Sidney? I hope you men don't think I'm on a man hunt?'

There was nervous laughter but no one answered her directly.

'No come on you lot, tell me. Is the woman always to blame?'

'I don't think that's what Sidney was saying,' interrupted Braithwaite.

'So what were you saying, Sidney?'

'The problem with you women with a bit of power these days is that you think we men are big, bad, nasty *badmashes*.'

'The question is what are we going to do about our principal?' asked Braithwaite. 'We can't ignore the events of last night; we would be encouraging such behaviour with the students. If we punish Kellor too severely, without due consideration of the provocation, we will be doing our principal a disservice. There aren't many around to replace him.'

'So then we should ask both Kellor and D'Silva as members of our staff to give us their version of events,' said Edna McFarlane and with a flourish she pointed to the door. Braithwaite and Carter looked annoyed at Edna's audacity issuing instructions for people to give their own evidence, acting on her own authority, whilst the other members of the board looked like they were thankful that they could now make up their minds on first hand accounts.

Kellor, their principal, arrived looking every inch the part of the accused who was trying to show his best side. He had shaved, carefully groomed his hair, wore a crisp white shirt with the school tie and a blue blazer, which, despite the muggy evening, he chose to keep on throughout his interview. He relayed his version of events with all the innocence of a man just having a good time. Both Braithwaite and Carter nodded vigorously as he recounted his story.

'Were you drunk Mr Kellor?' McFarlane's questions were blunt. 'Did you throw the first punch?'

'I'd had a few, but nothing I couldn't handle. It was the annual dance after all,' answered the principal in a sober, confident tone. 'I was pushed by Mr Storey from behind and lost my balance. I know he wanted to dance with Mrs D'Silva but that behaviour got my pecker up and I swung out in an involuntary action.'

Kellor did a good job of recovering his position with the board and he was pleased with himself as he left the room. Joan took his seat a few minutes later. She knew how vulnerable she would be in her position, as the woman who came between two upstanding men of the community.

'Has there ever been a relationship between you and the principal?' asked Carter to start the interrogation.

'No, never. Look he is much older than me and I only agreed to dance with him, as he was so persistent. It's hard for a woman to refuse someone like Kellor with his position and all that.'

'What is your relationship with Mr Storey, Mrs D'Silva?' asked Carter.

'We've been seeing each other recently, but I don't believe that is a matter of any interest to this board. Is it?' said Joan, looking towards Edna McFarlane for some help.

'When Mr Storey tried to cut in, was he aggressive in any way towards the principal?' asked Edna.

'No, not that I'm aware of. As is the custom, Mr Storey stood near us for a while and touched my dancing partner a couple of times on the shoulder. But he was either too drunk to notice or just didn't want to let me go. I was of course dying for Mr Kellor to let me go as I'd had quite enough of him for the evening. And then he just swung round to hit Ed and missed.'

'Did you encourage Mr Kellor, Mrs D'Silva?' asked Braithwaite.

'Not at all. He was quite insistent that I dance with him and while I was fine doing the quick step and the showy stuff, I found the slow waltz with him quite painful. You know, it is the dance for people who wish to be intimate and Kellor was the last person I wanted to be with in that dance.'

'My dear,' said Edna McFarlane, leaning over to her,' what did you do next?'

'I withdrew quickly to my table with my sister and brother-in-law. What followed looked ugly with the crowd baying for blood. I know Ed could have killed Mr Kellor last night as he is much fitter. My brother-in-law probably saved the day. Now I think I have said enough and must go.'

With that Joan stood up and took her own leave of the governors before they could ask her any more questions and Braithwaite stood up to acknowledge her leaving the room, a mark of respect that had been drummed into him.

'Well, I really don't know where we go from here. We don't know yet if he was genuinely provoked,' said Braithwaite.

'*Accha*, I know Mr Storey,' said Dr Ram Tiwari, a new recruit to the Board and an old Martinere boy who had so far said nothing. 'We play cricket for the President's Eleven in

Gaziabad every year. He is one of the most competitive sportsmen I have met. He'll appeal every decision and doesn't like to lose. I can see how Mr Storey would not allow Mr Kellor to get away with a provocation.'

'We men lose our minds when the provocation of a woman is involved. You know the sex drive,' said Carter.

'I also heard from some of the hockey players that there was some foul play on the *maidan* yesterday by Mr Storey when he tripped up Kellor to score a goal, one which the referee allowed,' said Tiwari who followed every sports fixture with intense interest.

'That seems clear to me then that Storey was goading Kellor off the pitch,' said Carter, clearly on the Principal's side.

'The point I'm trying to make is that both men had set bad examples and it would be wrong to penalise one man at the expense of the other.'

'I think it's very simple Brian,' said Edna McFarlane, 'we tell Kellor he has to find another job and look for his replacement.'

'I don't agree,' said Carter. There is no evidence that our Principal did anything to deserve the sack. Yes, he may have overstepped the mark with taking on Mr Storey but really, what else do you think goes on at those Anglo-Indian dances?'

Both Carter and Braithwaite considered themselves far too superior to be associated with the Anglo-Indians that went to the Institute. They saw themselves in a dwindling class of their own, determined by privilege and bloodline. Both could trace their parents back to England and that was where they believed they would eventually end up. They dreamt of an idyllic country cottage in Dorset surrounded by red roses and yet neither had visited their homeland. Their dreams of their eventual resting place were based upon pictures illustrating the tops of chocolate boxes and tins of biscuits sent by relatives. They spoke in clipped English accents more reminiscent of the British army than the Indian one.

'We have to make a symbolic gesture that such behaviour is not condoned by the governors,' said Tiwari. 'This is eventually about the abuse of power and we need to draft some guidelines for staff to follow in future. A written warning to Mr Kellor about watching his drink in public is also necessary. I would like to draft these guidelines and I suggest you Mr Braithwaite, on behalf of the governors, send Kellor a written note before close of play today.'

'I second that,' said Edna McFarlane and later that week a memorandum went out to all members of staff with 'general guidelines on decorum'. Kellor kept well away from Joan and from the school for most of the following week until the incident began to fade from people's memories. Even the gossip circuit got tired of circulating the same story over and over again.

Birthday

The earliest hint of the end of darkness came well before first light, with the raspy crowing of the restless cockerel that punctuated the stillness of the black, moonless night. His shriek would soon begin a cascade of noise from the awakening school compound.

The calm of the early morning persisted a little longer and the cock continued in his obstinate role as community alarm clock. It was still dark, far too dark in the early morning, making Joan snuggle the tip of her nose deeper into her soft-feathered pillow. Then a few hens decided their night of repose must be at an end and began to busy themselves with a clucking which gave way to further stirrings of human activity in the servants' quarters, making way to a cacophony of gargling, coughing and splashing, filling the air as humans went about their morning ablutions.

Now the early glow of the rising sun was streaming through the slats of her shuttered windows and Joan became more aware of her surroundings as blood began to pulse faster through her body and her eyes opened. She remembered her dream.

Even now in the reassuring light of day it made her shiver a little at the reoccurrence of her dream of seeing people suffering from being poisoned at a feast. They were dying and she was trying to resuscitate them with Storey's help. She put her hands to her face and they felt like ice. If this recurring dream foretold real events then she had to get to Storey immediately and tell him.

There was a knock on her bedroom door and in walked her son Errol.

'*Palung* k*a cha memsahib!* Happy birthday to you...' he sang smiling and offered Joan her best treat, a morning cup of tea in bed. Tea, which he had made by boiling the best Orange Pekoe in cardamom and ginger with a little condensed milk.

'Oh that's nice of you,' she said sitting up and reaching for his hand. 'Come and let me give you a hug for being so nice to me.'

'It's *holi*, I've got *chutti* today so we can do something for your birthday, *hah*?'

'Yes, yes, *Beta*. Ed is coming around later this morning and we can go out in the car and have a lot of fun. You could sit in the front with the driver and he'll show you how those gears work.'

Errol's expression dulled from a face reflecting the sunshine in his eyes to a look of dark, cloudy gloom.

'What's wrong darling? Wouldn't you like to come with us?'

'Ma, do you like Ed Storey?'

'Darling, well yes, he is a very good friend and has been very good for me ever since we came to Lucknow. You know how lonely it can be for your mum with you now as a boarder. Don't you like him?'

'Mm, not since I saw him cheat at the hockey game. He tripped Mr Kellor over and the ref didn't see his foul and then he scored the goal. They won by cheating.'

'Errol, you know the heat of a game. We forget sometimes and get carried away.'

'So is cheating alright sometimes, Ma?'

'No darling, but this was different, in the heat of a game sometimes we do irrational things.'

'Ma is it true he bopped the Principal?'

'Well it was a sort of scuffle, yes. Anyway if all these questions are worrying you about Ed and I then don't worry *beta*, you'll always be my greatest love. You know I think the world of you and I'll never do anything to make you unhappy.'

Joan sipped her tea. The first cup of the day was always the most welcome and Errol had made this one strong, allowing the tealeaves to infuse for quite a while before pouring and straining it. The looks of anguish on the faces of people in her dream came flooding back again. The muscles on her back tightened and she felt the dull ache of fear in her stomach. She hoped Storey would not be late.

Ed's car was there on the dot of twelve o'clock, just as he'd promised. The perspiring, black-capped chauffeur in his intensely white starched uniform complete with blancoed belt, shoes and gloves, smiled at Errol, who waved back, now quite excited at the prospect of an outing in such a posh car.

Joan had spent an hour deliberating on what she might wear having tried on her entire meagre wardrobe. In the end, she settled on a pure white cotton blouse with a shiny chilli-red belt.

'*Salaam* driver, *chullo,*' she said to the man as she slid into the back of the Ambassador car which was upholstered in old crackled brown leather giving the car a wonderful ageing smell which reminded Joan of Doctor Choudhury's bag.

'Is the *chotasahib* coming too?' asked the driver as Errol got into the front seat.

'You can help me drive,' he said mischievously, flashing another smile. With all the windows wound down, the movement of the vehicle began to blow air through it, providing cool comfort as they navigated through the stream of rickshaws, potholes and marauding cows. The only thing that marred her enjoyment was her troubling dream, like an indigestible meal it keep recurring, causing her the utmost discomfort.

'Joan!' said Ed coming out to greet her as they stepped out of the car. 'Happy birthday!' He kissed her on the lips and her red lipstick left its mark on his face. She laughed.

'You look gorgeous my dear, and those lips are far too tempting. I don't mind a bit of your lipstick one bit,' he said attempting to wipe his mouth. The chauffeur pretended to look away and Errol fidgeted with the car door handle, looking down at the ground to avoid embarrassment.

'Oh I hope you don't mind I brought my Errol along. He has *chutti* today.'

'Good morning young man, come and look at this cake.'

He led them to the veranda. There on a round cast iron table lay a large sponge cake with pink icing, a solitary candle and the words *Happy Birthday Joan* inscribed in white.

'What a lovely thought and such a beautiful cake.'

'I'm sure you deserve it. *Khansama* wanted to put your age on it but I didn't think ladies like to make things like that public.'

'Oh not at all, I'm thirty three today, and very proud of it.'

'Well there's a sort of neat symmetry to those numbers. Now make a big wish Joan before you blow out the candle.'

Joan asked Errol to join her and she held his hand.

'Why don't we all blow it out together then all our wishes can come true?'

They held hands and puffed up their cheeks to blow out the flickering flame.

'Make a wish,' instructed Joan and the candle's yellow light immediately succumbed to the puffs of air. A thin wisp of white smoke rose into the air.

Ed cut three slices from the cake. He put the smallest one on a napkin for Errol, a slightly larger one on a plate for Joan and picked up the largest one for himself, eating it with his fingers and catching the crumbs in the palm of his other hand. Errol had devoured his tiny slice before Joan sank her teeth into the layer of icing. She made a muffled sound of delight, her mouth stuffed full. Errol was not amused that he had been short-changed.

'Here *beta* have a bit of mine,' said Joan.

'No, there's plenty more here for a growing boy,' said Storey cutting Errol another thin slice. 'Better to have two helpings *hah*, than find out your eyes are bigger than your stomach.'

Errol's eyes widened as he stared at the fresh slice of cake, took it in both hands and wandered off to talk to the chauffeur about some aspect of the Ambassador's engineering of which the man had no idea but made up a good story to keep the boy engaged.

'Ed, I've got something on my mind.'

'If it's about the other night then I apologise unreservedly.'

'No, Ed it's quite serious.'

'That we regret our night of passion?'

'It was my dream last night. It was so realistic, like I'm talking to you now. People were dying from poisoned food at a feast. I swear it was so horribly real and almost a carbon copy of the first one.'

'Now look Joan, this stuff about ransoms should not be worrying you. We can sort these blighters out.'

'Ed, you don't understand, I've only had two other dreams like that in my life. And they both came true.'

'Joan I've read all about dreams from that fellow, Dr Freud. Those dreams are from your unconscious; they can't tell you anything about the real world.'

He clasped her right knee and moved his hands around them looking into her eyes, 'You look more delicious than that cake right now, believe me.'

'Ed really, I wish you'd take this more seriously.'

Just then Errol shouted out, 'Ma, are we going anywhere now?'

Joan noticed that the monochrome chauffeur was still stood awkwardly by the car in his gleaming white outfit, while they sat finishing their cake. 'Ed, are we?' she said.

'*Haan haan*,' he stood up and held out his hand for her to grasp as he pulled her up. 'We're going to have a bit of a surprise and Errol we're going to drop you at Mathur's house to play for a few hours with Vijay. He will be celebrating *holi* and I'm sure you'll enjoy the fun of throwing around those disgusting colours.'

'But can't Errol come with us?'

'I'm confident he'll be bored with our adult company. I know I'd have been when I was his age.'

Young Ashok Mathur was in fact pleased to see Errol with whom he could celebrate the festival of *holi*. Errol had never partaken in the delight of shooting coloured water at people and drenching them in colours of every hue and Joan was relieved that he would soon forgive her for being excluded from her outing with Storey.

The *chowk* was busy as usual with people taking advantage of the national holiday. Joan was cautious of her white dress which might attract an over zealous celebrant, but with Storey by her side she felt safer now than when she last wandered around the area. The shopkeepers were offering coloured powder to their customers in a more sedate form of greeting and every one there seemed to be in a good mood.

Ed attracted a number of *salaam sahib* greetings from the vendors in the market as they all knew that the managing director of the Apna factory was an important man. It was not unusual in these situations for him to be asked to consider giving a job to the brother or uncle of someone or the other as a favour. People like him were like fountains of hope from which flowed endless optimism to place a relative or *bhai* in a job.

A job in the Apna factory was a prized achievement and those who worked there were themselves looked on as being quite special people. A prospective bridegroom might be introduced as 'Mohan whose father is a respected employee of the Apna factory'. Even those that knew someone who worked at the Apna factory bathed a little in their glory and spoke of the glorious working conditions and how you could eat off the floor if you wanted to, as it was so shiny and clean.

It was when they stopped by a shop displaying gold and silver ornaments that Joan knew Storey had something more in mind than a gentle walk.

'Joan, I've seen something here that I'd like you to wear for me,' he said leading her into the shop. The owner seemed very pleased to see Storey and immediately began instructing his staff to bring teas and *samosas* for them. He began to pull out a tray of bracelets in stunningly dazzling silver and gold.

'I'd like to buy you a little birthday present,' he said talking softly into her ear.

'But Ed...'

'No buts, now let's see what we have here.'

Despite Joan's protestations and with the shopkeeper's constant interventions as to how nice each bracelet looked she was encouraged to try on a dozen of these ornaments. 'Now which one do you like?'

'Really Ed they're all very nice but I couldn't accept such generosity, really.'

'Now you're beginning to offend me. Please choose one.'

Reluctantly Joan picked out a modest silver bracelet, which she said she preferred to the sumptuous 24-carat gold offerings. She put it on and smiled with the pleasure of an excited adolescent. The shopkeeper found a camera and took a picture of her. He told Storey that he thought Joan was the most beautiful woman who had come into his shop for many years. She was still in a daze when they walked out holding Ed's hand.

'That was one of the nicest birthday presents I've ever been given.'

'Now what about a little *khanna* at the *chowk*?' said Ed.

'The street food for Nawabs?'

'And a feast for us poor,' replied Ed. 'Here, this is the best *chat wallah* in the *chowk*.' Ed stopped by an unshaven man with a filthy *pugree* and a torn singlet which had once been white. He sat cross-legged on a raised platform surrounded by a dozen stainless steel bowls. A couple of hungry-looking young men stood by the platform waiting for the man to mix up portions of the contents of the bowls into something that would transport them for a few minutes into a vortex of culinary ecstasy.

'You know what they say? The dirtier the stall holder, the tastier his food.'

'Tell him not to add too many chillies,' said Joan to

whatever Ed was about to order. 'These *chat wallahs'* idea of taste is to blow your head off with those green chillies.'

'The man took their order and began to work his way around the bowls adding a hand full of this and a pinch of that to two flat banana leaves on a mat. Gradually, the small pile of green coriander, chopped onions, puffed rice, crispy *pooris* and sliced potatoes grew to a respectable size and he sprinkled tamarind sauce and the *chat wallah's* own secret ingredient which always made his customers come back for more.

Joan and Ed picked up the banana leaves and began to scoop up the *chat*, tearing off a section of the banana leaf and using it as a spoon. It immediately attacked every tiny taste bud on her tongue, the spices, the flavours of the tamarind, the man's secret ingredient and of course the chillies. Every mouthful she took, the sensation became more intense, but soon the chillies were overpowering and every further delicious morsel she took, the pain of burning intensified until she could have no more. With her mouth on fire she asked for some sweet curds to put out the flames that had engulfed her tongue and brought a flood of tears streaming from her eyes. Ed laughed as he calmly finished off his banana skin and helped himself to the rest of Joan's uneaten portion.

She was still drying her eyes with her handkerchief when they heard the sound of jangling bells and singing. The *chat wallah* seemed oblivious to the approaching disturbance and soon it became clear that the noise was being made by two *hijiras* who were celebrating the festival of *holi* dancing through the *chowk* encouraging the stallholders and their customers to part with a few *annas*. Those that ignored them got doused with colour from a powerful water syringe whether they liked it or not.

Most of the men thought the *hijiras*, dressed up in their colourful saris and heavily made-up faces, were just a bit of fun but Joan could see Ed tense at the sight of them and perhaps the *hijiras* noticed his discomfort. They had soon encircled him and that was when Joan noticed it was none other than Lakshmi who was making sexually provocative gestures with her hips and her tongue very close to Ed. Her friend Pooja kept up the vigorous noisy dance that involved a lot of tambourine bashing, more sexual gestures and singing.

They sang of what a good-looking man he was and that Joan, his mistress, was the luckiest woman in the world. Joan encouraged them by clapping in time with the dancing. Then Lakshmi who had her head covered, held out her henna decorated hand asking for 'God's blessing.' Ed fumbled in his pockets but found that he had given all his change to the *chat wallah*. She kept her hand outstretched and Ed was beginning to look helpless.

For a very brief moment the sari covering Lakshmi's head fell to one side and Joan was staring at her giving her a look which pleaded discretion but the *hijiras* continued with their demand for money.

They were now getting angry with Ed for not producing any coins, having expended a good deal of effort in praising their rich benefactor. When nothing was forthcoming a few insults and curses began to flow; Ed's sex life would be damned, disaster would strike his business and his mistress would leave him for good.

At about this time they heard a loudspeaker declaiming something in Hindi. The calls for whatever it was became louder and soon Joan noticed a procession of around a couple of dozen people, all dressed in clean white *kurtas* with banners held high proclaiming the words 'Clean up *chowk*'.

At the end of the procession was none other than the Gonda *Gunda* with a megaphone stuck to his mouth and Jai-ice-blue-eyes strolling beside him holding up a card with the words 'Prostitution is anti-woman'.

The two *hijiras*, who were vastly outnumbered by the noisy protestors, disengaged from their humiliation of Ed Storey and turned to face their detractors. Lakshmi paled slightly as she caught sight of the Gonda *Gunda* and the ugly scar she had inflicted back in Calcutta, but he showed no sign of recognising her. The *Gunda* and Jai raged against the small group of dancers.

'Down with evil. Close the *chowk* brothel. Children of the devil.'

The *Gunda* was the first to break out of the group together with an accomplice bigger than him and began to manhandle the women, pushing them around and swearing all the time. They scratched, spat and swore in return. Even little Pooja who had her head covered kicked out at the neckless leader at chin height and knocked him over cursing and calling out to him 'Don't fuck with us Gonda *ke Goonda*.'

'Sirrah be gone you sons of whores,' yelled Lakshmi in the only Shakespearean insult she had learnt.

Lakshmi threw *holi* colours at his followers and Puja sprayed red water at them with her water gun rendering their white garments purple and red.

The protestors retreated a few feet in momentary recoil at the ferocity of the attack, but their bravado returned almost immediately and one enormous scuffle broke out as they fought back. Hopelessly outnumbered, both Lakshmi and Pooja were felled to the ground where they were kicked mercilessly by the *Gunda*, his thickset friend and a few of the other followers followed through to make sure they were true to their leader. Jai's beautiful spotless white sari was covered in blotches of bright red and pink.

It was Joan who called out to one of the shopkeepers to use his phone to call the police but no one in the *chowk* had one.

She turned to Storey, 'Ed do something, please. Stop them killing those poor women.'

'They were asking for a beating.'

'Oh really!'

Joan grabbed a bucket of the *chat* vendor's dirty water and emptied it over the *Gunda* in a frustrated attempt to quieten things down. The other vendors joined in with their buckets of indescribable liquids trying to stop the riot getting in the way of their business. The bucket of foul-smelling, chilli-infused washing up water from the *Pachowri* wallah had an immediate effect. The *Gunda*, rubbed his burning eyes with the sleeve of his *kurta*, cursing Joan.

Ed grabbed Joan by the hand to pull her away but she held her ground.

'No Ed, we've got to look after these two poor women. Just look at the state of them.'

The *hijiras* were still struggling to stand up after having received several blows in the attack; Lakshmi had a bleeding head which poured blood, and Pooja had more than one broken rib as she winced in pain trying to get on her feet. They held on to each other with the protestors still shouting abuse.

'What a *tamasha, ah yeh yeh yeh!*' said Ed to Joan as he shook his head. 'A man of peace indeed.'

'That was only a taster,' yelled the hoarse *Gunda*. 'God will have his eventual reward, you children of the unnatural.'

The shopkeeper, now concerned that his trade had come to a grinding halt, told his men to disperse.

Someone had found a phone and Mallothra and four policemen turned up in a jeep only to find the place back to normal with the vendors resuming business. 'Hello inspector, up for a bit of *chat* then? I'd recommend the *alloo papri* from my man over there,' said Storey.

'We were called to address some disturbances by the *hijiras* Mr Storey,' said Mallothra. Then turning in mock surprise to see Joan said,' Hello to you too madam. Back in the *chowk* again, *hah*?'

'Yes inspector that's me,' said Joan, 'you have a good recall of faces.'

Mallothra asked Storey if he could make a statement about the incident.

'Interesting, I was led to believe that the Swami and his followers were attacked viciously,' said the policeman having been fed one version of the story.

'Not really, you must know that *kutta* from Gonda. Ready to make political capital out of anything. He and his followers decided to give a couple of *hijiras* a bit of a kicking.'

'There's *garbar* going on sir wherever he is campaigning. I'm expecting this will not be the last altercation between his followers and the *hijiras*,' said Mallothra.

'Why has he got it in for them?' asked Joan.

'Politicians, madam, just want to have campaign scapegoats. But I'm a policeman and I shouldn't be expressing an opinion on these matters.'

'And no doubt also wants to develop the brothel area with some of his *Ashram* loot,' chipped in Storey.

'That could make him enemies amongst the VIPs. Many go for comfort evenings and conversations to the *hijiras*. That would not be an amenity that they would wish to give up. They won't want to be causing any trouble there too soon.

But as far as I'm concerned they are still number one on my suspect list for the ransom of your factory sir. Have there been any more demands?'

'No, nothing of late. Mathur is still trawling through those batches to see if he can spot anything.'

'I hope it's a hoax, Sir.'

'Well, Inspector I'm sure you have a bit more work to do this evening developing your Mickey Spillane theories. The *Memsahib* needs to get back home now.'

'Goodnight sir. Madam, it was nice to see you again.'

It was time for them to leave Mallothra and the *chat* vendor who was now in full flow with several customers waiting to have their taste buds assailed with the pungency of his chillies and tamarind water. Ed led Joan out of the *chowk*, his firm hand guiding her back quickly to the car.

'Ed, could we take these two *hijiras* back home? They can hardly walk.'

'Not in my car, I can't. Really Joan, that is asking far too much and my driver would be appalled.'

'Well in that case I'm taking them in a rickshaw.'

It was just a few hundred yards to their house but Joan saw the pain that Lakshmi and Pooja were in. She called a rickshaw and helped them in, giving the puller a few rupees with instructions to take them home.

The other side

Joan walked through the entrance of the centre for Universal Light once more after holding her last class for the day. The American man with a shaved head who called himself Bahadur was there.

'Good afternoon sister,' he said, 'the Swami welcomes you back to the Ashram of Universal Light. Too late for *darshan* today but you're welcome to go and visit the meditation hall, we have a recital of *Bharatanatyam* dancers.'

Ice-blue-eyes Jai in the white sari was with Bahadur, engaged in what appeared to be stuffing envelopes with literature about the Ashram. She hugged Joan.

'It's nice that you crossed the worldly threshold out there again to join us. I'm sorry some of our fundraisers lost control of themselves last week. I apologise on behalf of the Swami.' As she spoke she dropped her embrace to give Joan a comforting couple of strokes down her spine as if offering an additional reward for coming back so soon.

'Being sorry doesn't help mend the bones and the bruises of those poor women who were just begging for a few rupees. But perhaps you can help me. I've come to see the Swami personally for a few minutes of his time,' said Joan.

'The Swami's day is fully booked sister, as it is for the next month,' said Bahadur. 'He's a real busy guy right now given his political campaign for the election of Sri Shivaji. The programme is now full speed ahead and he spends most of his time out of the Ashram helping the campaign. Anyway, I humbly suspect that you will find the donation to the Ashram for his personal time unaffordable.'

'The Swami is helping the Gonda *Gunda* to become an MLA?'

'Sure thing sister, but the label isn't very helpful. Sri Shivaji has impeccable credentials and is a big supporter of the Swami.'

'How do his disciples like you feel about a convicted criminal in your midst?'

'Oh, like real positive sister! We have to spread the word of love faster than we have been able to do so far and the Swami is on the right track. Swami says he'll have the entire Legislative Assembly in here one day. Many of them have been to prison.'

'Jai, that was a terrible fight in the *chowk*. You must have been very scared?'

'Sometimes the Swami's followers get carried away with their message sister, but our general aims are the same. He is a man of peace.'

Joan thanked brother Bahadur and went in search of the meditation room where she hoped she might salvage something of her visit by taking in the tranquillity of the environment. She wished she could make the Swami see the error of his relationship with the Gonda *Gunda*. Was he knowingly part of the campaign or just a naïve man so locked up in his belief that all people were inherently good and that his job was to bring out their goodness?

There in a cool dark corner of the hall was a small group of people sat on the floor with their legs crossed and eyes closed, engrossed in their personal meditations. Joan had never done a meditation on her own before but thought she might sit with the group and close her eyes to see if she could be transported again. She carefully spread her skirt out on the floor arranging the pleats around her creating the effect of a grey chrysanthemum.

It must have been several minutes after she had her eyes closed that she heard a voice whisper in her ear.

'My child, come with me.' She opened her eyes to see the Swami tilting his head to one side holding Jai close to him with his arm around her waist. She indicated that Joan should follow them. Joan arose and smiled too.

'Thank you for coming. I came to help you.'

The Swami kept his fixed half-smiling expression as they walked together out of the hall in silence into a small circular garden where a *peepal* tree occupied the centre of an area of hard bare earth and three large stone boulders had been placed around the base of the tree to act as seating. Three incense sticks slowly smouldered from a brass holder as their smoke rose gently skywards in the still, windless evening.

Suddenly Joan felt she wanted the Swami to hold her forever and never let go. Jai's silent presence seemed to complement and enhance her sense of well being.

'Please sit with us,' said the Swami still with a fixed half smile on his face, which Joan had begun to think he had been born with. 'I remember you when you first came to our *darshan*. We have many people here every day of course but you were distinguished by the dazzling light coming from your forehead, your third eye.'

Joan looked at him, her eyes widening. 'A light from my forehead?'

'Yes most certainly, I will never forget it. Just like the sun was reflected in a mirror attached to your head. It happens sometimes. Very rarely, that's why I remember you so well. It usually happens to people who have released their *kundalini* in their base *chakra*. My child, you don't mind me asking but did you have pleasure during the *darshan*?'

'It was pleasurable, yes.'

'But did you have orgasm?'

'That is a very personal question Swami which I don't feel like answering,' said Joan.

There was an embarrassing pause which Jai eased by stroking Joan on the face with the back of her fingers and followed up with a hug.

'Never the matter my child, *nahi*, *nahi*, never the matter,' he replied with a leaning of his head to one side. 'But now tell me, today you look like a frightened doe, timid and edgy. Your forehead is dark and your third eye crowded. Your aura is a dark mauve colour. What has gone wrong?'

'Swami, I came here the last time out of spite for a priest who was arrogant and wanted to make a fool of me. Your *darshan* and meditation triggered a transformation, bringing my confidence back and demonstrating that my fear was just imagination. But there have been strange things still haunting me. There was this terrible dream in which people were poisoned. It felt so real.'

'And has this any basis?'

'Well it could. You see someone has blackmailed Mr Storey, the factory manager and threatened to poison the production. I dreamt that people were dying from the poison and I want to stop this happening if this were true.'

'I can see that being disturbing. Did you tell anyone? Did you try and get the dream investigated?'

'Yes I did. I told Ed Storey. I think he may believe I'm some sort of crank.'

'No, not at all. Sometimes God speaks to us through the most mysterious channels. You should trust your dreams and see what they are really trying to tell you. It might be that you have not fully expressed yourself sexually. Is this Mr Storey your lover?'

'I'm not sure. Well, we've been intimate and he's been very generous to me but I'm not totally sure about him.'

'Would you like to be his full lover then?'

'Swami, when I left you last time, I went away looking to give myself to someone and to conquer my fear like I did in my meditation.'

'Ah, I see, it worked. But my dear sister, I hope you don't mind me calling you that.'

'No, not at all.'

'I'm always available if you wish to give yourself to someone. That is my role as your Swami. Use me if I can be of service to free the energy and the fear trapped in your beautiful *kundalini*.'

'I don't understand,' said Joan. 'You would offer yourself to me sexually? But you're a man of God?'

'The words are metaphorical,' he said smiling and allowed Joan to relax a little. 'You're in a mess in that worldly world out there?'

'Yes, that just about sums it up,' acknowledged Joan.

'There is only one robust way of securing your future my child.'

'And what is that?'

'It's to renounce your material self and do what hundreds of others have done. That is the only way. Join this community and make a new life for yourself.'

'Oh, I can't do that. My son depends on me. He is all I have in this world and I need to find paid employment to provide him with a future.'

'That is your choice sister, and Jai is always here to help you reach your decision if I'm not available. In the meantime you need to confront the source of your fear again. So make a meditation here in the garden of the *Shakti* and your way ahead will be clear. Please close your eyes and think of being in a beautiful garden.'

'But Swami, I wanted to talk to you about your fundraiser, Sri Shivaji. He's not a good man and he's acting in your name.'

'My sister, God loves everyone even the sinners, *hah?* Why can't I try and practice a little bit of God's principles. I hope the Universal Light that shines down on us all will touch him like it does you and me. Now let's do a little meditation.'

Joan closed her eyes shut, put her hands on her knees, just like she had done at her first visit to the ashram. The Swami put the palms of his hands on the top of her head and she felt the blood from her body rush to meet her scalp and in minutes she had lost consciousness of where she was. She was not sure how long he had held his hands in that position or when he had left her side, but when she opened her eyes it was dark. The familiar smell of burning kindling filled the evening air as hundreds of dwellings across the city stoked fires to prepare family meals. The sticks of incense still burned, now glowing in the dark.

When Joan had become fully aware of her surroundings she noticed the figure of Jai sat on the floor a few feet away from her; ever watchful, protective and reassuring.

'Oh Jai, thanks for staying. I was lost in my meditation. '

'That's cool. I needed to be with you.'

'Jai, what's wrong? You look sad, or are you just tired?'

'I'm… just,' Jai paused then began to cry. 'I'm so fucked up, literally, sorry, sorry.' Joan put her arms around her.

'Tell me Jai, what's happened to you? You, the lovely disciple with the ice blue eyes.'

'Joan, I need to go home. I don't like it here anymore. I'm pregnant.'

'Oh my God! Are you sure?' Jai nodded. 'Do you know the father?' She shook her head.

'Shivaji, the big bully, won't give me back my papers and I have no money. I need the fare to get back home and it's hundreds of rupees. He says I need to work out my contract with the Swami. I didn't know we had a contract.'

'Well, we'll see about that!'

'No Joan, no. Shivaji is one bad man. I'm really at their mercy on this one. Can you find me the fare home?'

'Jai, I'd love to but I'm broke. I barely have enough to live on myself. I can ask someone, someone who may have some money.'

'Thanks Joan, thank you. Be careful who you tell, I don't want to get the Swami or his bully boy sore.'

'I'll be discreet. Does Bahadur know?'

'No.'

On the way out she saw Bahadur still stuffing envelopes.

'It's gotten real dark out there sister, sure you wouldn't rather stay the night with us?' he asked.

'I'll be fine, but thank you for the offer,' said Joan.

As Joan pedalled her bicycle home in the pitch black night, accompanied by the hum of the dynamo taking its power from her front wheel, she navigated her way around the pot holes with the help of the spot light fixed to the handle bars. She had no recollection of the time between light and dusk. Had she sunk into such a deep trance to obliterate any memory of her thoughts or any of the sounds or smells of her surroundings? Her confidence had returned and the fears of her dream had receded.

Alpana's wedding

News of the wedding of Alpana, the only beloved daughter of Ashok Mathur, had spread far and wide throughout Lucknow as the groom's father was a senior civil servant in New Delhi and therefore well-connected with the political elite in the Congress party. Their guest list included the eminent, the crooked and the moneyed voyeurs of Lucknow, far surpassing the status of anybody the Mathurs knew. He had spared no expense and to heighten his guests' sense of self-importance, the chief of police had also received an invite as he always came with at least half a dozen police constables to ensure that everybody felt they were all in the company of extremely important people.

Unfortunately for Mr Mathur, one of the people he despised most, Sri Shivaji, was on the guest list, invited by the groom's father who hoped to gain favours after his success in the election. He talked to his wife about objecting to the presence of a man he considered to be a *pukka Gunda* but they decided not to risk the future happiness of their darling daughter through any early disagreement with her in-laws.

So Mathur had tipped off the *hijiras*, who were bound to make an appearance, that if they wished to make a spectacle of anyone to enhance the evening's entertainment then it should be the *Gunda* and they seemed prepared to indulge their patron. For he was now their most hated enemy and Mathur had just handed them the prospect of priceless and legitimate humiliation.

The Mathurs had set their ambition at Himalayan heights to make this the wedding of the year and the sari shops in the *Gunge* had been busy entertaining ladies with their latest silks and textiles from Bombay's finest suppliers. The *durjees* had been working through the night to the rattle of their Singer sewing machines and the hiss of their hurricane lamps, tailoring dresses for the few Anglo-Indian guests who wanted to look their best. Even Joan had summoned up the courage to find enough from her first month's salary to have a striking lemon-coloured dress made for herself, borrowed from the famous *Jiffy* patterns promoted by the Singer Sewing Company.

The Mathurs were a large sprawling family of seven brothers and sisters and with his wife's ten siblings there was a small army of relatives. Each brother and sister had their own family tentacles that extended to the far reaches of the Mathur clan. As head of this empire of relatives, leaving any member off the invitation list would be highly offensive to the individual, so he had been obliged to borrow substantial sums of money from family elders to fund this spectacle.

The Mathurs had been preparing for this event well before Alpana became eligible for marriage. She had been given a decent education, having attended The Martinere School for girls. She was tall, good-looking and so commanded the best of the available bachelors her parents and family matchmakers could find. Mrs Mathur had sent out signals about the family's intentions to find a husband for their daughter on the marital long-range jungle drums. There were photographs of Alpana taken in both Western dress and a sari and compiled together with her certificates of school education and the headmistress's final glowing report on her. Any prospective in-laws would have begun to get a very good idea of this young woman's excellent credentials, well ahead of actually seeing her in person. This attentive, intelligent and attractive woman would be an excellent wife for their son.

Finding and choosing a husband was a decision Alpana had vested almost entirely in the hands of her father and mother who would choose from a range of attributes. Perhaps most importantly, would their son-in-law be able to take care of their daughter financially, support her and perhaps them in old age? The compatibility of the two families was also an important consideration in arriving at their decision, for the Mathurs would often find themselves in the company of their in-laws; getting on with them would make life much easier for the families and their beloved daughter.

Alpana had no hesitation in approving her parents' choice when she first saw her husband-to-be at a pre-ceremony arranged for the prospective bride and groom to meet each other in the company of the two families.

'When I got married,' said Mrs Mathur to Alpana, the night before the ceremony, 'I had never seen your father ever in my life. My brothers and sisters were wishing me a nice surprise; such was the faith I had to put in my parents.'

'*Arey* ma, that was in prehistoric times, *hah*?'

'You young people don't know how lucky you are.'

'Are you saying that *papi* was a good choice or not, made by your parents?'

'*Hah* of course, he is now my husband. But then I must say I was a little disappointed when I first saw him; this short little fellow who looked like a boy rather than a strong virile man that I was expecting.'

Alpana laughed at the description of her father.

'So when did you get to like him?'

'Oh, very soon after the ceremony and we were shown to the marital bed and were supposed to consummate our marriage straight away. I just didn't want to sleep with this short man who looked like a boy and your father was very sensitive and told me that it would all be in good time, in my time and when I was good and ready. After all we were to spend a lifetime together so why hurry. That immediately changed my mind about him.'

'Ma, that's a lovely story.'

'Yes, I wish you a good sensitive man. That would be the best surprise.'

Mathur had acquired the grounds of the prestigious Cantonment Club with the help of his boss, Ed Storey. The club committee had to be convinced that the VIPs being invited would not lower the club's reputation. Prior to Independence, most of them would have been barred from the club because of its strict 'Britishers only' policy. Braithwaite, their new chairman, was now keen to open up its doors but restricted membership to well-heeled and well-connected Indians to keep out what he described as the '*loonghi* wearing riff raff'.

A *shamiana* had been erected to accommodate several hundred people and catering equipment, waiters and cooks. Coloured lights and paper lanterns were strung out everywhere inside and outside the large tent, powered via a makeshift illicit connection to the electricity supply cables on the main road.

The *Jaimala,* to which the guests had been invited, was to precede the actual wedding after most of the guests had departed. The Police had visited days before to discuss the control of the cars, rickshaws and *tongas* that would arrive at the club. Getting these people in and out of the Cantonment Club, fed and watered, in three hours was quite a feat and Mrs Mathur had thrown every ounce of her ample self into planning it all down to the last detail. After all, there was nothing more worthy of her time than to devote the year to assuring the future happiness of her daughter.

She'd consulted for weeks on organising the seating arrangements for the dinner, as there were certain people who would rather not be near those to whom they considered their inferiors or where there might be long-term enmity. These were complex threads that had to be untangled from a web of rumour, hearsay and gossip which thrilled Mrs Mathur in her endless rounds of unravelling *chai* mornings, phone calls and casual chit chat.

It was the Anglo-Indian guests who had given her the biggest challenge as she never did quite understand why a community so small were quite so fastidious about the friends they kept. Quite logically she had put them together near the main dais where the bride and groom would exchange garlands and receive presents. Amongst these guests were Dougie Kellor and Ed Storey, past enmities temporarily suspended to avoid giving offence.

The brass and pipe band played 'Scotland the Brave', a keen favourite at Indian weddings acquired from the days when the band master Mr Lobo was employed by the Indian Army in a pipe and drum band. They played remarkably in tune this evening as it seemed most wedding brass bands were composed of *bajawallahs* who played in a slightly different register to each other, rendering a wall of sound that bore only a passing resemblance to their original tunes.

Tonight was different, for Lobo had chosen his musicians well and even Mr Braithwaite approved as he tapped his toes on the ground in time with the music. Somewhere far away in his Scottish ancestry, a forefather in a Tam o'Shanter jigged about deep inside him to the rhythms of a highland fling.

The marquee was a sea of vivid purple, mauve, lime green and yellow, mixed with red, indigo and saffron and of course the shiniest twenty-four-carat gold. Here there was more gold festooned around women's necks and ears than in the entire collection of jewellers in Charbagh, the ornaments gleaming a deep amber richness as they caught the illumination from the multicoloured lights hanging from above. The almost suffocating surfeit of colour was punctuated every now and then by men in black or white *kurtas* and jackets. Lobo struck up another tune with the current Hollywood favourite, 'Come September'.

Ed Storey smiled at Mr and Mrs Mathur who were at the entrance to greet him and Mrs Mathur displayed a perfect set of *neem*-brushed teeth.

'I'm so happy today Mr Storey and now even happier to see you at our daughter's wedding. Thank you so much for helping us to be here.'

'Oh, the least I could do for you, my loyal friends.'

The tables had been set out in long endless banqueting rows, each row reaching out in the straightest lines. Banana leaves, to eat the food on, had been laid out at each place setting and stainless steel cups had been set with military precision like *javans* in a parade line on Republic Day. The Anglo-Indian guests were the only ones with cutlery and napkins and they were directed to their appointed place by one of the club bearers.

'That Mathur's done the club proud, eh Storey?' said Braithwaite as he wiped his perspiring head with a large white handkerchief.

'I had no idea he was planning such a spectacle on his

monthly salary,' said Storey. 'He'll have to work till he's in his dotage to pay this lot off.'

'Must mean a lot to bankroll the rest of his life in a false show of wealth.'

'And most unlike the man who is so humble and modest,' said Storey.

There was a huge buzz of excitement amongst the mass of people ready to sit down to eat with each one having a word to say about the bride, the groom, the surroundings of the club and of course the general tittle-tattle about those assembled for the evening.

Detective Inspector Mallothra, stout and mustachio freshly waxed in his black *kurta* suit, stood alone with his wife, a short lady in a purple sari, looking slightly uncomfortable. He fiddled with his whiskers wondering if his boss the Chief Inspector, also present, would acknowledge him and he was not sure if he should take the initiative and engage him in polite conversation. Ed Storey approached them.

'Mr and Mrs Mallothra, good evening, *namaste*,' he said and the couple seemed relieved that they had company. 'Lovely to see the ladies looking so colourful *hah*?'

'Ah yes sir, weddings are an occasion of great joy!' He then lowered his voice and spoke at the floor in a serious tone. 'Please may I ask if there has been any very recent contact with the blackmailers?'

'No, nothing, just stalemate. According to your Spillane theory, at this point in time something happens, either the *Gundas* declare themselves and get caught, or the stalemate breaks down and someone gets hurt,' said Storey.

'I'm hoping we can apprehend them before it is too late sir.'

'Indeed, and I hope we can count on the force to help us Mr Mallothra,' said Storey.

'Certainly, of that you have my maximum guarantee.'

Just then someone came barging into their conversation.

'Ah *Storeyjee*, I'm Sanyal, a very good family friend of Mathur. You may remember me when I visited the factory a year ago,' said a man in a sports jacket and a red kerchief with a plump woman by his side.

'*Hah, hah*, I think I remember.' It was clear that Storey had no idea who he was.

'My son has recently graduated in Chemistry with distinction from Lucknow University and my wife and I would respectfully ask you to consider him for a position in your very excellent factory.' The woman by his side beamed in acknowledgement of her son's achievement.

'You must be very proud parents.'

'Oh yes he is our eye's apple, I think you say.'

'*Achha* now, what you should do is contact my Personnel Manager Mr KP Singh. He handles all recruitment and I'm sure will give your son due consideration.'

'Thank you very much, *Storeyjee*,' they said in unison and withdrew, nodding all the time as if underlings in some Nawab's court.

'He's probably as thick as donkey dung Mr Storey,' said Mallothra mumbling without moving his lips.

'Ah yes Singh deals with them all politely but firmly.'

The conversation was in full flow when a few firecrackers were set off in the tent accompanied by squeals of excitement from the children. The *Baraat* could now be heard coming through the Cantonment. The bridegroom, accompanied by close friends and members of the family, was riding a fine white Arab stallion, resplendent in a white turban and tunic. The strains of another less proficient wind band could also be heard this time with gaggling discordant bagpipes out of tune with the horns but the booming drums drowned out the worst of the disharmonious undertones. As they neared the marquee the guests became expectant of the groom's entrance and the noise of the conversations fell to a murmur. Lobo stopped his band playing so as not to mix his group's melodic perfection with the discordant cavalcade of processing musicians.

The *Baraat* wedding party entered the *shamiana* to the beat of the syncopating drums, the bagpipes and horns filled the tent with a cacophonous but exhilarating sound. The groom entered, still on the white stallion, having to hunch over to avoid hitting the roof of the tent. The bride Alpana, in a red and gold sari with exquisite jewellery decorating her neck, nose and ears, looking like a picture book bride, was now on the dais to greet her soon-to-be husband. Once he had descended from the horse and risen up the steps of the dais a spontaneous applause erupted from the guests in the *shamiana*. Mathur was on the platform grinning with sheer delight at the spectacle of his daughter's special day, giving a string of continuous *namastes* to the crowd. Women cried, children squealed, men grinned at each other nodding their approval.

Garlands of marigolds were exchanged between the couple and then began the customary female mouth warbling which wafted eerily at first and then joyously as the sounds circled around the enclosure increasing in intensity until the couple sat down on their thrones, bedecked with silks and flowers of every shade.

The general ambient noise was now punctuated with the sound of tambourines and singing coming from the entrance of the *shamiana*. The band responded to the dancers entering the enclosure by playing in time with the tambourines and soon it became clear that the *hijiras* had come to pay the wedding guests a visit.

Singing and dancing at weddings was a major source of income for *hijiras* for many centuries but the sight of them made some of the male guests uneasy and they moved uncomfortably in their seats; for these were the men who had at times frequented their brothel and the *hijiras* were not known for their discretion.

The new arrivals dressed in ludicrously provocative female clothing launched themselves fully into the dancing, with the band swaying and egging them on to become more outrageous with their hips, arms and bodies gyrating in sexual depictions of some Bombay film hit. The audience was soon swept up in the display as they clapped them on with a few of the extrovert men getting up to dance with them on the dais.

They headed straight for the Chief Inspector who was dragged onto the dais to dance until he was exhausted from the gyrations and flailing arms. Then it was the turn of the groom's father who just shook his head until he was carried off and made to go through the motions. He smiled as if he was enjoying the exercise and the crowd roared their approval.

Lakshmi was leading the *hijiras*. She was by far the biggest of them all, her muscular arms, the henna coloured wig and the big pouty lips marked her out unmistakably. She led the troupe off the dais followed by the band processing between the tables until they got behind the main target for their evening's foolery, the Gonda *Gunda*.

He sat with two other men dressed in black. The mock smile on his face turned to horror as Lakshmi gyrated her pelvis just over his head. She touched him and caressed his face with her overlarge false breasts and the crowd roared with laughter. One of the men with him arose as if to intervene only to be held down when one of the bigger *hijiras* sat on him. There was more laughter and applause and then in a departing defiant gesture the dancers sung out the words:

Watch out for that fake from Gonda
He's a neckless, reckless Gunda
His Dick's so small, hardly anything at all,
And his head is as thick as a dunda.

They repeated it as they withdrew. The crowd roared again at the irreverent dig at the would-be MLA. He grinned as if to accept the good-humoured jibe at his expense, which was not shared by his surly accompanying friends. And then something seemed to flick a switch in his head as he gazed at Lakshmi. He stood up in a rage but the man with him held him down and tried to pacify him.

'Wouldn't like to be in the sack with her eh Storey,' said Braithwaite quite enjoying the spectacle. 'That Gonda chap has been in league with the local *Gundas* and wants to stand for the Assembly in the 1962 elections. Been in prison twice, once for aiding and abetting a murder and there he is as if nothing happened. I tell you I wonder about this country sometimes.'

'They deserve to be locked up those perverts. Don't know how this club let them in,' said Storey, looking disgusted.

'Steady on Storey old chap. It's just a bit of fun for these Indians. Stop taking it so seriously,' said Braithwaite.

Several of the guests breathed a collective sigh of relief when the *hijiras* danced out of the tent and away from the wedding party, hopefully to give their blessing to some other bride and bridegroom on this highly auspicious day in the Hindu calendar.

The dancing and the hilarity now gave way to the delicious smells that wafted through the tent, presaging the serving of the wedding feast. Bearers could be seen coming down the aisles dropping *samosas* on each banana leaf with a red dollop of tomato chutney followed by a second wave of *alloo dum*, the spiced potato slices in tamarind sauce appetiser that was so popular with street vendors.

Wave after wave of small portions of vegetarian accompaniments appeared in front of each guest and they cleaned their banana leaves every time.

'This is the best food I've tasted in ages,' said Braithwaite and everyone nodded in fierce agreement.

'All supervised by Mrs Mathur herself, I believe,' said Storey.

Just when they thought they were done, another course arrived with the servers asking guests if they preferred vegetarian or non-vegetarian.

'What is the non-vegetarian?' asked Ed Storey.

'Goat curry *sahib*,' came back the reply.

'Vegetarian for me then,' he said. Only Braithwaite chose the goat, as most of the Anglo-Indian guests knew that at a Hindu wedding the meat curry would be tough and unpalatable.

'I just adore goat curry with rice. It's my favourite. We're carnivores you know, as a species. That vegetarian stuff is alien to our constitution. This smells exquisite,' Braithwaite said, taking in a big sniff to absorb the flavour before the rest of the diners had been served.

The vegetarian option was a combination of chick pea, potatoes and cauliflower cooked in a thick, viscous tomato and turmeric sauce; one of Mrs Mathur's traditional recipes, but Braithwaite would not be tempted by what he referred to as '*ghassi*' food.

Young Ashok had asked his mother if he could eat the goat curry and she had reluctantly agreed to let him try it. The boy was quite frail for his age and his friends at school, most of them meat eaters, told him that he'd never be big and strong if he didn't eat meat. This was the first time he was being allowed to sample the dish that had never featured at home.

There was some more movement from the first row of tables as guests lined up to give their presents to the bride and groom. They carried boxes large and small, usually gifts for the home; crockery, towels and bed linen were the usual gifts which looked acceptably voluminous for someone to be seen with; size made a clear visual statement about their generosity towards the couple.

One by one they went up on the dais and congratulated the bride and groom, placing a box or parcel at their feet. Two bearers were on constant duty removing the piles when they grew too large. Gifts from hundreds of people were a lot to assimilate in an evening and yet for the guests this was the most important part of the ceremony. For them there was far more pleasure in giving than taking hospitality and the public shows of generosity showed how well off you were and how much you cared about the bride and groom. Ed Storey had chosen as his gift the latest household gadget, an Electrolux iron. This was at the cutting edge of consumer technology especially designed to make life cleaner, easier and quicker for every American housewife.

Just as he handed it over, there was a shout of confusion along the front table. It was the young Ashok Mathur who was groaning with what appeared to be acute stomach pains.

'*Arey* someone help! I'm dying, my stomach is on fire. I

can't bear it. Help me!' he shouted. An adult tried to haul him to his feet, taking him away where he could lie down and rest.

'That's what happens when you eat meat,' someone whispered.

One of the guests was feeling Ashok's pulse and asking him questions, but he kept shouting the same answer, that his stomach was on fire. The commotion had silenced all other activity in the marquee, even the music from the wedding band. and now all eyes had turned to Ashok. Was it possible that the Goddess Kali had come to claim this young life so early for eating meat?

Then another man had spewed out the contents of his stomach and collapsed on the banquet table over his banana leaf. A woman near him was screaming at the horror of having her turquoise silk sari bespattered with lumps of his foul-smelling vomit. An immediate hush fell upon the crowd followed by a rising hum of whispers and low-level chatter. Mrs Mathur had heard what was going on and rushed to the scene.

'*Arey* is there a doctor anywhere?' she shouted out. Apparently the man feeling Ashok's pulse was not a doctor. But strangely nobody was rushing to admit their medical credentials amongst the middle-class guests where there must have been at least a dozen doctors. She helped lay the still comatose man out on the floor until help arrived and the person feeling his pulse said that his heartbeat was slow and irregular. The woman in the soiled sari had left with her husband after being offered profuse apologies by Mr Mathur and attempts to diffuse her anger by agreeing to buy her a new garment, probably worth another week of his wages.

No sooner had this confusion abated than in another part of the *shamiana* a woman stood screaming with a man emptying out his insides. Again this had been preceded with shouts of his stomach being on fire. Soon there were similar incidents happening all over the marquee and screams could be heard all around. There must have been at least a couple of dozen men who had now become afflicted and Braithwaite was one of them.

Joan had been watching the events unfold. When she saw little Ashok fall ill, she felt sympathy for him, when the second and the third incident of vomiting took place she began to be alarmed and by the time Braithwaite collapsed in front of her, she was consumed with fear. Suddenly the scene in her dream came flooding back to her. This was it, this is what she had dreamt about twice and no one believed her.

'Braithy, Braithy, what is going on? Don't do this to me here in front of everyone,' bawled Mrs Braithwaite.

'Ed, the dream, the dream. This is it,' shouted Joan. Ed stood stock-still, his face ashen.

Braithwaite collapsed in front of Joan and Ed, vomiting out a black substance tinged with what looked like blood. Joan screamed. Braithwaite's heavy six-foot-four frame lay slumped over the rickety wooden trestle table and Storey managed to get him off the chair onto the grass floor of the tent. Braithwaite's eyes were shut and be mumbled something about 'bloody oats' then heaved up another dollop of nauseous black liquid and fell back unconscious. He repeated this twice until he lay worryingly still for over a minute.

'This is just too terrible. Oh God, what have I done to deserve this?' continued Mrs Braithwaite.

Ed felt Braithwaite's pulse and put his ear to his chest.

'His heart's stopped, oh God,' he shouted. Storey put his hands on the old man's chest and heaved a few times, as if trying to crank a reluctant combustion engine into life, but to no avail.

'It was poison, the food was poisoned by someone. I saw it in my dream,' Joan was saying.

'Did we all eat the same thing?'

'No,' said Mrs Braithwaite. 'It was that blinking goat curry, the goat curry. My Braithy ate the goat curry.'

'Good God, there must have been something horribly wrong with that meat,' Kellor shouted, running to Mrs Mathur who was reduced to a quiver. He yelled, 'Get the hospital; we have a mass case of food poisoning. *Jaldi, jaldi*! Where is the phone?'

There were two people amongst the guests who finally identified themselves as trained doctors, but there was very little they could do. One said, 'Definitely poisoning, but we need to pump out their stomachs immediately before it gets absorbed. The ones who have vomited are in a better position long term.'

Most of the wedding guests began to feel nauseous whether they had eaten the goat curry or not and the two doctors were telling everyone who felt sick that it was better to go outside and bring up the contents of their stomachs by whatever means they could. The inside of the *shamiana* stunk of bile and stale vomit. Outside too, the lawn was covered with people trying to void the contents of their stomachs.

Ashok was now on his feet, still moaning with pain but was able to walk. His mother kept fussing around him blaming herself for having let him eat the goat curry. The bride and groom could not be seen anywhere but the groom's parents began to shout abuse at the Mathurs.

'You, your daughter and those *hijiras* have brought a curse on our family. We shall never forgive you for this. Your daughter will never complete the marriage to our son.'

In a system of arranged marriage suddenly the future did not look good for Alpana, for she too would bear the stigma of a death at a disastrous wedding ceremony for the rest of her life.

Joan saw Mrs Braithwaite now cradling the head of her husband. His eyes were closed and one of the doctors was bending over him trying to restart his heart again. The doctor pushed hard on his chest and puffed air into his lungs. Each attempt seemed to gain a little response but soon faded before another round of blowing and heaving until the doctor gave up.

'It affects the elderly most,' he said. 'But this seems very different to just salmonella or cholera. It looks like a poison; the speed with which it has acted.'

It was less than an hour earlier that Braithwaite had been enjoying the music of his ancestors. Now he lay still, at rest on the soil where his parents and their parents had been buried. His ambition to walk the green rolling hills of Banchory, fish by the Dee and wear the red tartan of his forbearers had never been realised.

Mrs Mathur, his host, seeing the cruel destruction of her daughter's wedding day wailed out, 'Why, why, why us, God why us, what have we done?'

The doctor had given up on Braithwaite as the two police vans arrived to ferry the worst victims to Lucknow General Hospital. The ambulances still hadn't arrived. Those who were fit to walk helped carry the people who had passed out on makeshift stretchers and table boards. There must have been at least a couple of dozen guests who were on their backs either crying out in pain or comatose, limp lifeless bodies reflecting the horror of the unfolding tragedy.

Four men struggling with the weighty Braithwaite, put him in the van with his wife joining the driver in the front seat and Storey made the sign of the cross as it pulled away. Inspector Mallothra was giving orders to Mathur.

'I want all the servants and employees of the club to be held for interrogation by me and this club is to be sealed off to the public until further notice. *Jaldi*, *jaldi*.'

'But I don't have the authority, I'll have to find an official of the club.' Braithwaite was the only one Mathur knew with enough authority at the club and he was no longer of this world.

'We'll find someone now. At least one person has died from some suspected form of poisoning tonight and we have to make sure we don't have a murder investigation on our hands, Mathur,' he said. 'The speed with which the vomiting attacks happened after the meal is very worrying, I must say.'

'We used only the best ingredients *Inspectorjee*; my wife personally supervised the cooking.'

'Just do what I say. We'll see what the medical analysis says. *Hah*? I'd better see if I can find someone in authority.'

What was next to happen had not appeared in Joan's dream but it would forever leave an indelible mark in her memory. First she detected the smell of burning kerosene and then to her horror in the centre of the dais she saw Alpana's beautiful red sari in flames with the young woman's eyes closed to avoid the plumes of black smoke which swirled around her. As the flames took hold like a fiery python climbing around her torso, she screamed, falling to the ground, and several guests jumped on the platform to douse out the flames with anything they could lay their hands on.

'Let me die, let me die,' were her last words before she passed out.

Joan also rushed onto the dais to join the others who had now put out the flames but Alpana was past saving. The several yards of her voile sari had been the perfect funeral pyre and was now a black tangled mess stuck to her skin. The foul smell of her burned hair lay heavy in the air.

Batch 7014c

Mallothra's whiskers twitched a little when he entered the Chief Inspector's office the next morning; a boxy glass enclosure which stank of stale *Charminar* cigarettes. His boss was in a foul mood having received several calls by nine-thirty from the chief minister and other high ranking officials telling him that they expected him to clear up the poisoning incident and have the perpetrators behind bars no later than the end of the day.

Alpana's injuries had been fatal and she died in hospital. The young woman had been told by her groom that he was going home with his parents and that the wedding was over. In desperation she had grabbed a kerosene lantern, emptied its contents onto her sari and set light to it. In the commotion no-one had seen what she was doing until it was too late.

'Mallothra these bloody bastards are making *bundders* of us. What did you come up with last night?'

'Sir, I do not have a single confession or even a lead to follow.'

'*Arey*, how is this? After a night of investigation how are you not able to carry out a simple task like this? You were at it all night I assume?'

'It seems Mrs Mathur supervised all the food preparation herself and she is a most exacting lady. My attention has been

189

focused on the *bakri* curry from its procurement to consumption and she remembers very clearly how each stage was completed.'

'Any of the servants seem at all suspicious?'

'No sir, all long serving people with good records of serving family and club.'

'That is not looking very good for you and me Inspector. The Chief Minister wants a conviction. We must get one quickly or you will be finding yourself a post in the Andaman Islands Police force.'

'Oh sir no, that will not be necessary. I will turn out the *hijira* house today. My current suspicions are that one of them poisoned the curry when they came to make a *tamasha*.'

'The *hijiras*, how can that be? Don't be such a fool, they were nowhere near the kitchen.'

'Sir they have a motive. They are prime suspects in the Apna blackmail. Don't you see it sir?'

'You've been reading too many Mickey Spilligan novels.'

'Sir, respectfully, its Mickey Spillane.'

'Spillane, Pillane, I don't know. Just get me a conviction. But don't go upsetting the *hijiras* for nothing.'

'Sir you are tying my hands unnecessarily.'

'There is nothing in the *hijira* house other than a lot of trouble for you and me. Believe me, I'm many more years in this job than you.'

'*Sirjee*, there is one more thing. This Mrs D'Silva who is the lady friend of Mr Storey, says she saw it all happen in a dream and I found her in the *hijira* house a few days ago.'

'So now what fantastical story are you telling me, that his fancy lady has teamed up with the eunuchs and has poisoned the wedding guests? Really Mallothra, come to your senses if you want to stay in your job.'

So Mallothra went about his day with the impossible task of getting a conviction for the poisoning without the freedom to search and question the people he regarded as prime suspects. The hospital had worked around the clock to analyse samples of the goat curry to trace the cause of the poisoning. Salmonella was ruled out early, in fact none of the tests for common bacterial infection showed up as positive. The cooks, who had been closely questioned by Mallothra on the method of preparation, were hauled into the *thana* again to see who was involved in the cooking of the food and each process from acquisition of the meat to the final serving was examined in detail. Each ingredient was listed and the detective went through each one with the doctors and Mrs Mathur again.

Mallothra was now facing the most stressful challenge yet to his competence. The Andaman Islands was not his favourite list of places to spend the rest of his working life. The natives were naked, unpredictable and known to be hostile to any rule of law and order. Policemen there lived in fear of being shot in the neck with a poison dart then speared and disembowelled while still alive.

The morning after the calamitous wedding feast, Joan went to visit the Mathur family, still in a state of shock.

'It was our fate Miss Joan, you see. She'd never have been married again as no family would have touched her for the bad luck she might bring. So by killing herself she was trying to make it easy for us but nothing could be harder than to have your daughter commit suicide. And fate has been doubly cruel to us as we are quite ruined too; all that money my husband borrowed for the wedding will have to be paid back.'

Mrs Mathur spoke with little emotion in her voice. She was not yet reconciled to the tragedy that had befallen her family.

'Mrs Mathur, don't be so hard on yourself. Yes it is a tragedy but you weren't to blame. These things are not generally just fate, they're man-made disasters. You have to think back, did you buy anything from anyone suspicious?'

'Why does God choose us for this misfortune, why us? We are good people and I pray every day.' Mrs Mathur took a deep shuddering breath. 'No, Miss Joan, I did everything personally.'

'Now, let me see, the meat was procured from the *moselman* butcher in your road?'

'Yes, we don't eat meat but it is said that his is the best available.'

'*Achha*, what about the water for the cooking?'

'Our *chappa cul*, cleanest water you can get.'

'The *garam masala*?'

'Ground by hand that very day. My *ayah* who has been with the family since she was a young girl, did it.'

Joan tried to recollect her dream again but there was nothing she could recall that might help Mrs Mathur.

'You didn't by any chance use any Apna to fry the spices, did you?'

'Yes, we didn't use *ghee*.'

'*Hah, hah*, where did you buy it from?'

'Well, not exactly.'

'*Hah*?'

'Well my husband brought it back from the factory after they had done some tests and he said that it would be okay to use and that it was immoral to throw away perfectly good Apna.'

'May I see the tin please? I'm going to call Mallothra to take it away for some tests in the hospital laboratory.'

Mallothra took the can and recorded its batch number as

7014c. The hospital was asked to test another can from the same batch for all common poisons or pathogens. By the end of the day the hospital had identified a rare pathogen which Mathur's own assay chromatographs had been unable to detect as his assay procedures had being designed for accidental bacterial contamination. He called at the factory to give Storey the news.

'Mr Storey, we now have the source of the poison, but you must shut down and isolate the whole factory until we have eliminated the entire consignment of Apna.'

'Do we know if this was introduced deliberately?' asked Storey.

'Oh, I'm being one hundred percent sure. They will take a few more days to confirm but I talked to the lab and they said that the poison was probably Amatoxin, which is not available as a contaminant. I believe it is commonly extracted from a variety of mushroom.'

'I've never heard of it.'

'Looks like our blackmailers are quite sophisticated people, of a good education maybe. Apparently it is lethal if taken by animals but shouldn't kill humans unless in exceptional circumstances such as a weak heart condition. I believe that Braithwaite had been having heart problems.'

'But we are now looking at a murder enquiry aren't we Inspector?'

'Yes, definitely.'

'Shouldn't we lure the blackmailers? Set up a trap for them? How else are we going to get them?' asked Storey.

'And how are you proposing to do this Mr Storey? I've said before that we would have no surety of nabbing them in that maze of tunnels.'

'There is only one way in and out Inspector. All you need to do is keep enough men around to monitor who goes in and out.'

'I'm still not sure how that would work. There are many visitors who come to the *Imambara*. By the time we've followed them all, we might as well shout from the loudspeakers of the *Imambara* what we are doing.'

'You're just thinking of problems. I'm paid here to find solutions Inspector. This stoppage is costing us Lakhs every week.'

'And I'm paid to make sure no one else gets killed.'

All the other batches were sent for thorough testing in the hospital lab and the entire consignment of stock could now be impounded. The local newspapers had picked up on the story which gripped Lucknow for days and the future for the Apna company, Carver Brothers, hung in the balance. The whole Mathur family descended into a dark oblivion. Mr Mathur couldn't forgive himself for having instructed his wife to use the test cans of the cooking oil and she blamed herself for having accepted the ingredients unquestioningly.

APNA FEAR

The entire U.P. is seized in the grip of Apna Fear after it was discovered that a contaminated batch of Apna led to one death at a wedding feast and the hospitalisation of eighteen adults.

It is believed that a mysterious poison was involved. The detective inspector handling the enquiry says he thinks it was the work of an extortion racket organised by a local criminal gang. Sources say it involved a Rupees 20 Lakhs blackmail demand to release the number of the infected batch. The management refused to give into the demand saying that it would create a precedent and handed the matter to the authorities.

Now consumers of Apna are boycotting the product and the tin cans supposedly free of any contamination lie on shop shelves. The company said that the infected batch 7014c was never released from stock and that all other stocks are perfectly safe.

Swami Naik, whose pioneering work at the Ashram of Universal Light has brought him international fame, said 'It is time we drove such people who contaminate and corrupt our lives out of our city.' He is supporting Sri Shivaji the Independent, for election as an MLA.

At Braithwaite's club the *chakra* flew at half mast to mourn the death of their chairman. At the parish church many of the elderly Anglo-Indians gathered to mourn the passing of a staunch member of their community. Each such death reflected the rapid demise of their way of life and the funeral service was more a ritual of a people fading away into the mist of time.

'Brethren, it is with great sadness that I have to stand up today and tell you of the death of one of our own. Through no fault on his part he met his death, it was just one of those unfortunate but inevitable occurrences which comes to us all. Destiny picks one of us at random and deals its deathly blow.

'We should reflect on the happy life that Mr Braithwaite lived in his short time with us and of those who had the opportunity to study with him, to play with him and enjoy his life with him. Let us spare a thought too for his sad wife and those near and dear to him.

'Let us also think of those of us who are fortunate to live on this planet and in this beloved country of ours and let us promise to make the most of our lives, which I hope will be many more years to come.

'To honour one of our own, his club will be holding five minutes of silence at 2pm this afternoon. Both members and non-members are welcome to attend. Please observe the silent ceremony respectfully and pray, meditate or spare a few minutes to reflect on your own life, in whatever way suits you best.

'Now let's stand and sing hymn number 197.'

The organ played and a few dozen shaky voices sung out with all the feeling they could muster.

I fear no foe with Thee at hand to bless;
Ills have no weight and tears no bitterness.
Where is death's sting? Where grave thy victory?
I triumph still, if thou abide with me.

Joan and Ed offered their condolences to Mrs Braithwaite, dressed in black taffeta, after the burial.

'I'm done in Lucknow now Joan, and in this country. I'm going to get my papers together and go and live with my sister in Brighton.'

'Oh Mrs Braithwaite, we'll miss you. Won't you miss the sun and your friends at the club?'

'My dear there're very few of us left now and getting fewer every day. My hubby's awful death has been a message to me from the Almighty that it's time to get out now. There's nothing left for us any more and I've got a few more years to live, so I'd rather spend it with my near and dear.'

Joan smiled and said she understood. But she feared that the septuagenarian woman would be dead in a couple of years after getting to England, like so many others before her.

'Will you walk with me Joan?' said Ed. She took his hand and they walked through the cemetery passing dozens of gravestones of every shape and colour and which marked the passage of time of the British in India. This is where the ruling class had buried their dead for the last two hundred years and the epitaphs echoed memories of both sorrow and triumph in the lives they had led.

'Joan, I need you to help me rescue my factory.'

'Ed?'

'No really, I mean it. I've thought long and hard about this ransom and now I think is the time to give in. We can't go on killing people like this.'

'But Ed, how do I fit with this? Why me?'

'You're the only one I trust now, Joan. Look the last ransom note gave precise instructions of where to leave the money in the labyrinth at the *Imambara* and we have one last day before the deadline runs out. I couldn't be seen to be going in there with the money. Please Joan, help me, I have no one to turn to. Help me stop this endless dying and misery.'

Entrapment

Joan alighted from a rickshaw by the entrance to the *Imambara* at half past four in the afternoon with a canvas bag which contained a ten-pound can of Apna, the biggest size you could purchase. She walked directly towards the maze, which would stay open for another half an hour before the *chowkidar* would ring a hand bell to signal its closure. She walked slowly, not looking left or right, and kept her gaze firmly in front of her pair of patent leather beige shoes with sensible heels.

There were twenty deep steps up to the maze in a circular staircase and Joan mentally counted each one, swapping hands to carry the dead weight of the Apna can. The single lamp which lit the stairway faded once she got to the top and it was from there she began to count her forward steps in a soft whisper.

She paused to acclimatise herself to the cool, clammy darkness but she could see nothing ahead of her. Her hand touched the wall to her left, wet and slimy, as she walked on for twenty-seven steps. At precisely the twenty-seventh, she felt an opening to the tunnel turning left. She took this turn and proceeded, this time for thirty-four steps, until she came to an opening to her right. She turned to walk for another forty steps and turned around to see if she could see anything behind her. There was only blackness.

When she had advanced the next forty steps she felt a door which opened easily into what was a chamber and it was there she deposited the can of Apna on the floor in the canvas bag. She turned around and walked back in reverse order of the way she came, remembering the steps she had taken at each turning. In a few minutes she was out in the glare squinting at the light of the afternoon sun. The rickshaw was waiting for her. She left, not looking around to see if there was anyone else following her.

'*Chullo*,' she said to the puller and off she went to her rendezvous with Storey at the club.

Back in the tower of the East Wing of the *Imambara* where Inspector Mallothra had a bird's eye view of the entrance to the tunnel he kept a close watch through his binoculars. He had men posted at every exit from the building to catch whoever emerged from the tunnels with a canvas bag. He saw Joan go in with one and come out again without it. He waited. There were less than half a dozen people in the building at the time and the guards were ringing their closing bell but no one entered or emerged from the tunnels carrying anything suspicious.

At five o'clock the guards shut all doors and entrances to the *Imambara* and Mallothra ordered his men to thoroughly inspect every part of the building for intruders or unauthorised persons who might have chosen to hide somewhere until dark. When he was satisfied that there was no one in the grounds or in the building he ordered his men to search the chamber behind the secret door and recover the canvas bag containing the tin of Apna.

To Mallothra's disbelief they couldn't find the canvas bag

or the tin in the chamber or anywhere in the labyrinth. He decided to go and look for himself only to confirm that in all probability it had been taken by someone who was no longer in the maze.

'Did you order a thorough inspection of the maze, Inspector? The rogues could have been hiding somewhere before Joan went into the tunnels,' asked Storey when Mallothra went to debrief him at the Cantonment Club later that evening. Joan, also keen to know the outcome of the proposed entrapment had joined them directly after placing the ransom in the labyrinth.

'Yes absolutely our maximum efforts sir from nook to cranny.'

'But that is impossible, just impossible Inspector. I knew we couldn't rely on you and your fools to do anything.' The detective winced at the outburst.

'Ed, there is no need to be offensive towards the inspector, the whole thing was your idea,' said Joan.

'Yes and I've got to explain to my Head Office why I put such faith in the police to get hold of these criminals.'

'Sir, am I understanding correctly that you actually had real money in that bag?'

'Yes, of course. We had to make this an authentic exercise. We're not dealing with amateurs you know. Mrs D'Silva agreed to help me to place the ransom in the maze according to the directions set out in the note.'

'But respectfully sir, real authentic rupees is not what we agreed. I said I could not guarantee the success of this plan because the *Imambara* is one of the most difficult places to monitor.'

'Damn, bugger it! Now I'm finished.'

'Sir, did you obtain the cash from a bank?'

'Why yes, we don't keep that sort of money in our safe.'

'And did you ask the bank to record the serial numbers of the notes?'

'Oh don't be so ridiculous Mallothra, of course not. There were too many, besides I was sure we would seize the ransom soon after Mrs D'Silva had left the *Imambara*. At least that was assuming you had done your job.'

'Ed, please!'

'Now sir, it makes it most difficult for us to trace the money. Will you be opening the factory again now that the ransom has been paid for real?'

'Why yes of course, why not? I suppose we're going to be in the clear until someone else decides to hit us up again.'

'And I believe they will sir, now they have a taste of victory over capitalism.'

And so the next day Storey had the gates lifted and declared the factory open to commence production. The staff returned and the production line resumed its familiar hum. Storey now had to tell his superiors that he had squandered twenty Lakhs, against their wishes, to get the production lines running.

Escape from the Ashram

That night Mallothra made several sweeps of the *Imambara* with two of his men in the faint hope that they had missed something or that someone had hidden the bag somewhere in the hope of collecting it later. He ensured that they turned every piece of furniture over, searched every cupboard or storage space and looked under tarpaulins.

Joan knew Storey was in a vile mood and decided to return to her bungalow only to find Bahadur sat on her veranda. The young American was out of his Ashram garb and wore a check shirt and trousers with sandals. She had not seen him for a while and it took her a few moments to make the connection between the casually dressed person on her porch and the devotee from the Palace of Universal Light.

'Hi Joan,' he said in his Californian drawl, opening out his arms to hug her and not letting go. The blast of the horn of a diesel locomotive reverberated as it crossed the Gomti in the distance pulling a dozen carriages across the tracks away from Lucknow station. Then Joan heard him gently sobbing in her ear.

'Bahadur, what's the matter?' asked Joan disengaging from the young man.

'It's the end of the dream Joan. They're killing Jai, I think. She needs help.'

'Jai? What have they done?'

'Given her something, I think.'

'Given her something, what do you mean?'

'Something awful. I just found her in her room on the bed, face down. Oh it was terrible, blood everywhere. Her bed, her room, it made me sick just seeing this sea of blood.'

'Oh no! Was she breathing?'

'Well yes I think so. But she needs help real bad. She told me to reach out to you. This guy, the fundraiser fella Shivaji, found out she was pregnant and there was one hell of a row. I think the Swami suggested that she take this stuff to abort the foetus.'

'Oh no.' Joan looked pale. 'When was that?'

'I don't know exactly but I saw her last night and she hadn't taken it. I told her to run away but she said she couldn't. They had one of Shivaji's men watch her closely.'

'Bahadur, we have to get her out of there if she's still alive. I'll call the Police right away.'

'No, that will make matters worse. Shivaji will get her back in seconds. You have to get her out of there under cover of darkness or something. But we'll have to be quick.'

'Okay, then help me Bahadur, let's find a way.'

Later that day at dusk a new novitiate in a plain white sari with her head covered arrived at the gates of the Ashram in a rickshaw. She was greeted by Bahadur who completed the necessary preliminaries of form filling and directed the rickshaw driver to take her to one of the accommodation bungalows. Joan could hear the sound of a *sarangi* playing in the Hall of Enlightenment and a hundred devotees were gathered for the commencement of evening *darshan*. The living units were empty and deserted. Bungalow 'B' was a brick and timber block, made up of four units each with a solid wooden door secured with a heavy metal latch.

The latch to number 4 had not been padlocked and Joan knocked on the solid teak panel which made a dull muffled sound. She knocked harder in an attempt to be heard. There was no sign of any movement from within so Joan slid aside the latch and cracked open the door to let herself in. An acrid rotten smell fell out of the pitch dark room and Joan called out Jai's name, once, then twice. There was a hint of a groan in response. She fumbled for a light switch but could find none, then ran out to the rickshaw *wallah* for a box of matches. The first match revealed a human figure lying on the floor a few feet from the bed. It was Jai on one side, eyes closed, her hair was matted, her clothing blood stained. As the match died away Joan felt Jai's pulse. She still had one.

Joan undressed, taking off her sari and in the darkness wrapped it around Jai. In her bag were a pair of black slacks which she put on then called out to the rickshaw *wallah* to come in and give her a hand. She lit another match as the man entered and he held his nose at the smell and sight of what he saw.

'*Arey memsahib* she is very sick.'

'*Chullo* help me get her in the rickshaw. She's coming back with us.'

Minutes later, under cover of darkness, the rickshaw left with two passengers, one in the same white sari still with her head covered and the other by her side in black slacks and a sleeveless blouse, holding her companion upright. The two security guards were lighting up each other's *bidis* at the gate and waved the vehicle on without paying much apparent attention.

With Jai slumped on her lap, the journey back to Joan's own bungalow seemed interminably long. Each pothole, each lump in the road was met with a painful groan from Jai and Joan could tell she was in agony. They stopped by the infirmary and called for the Matron's help.

'Matron, you've got to help this young woman who is very ill.'

'I'm not allowed to treat anyone other than the boys here in my infirmary Mrs D'Silva,' she said stiffly without even looking at Jai whom she assumed to be one of the servants who had been beaten by an abusive husband, something that was all too common amongst the servant *Bhanghi* castes.

'Matron, may I appeal to the good Samaritan in you for a few minutes to help me take her into my bungalow to get her comfortable?'

Joan's biblical connection seemed to appeal to Matron and she helped carry Jai into the bungalow.

'Who is this woman, Joan? She's not one of the servants?'

'She's an American who has been in quite a bad way. It's far too long a story Matron but she needs some medical attention. She's been bleeding from her womb and I'm sure needs a drip or something.'

They laid her on the bed and set up a saline drip acquired from the infirmary. Matron scurried around for several minutes with towels, gave her a shot of something and Jai passed out again.

'She's going to need a lot of rest and rehydration now. I've given her something to sleep. You should call the police Joan.'

'I'm afraid that will probably put her in more danger. No, we just need to get her out of here as soon as she gets stronger.'

'I'll check on her in the morning.'

'Thank you so much, Matron. I'll get her cleaned up. She won't want to wake to see herself in this state.'

Together they took off her clothing and cleaned her with wet towels. Joan wiped and combed Jai's hair and gradually the horror of the evening crept up on her like the chilling river fog that rolled over the Gomti in the winter evenings. Matron was full of questions about Jai and Joan was vague. Soon her murmuring faded away as background and Joan could only remember the last encounter with Jai, when she seemed desperate to get out of the ashram and back to California. She remembered the pleading sorry face, the tears and the distress of the young American woman. Joan now wished she had some money to have helped her or could she have tried harder at shaming the bully Shivaji, or provided more words of support to the woman with ice blue eyes who must have felt desperate, lonely and abandoned.

When Bahadur turned up later to check on Jai he reported that there had been a terrible commotion after *darshan* when someone found out that Jai was missing. He had slipped away knowing that the finger of suspicion would soon be pointed at him.

'It's not safe for her here. Shivaji and his fundraisers are going to be furious that you have taken her away.'

'Who are these fundraisers Bahadur? They keep coming up.'

'Joan, they've taken over the Swami. Just mean guys who manipulate the Swami. At first I believe they came to manage his business interests as the Swami was terrible at handling the money the Ashram receives from devotees like us. Now they have their tentacles into everything.'

'And how did Jai get mixed up with them?'

'She never talked to me about it but she was always in

heated exchanges with them. The other day she was in sunglasses, which she never wore. I discovered that she had a black eye which she said came from a fall in the dark.'

'Beaten, no doubt.'

'There was a time we would have done anything for the Swami, even if it meant giving up our life for the Ashram. But gradually it seemed we were being used to do bad things in his business interests.'

'Now you need to get out of town quickly, Bahadur.'

'Hey, I'm a guy, and six foot three. That helps. I have the protection of my Embassy. That sort of thing helps when you have the US of A behind you. I'll be outta here by tomorrow as soon as my folks can wire me some money.'

'I'm sure my house is being watched. The police are keeping an eye on me and the Swami or his fundraisers will eventually find out for sure. You need to take the night train to Delhi and go directly to your Embassy when you get there.'

Joan emptied out the contents of her purse and gave them to Bahadur which he took with an embarrassed shuffle of his legs.

'Gee, Joan, you sure you can spare this?'

'Take care Bahadur, and thanks for helping to rescue Jai. Let us know when you're safely in Delhi and see if the Embassy can offer her any financial help to get back home. I know her parents have disowned her so no help from them would be forthcoming.'

'I'll be right onto it, Joan.'

'Oh, just one more thing. These fundraisers, are they likely to be engaged in extortion, blackmail, that sort of thing?'

'Hell, they've been pretty mean to Jai so I guess so. I've kept my nose outta their business. Why, have they been on to you?'

'Never mind Bahadur, just asking.'

The letter from Jai, posted by Bahadur a day earlier, arrived early the next morning while Jai still slept under her saline drip. Joan ripped open the flap sealing the envelope hurriedly to read the note.

Dear Sister Joan,

I may have managed to convince the Shivaji to part with some money to get me back home to California.

I hate where things have ended up and I don't know who I should believe any more. I'm convinced that Shivaji is some mafia sort of guy, up to his neck in criminal activity; the Swami says that it's all made up stuff by ungodly people.

Now Shivaji thinks he can give me something to abort the baby. I really don't know if I should, but a kid will be curtains for me back at home.

You've been such a support to me and I consider you my first and last success as a novitiate. I hope you continue to meditate and get enough refreshment from it. I'm already getting the pangs of motherhood and I wish there was a quick way out of here. I don't have your address but will give this to Bahadur who will hopefully be able to get this message to you.

Thanks for listening to me and being such a good 'sister',
Loretta (the novitiate previously known as Jai).

Joan read the letter over and over to make sure she understood the full horror of what the Swami's fundraisers had been up to and their deception of a young vulnerable woman who still held on to an illusion that the Swami was on her side. She was convinced that the Swami through his naïvety was an unwitting accomplice to the Gonda *Gunda* and his criminal activities.

Bahadur managed to catch the late night train to Delhi, sharing a crowded third class carriage with dozens of sleeping families sprawled out on the benches, floor and some even tucked away in the upper luggage rack. He dug out a small area by the door to sit on and nodded off, the tiredness overtaking him in a few minutes of the train setting off its rocking motion. Few foreigners travelled in third class and at daybreak, when most of the children were awake, there were giggles of amusement at the sight of Bahadur, head drooped over the shoulder of a fellow traveller, an elderly man in a *pugree,* who was happy to offer himself as a headrest. The train jolted to a stop at signals and Bahadur awoke rubbing his eyes to more merriment amongst the children. The man in the *pugree* offered him a cup of sweet tea from a flask and Bahadur sipped the drink thanking him and waving to the children who burst out into loud laughter.

The sack

Mathur had been sleeping poorly since the death of his daughter. The combination of personal loss and the huge debt he had to pay for the wedding feast hung heavy on his mind. He awoke at the first hint of daylight to take a walk in the comfortable early morning air and stumbled from his bathroom towards the front door. There amongst the pots of dahlias outside his door he noticed a large brown paper envelope in full view of the front entrance but hidden from the street.

He rubbed his face to clear the sleep from his eyes and picked up the package. It was heavy, stuffed with loose documents or papers. He tore open the flap and saw to his surprise that it contained bank notes. Mathur looked around him to see if there was anyone around in the street outside, then hurried inside. He emptied out the contents of the envelope onto a coffee table and took a deep breath when all that seemed to be in it were bundles of notes in thousand rupee denominations. Then he noticed a slip of paper typewritten in the same typeface as the ransom notes. It read:

My dear friend, please accept this gift of two lakhs as an expression of our guilt for the harm it has caused you and your family. We hope that it will help to pay off your debts. We strongly advise you to keep this in confidence between ourselves.

Back at the Apna factory a peon knocked on Storey's office door at nine o'clock in the morning.

'Sir, it's a head office *sahib* who is on the phone for you.'

'Oh, okay, very well, put him on. Always got to speak to the higher paid helpers.'

'Storey, this is Sanyal, head of production. I need to convey some unhappy news, I'm afraid,' said the voice in a businesslike tone.

'*Accha*, more doom?'

'Yes. You see the Board met early this morning to review the already dire state of affairs at your factory and has come to the conclusion that we need a new man in charge.'

'A what? A new man! Am I being replaced?'

'I'm really sorry Storey, after what you have been through, but I hope you will understand the position of the Board. They have to be answerable to shareholders and the position has been gradually sinking into the mire with your production numbers.'

'Yes, but was there no one there to defend my position? The need to uphold the rule of law. The extortion. Don't they understand the crisis we're in?'

'Yes indeed, that was talked about and we decided that a fresh set of eyes, a new brain and new energy might resolve the impasse.'

'I can't believe this!'

'We also heard that you drew out an extra large sum of money from the company bank account without the knowledge of our accountant or your Deputy, Mathur. That didn't exactly help your case.'

'Don't you people get it in that ivory tower of yours? Don't you understand that we have to keep this factory running and that I acted in the best interest of the company? These are vicious people; they kill. They mean business.'

'I'm really sorry Storey. Mr Siddiqui will be at the factory this afternoon for you to begin your handover. You will be paid your month's notice period but we ask that you vacate by this evening.'

And that was it. Storey called his key personnel together to tell them the news.

'Friends, colleagues, I've just received some bad news. You have been loyal and steadfast with me over this crisis we have faced with the blackmail. I may have made some mistakes in the past or errors of judgement that will be for you all to decide. I took some initiative to save this company by trying to trap the *Gundas* and failed and now I've been made a scapegoat.

'The Board have decided to replace me and I ask that you give the new man your full cooperation. He will be here this afternoon and I will bring him around to meet you. In the meantime please continue as before and my sincere best wishes be with you. *Dhanyabad.*'

There was an uncomfortable silence, no quiet exclamations of shock or surprise, almost as if the staff were expecting the news.

Mathur was the first to come to his office as Storey, still reeling from the call, was collecting the few personal effects he had.

'Sir, I'm so embarrassed to see what has happened, please accept my condolences.'

'Good God, Mathur, I'm not dying, just leaving this job. Essentially this is an excellent factory with good people and it will continue to prosper whoever is in this office, with men like you Mathur who do your job with such meticulous care and attention to detail.'

'But sir it's the principle of what they're doing to you that is morally wrong.'

'No Mathur, they are so far removed from what is really happening on the ground. That is the issue. Anyway, you need to educate the new fellow quickly and convey some of your very sound ideas to him.'

'Mr Storey, there is something else I need to...'

The peon interrupted, knocking on the door and entering. '*Mathursahib*, a Mr Siddiqui would like to speak with you now.'

'Here already?'

Ed lost his job and his bungalow along with the benefits of the considerable entourage of servants, and help that he enjoyed. By the time he had introduced Mr Siddiqui to the staff and collected his belongings, it was near the end of the working day.

Ed walked out of the factory gates unemployed for the first time in his working life. In the bungalow he packed a tin case of his possessions, stopping only to collect his Holland and Holland shotgun. Striding back through the garden with its bright red cannas and rows of marigolds, he went to his Royal Enfield, then with one kick of the starter, he and the machine were thundering out of the grounds leaving the factory and its surroundings for good.

Joan heard the distinctive sound of the Royal Enfield with its engine misfiring entering the grounds and then stalling. In the gloom she saw him pushing the vehicle up the track towards her. She ran out onto the veranda delighted to see Ed with his shotgun sticking out of the sidecar.

'Funny time to be going for a shoot *hah* in that sickly sounding machine of yours?'

'Oh, you haven't heard?'

'Heard what? I've been in classes all day.'

'They gave me the sack, Joan.'

'The sack!'

'*Hah* that's me finished,' he said, a little out of breath. He kissed Joan and they shared a long silent embrace.

Joan was the first to speak.

'You're always welcome here Ed, while you sort yourself out, you know. No strings attached on my side. We've got to show those *Gundas* we can't be beaten.'

'I wasn't sure about coming here to burden you, but I'm pleased I did. The bike took me here, like a trusted steed.'

'And I'm so pleased you came. Is this all you've got?'

'This and this,' he said pointing to his material possessions and himself.

'Well that's good enough for me, let's get you settled. I was just making some *fulowris*. Bring your stuff in.'

'I tell you what,' he said taking his gun and a suitcase out of the sidecar, 'why don't I take you out for a real treat?'

'Well, I have a sick guest to tend to Ed.'

Ed paused at the door and entered cautiously at the mention of the guest. His eyes fell on Jai who was propped up on the only bed, the saline drip still beside her. Some of the colour had returned to her face but the shadows cast by the neon strip light had aged her by several years and her once ice-blue eyes were dark and sunken, her thin blonde flowing hair was a matted unrecognisable brown mess. She saw Ed and managed a faint smile.

'This is Jai, Ed. From the Ashram of Swami Naik. They tried to kill her. I rescued her yesterday. But we're doing much better now, aren't we Jai?' said Joan, tucking her pillows in by her bed to make her more comfortable.

'Does Mallothra know?'

'No, I'm keeping her away from officialdom. Its all too complicated.'

'Are you sure you know what you're doing?'

'Not entirely but its the best I can think of. She's not safe out there in a hospital, she can't go back to the Ashram and she has no home. So this is it.'

Storey still stood awkwardly near the doorway until Joan asked him to sit down. Jai began to talk about the magnetism of the Swami and how he was well practiced at reaching out and capturing the hearts and minds of a generation of people looking for a deeper meaning to their lives and how Jai and Bahadur had been two such individuals caught up in the Swami's typhoon of evangelism.

Jai had been picked out early on as one of his 'most favoured' novitiates, presumably because she was not only the most vulnerable but because her ice-blue eyes and blonde hair made a fine exotic trophy captured by his Eastern thought and teaching.

'So all the rumours were true then,' said Storey, giving Joan a supercilious look.

'The Swami is a wonderful man,' said Jai, 'but his fundraiser... Sri Shivaji could never get enough money. There must be millions pouring into the Ashram every month but he's always begging for more.'

'So Jai who are the fundraisers? Because they looked to me like nasty people.'

'One day two men turned up at the Ashram who he

introduced as his disciples to help him with his finances and to accelerate his fundraising activities for the oncoming elections. They were mean guys who made me and Bahadur write letters all day to benefactors claiming that more money would accelerate their achievement of eternal happiness.'

'And you just went along with it?'

'Yeh, I guess we were mugs. We would have done anything to please the Swami. But I stopped short of blackmail and coercion.'

'Blackmail?' cried out Joan.

'Well, yes. The fundraisers seemed to have pictures of powerful men with their pants down so to speak, taken I don't know where. I showed them to Bahadur who just laughed but I was not going to be part of that. I got whacked by the big one for disobeying his orders and that was when it all went downhill for me.'

'Didn't you tell the Swami?'

'I daren't Joan, I would have been whacked again. So I asked for my passport to go back home.'

'Did they ever mention the Apna factory, Jai?' asked Joan.

'No, but I was told to find out more about your relationship with Ed. They said he was a rich guy with important connections.'

When Matron arrived late that evening to check on Jai and give her a sedative to help her get a good night's rest, she couldn't miss Ed's Royal Enfield parked outside Joan's bungalow. First Jai and now Ed, the school governors might have something to say?

Tongues had already started wagging as soon as news of Storey's dismissal spread in the Anglo-Indian community. Was this another example of one of their own being victimised?

But then he hadn't made a lot of friends with his superior attitude towards them and the consensus was that he'd probably deserved the sack. There was much speculation that he might seek refuge with Joan and now Matron would ensure that the latest development of both Jai and Ed Storey lodging with her would spread like dengue fever.

Joan saw herself as protector of a woman in fear for her life and a provider to the man whom she loved. The more she thought about her actions the more she remained convinced that she was doing the right thing.

'I should be going to find somewhere for the night as I'll just be getting in the way,' said Storey in response to Matron's obvious disapproval of his presence in the bungalow.

'Not at all. I won't hear of it. And I'm sure I could use a little of your assistance in getting Jai back on her feet again and helping us to nail that wretched Swami. I'll make up a little field bed on the floor for you in the box room. You don't mind sleeping a little rough do you, with two vivacious ladies for company?'

He laughed.

'You know what? If you can get that machine of yours restarted I'll take you up on your offer of a little *chat* at the *chowk*. We won't leave Jai for long.'

The school kitchen had made a chicken mulligatawny soup which she had watered down for Jai and she seemed to finish the entire contents of the bowl. Ed's bike fired at the first kick, and they set off into the darkness.

Witch hunt

The *chowk* was quiet that evening as they found the *chat wallah* without the usual circle of customers around him. He had memorised their order from the time before which impressed Joan considering he served hundreds of people every day. Soon he was doling out copious amounts of tamarind water and potatoes laced with the crushed coriander and cumin. Storey and Joan both made appreciative noises which egged the *chat wallah* on to give them more of the same. In time the chillies had got to Joan and she had to give up. While Ed reached into his pocket to pay the man, Joan noticed a *fakir* sitting on the pavement cross-legged against the brick wall. She realised it was Lakshmi and went over to her.

'Please give me your right hand,' said the *fakir*.

She took Joan's hand and squeezed it once then stretched it flat and spoke so softly that Joan had to get closer to her to be heard.

'You're in grave danger, you and the *sahib*. Please be very careful, the Gonda *Gunda* and the Swami's men are out to get their revenge on you both, probably as early as tonight. Lock your doors and be ready to defend yourself. Tell that useless inspector to put a guard on your bungalow. There could be trouble.'

'Lakshmi, thank you for the warning but I think we can look after ourselves.'

'Please take me seriously, we have our informers as they have theirs. Now please give me some money, anything. I'm afraid we are being watched.'

Joan fumbled in her bag and put some coins in her aluminium bowl which she acknowledged with a *namaste*.

When they got back to Joan's bungalow Jai was still asleep. The kerosene lamp she had lit flickered with a smoky orange sooty glow as it struggled to be seen through the blackened glass shade. The smell of partially burned paraffin filled the room.

Storey unpacked a few of his clothes.

'Put them in the bottom drawer Ed,' said Joan, 'It's empty. I've been saving it in case I got some new things to wear.'

'Thanks, can't see me wearing anything too formal for quite a while,' said Storey.

'Oh! Now, what are you going to do tomorrow, *hah*? Your first day of being without work.'

'I'm going to see the British Consul.'

'About what?'

'About emigrating. I'm finished here, *khatam*. No one is going to employ me no matter what it says that I have done on a piece of paper. My judgement on taking on the blackmailers was flawed. I need to go to a place where principles of honesty and decency are valued and upheld. There doesn't appear to be room for that any more in this country. I need to get out of this crumbling wreckage of a nation and I'd like to take you with me Joan. Please come with me.'

'Ed, Ed, *asté*, please slow down. I didn't run away from

Calcutta and I'm not about to change my mind now, as much as I like you and want you with me. You think England is so easy do you? From the time you get off the boat or the plane people are looking at you as though you shouldn't be there. You'll be wiping bums in some government hospital and they'll treat you like *bhunges*. Is that the life you want?'

Their conversation was broken by the sound of a dog barking outside in the darkness, and then its shriek as someone silenced it. The pariah's instincts to preserve and guard its own territory was not with the approval of someone outside. Sweet silence followed and then the sound of crashing glass, a bang and Joan saw a mass of flame light up the end of her veranda, the strong smell of kerosene indicated a makeshift firebomb had been thrown from the darkness.

'My God, they're here for us Ed,' shouted Joan throwing on her dressing gown and running out into the veranda. She doused out the flames with her feet in a few seconds and yelled out into the darkness. 'Come on, show your faces, you swines!'

'Who, what's going on?' called out Ed.

'Looks like the Swami's hard men have organised a lynch mob for us.'

There in the darkness, they could now see a dozen or so people, a few with flaming torches, others with large bamboo *lathis* and at least one with what looked like a machete. They were all men, looking menacing, bare-chested, just in their *lungis* walking up to the bungalow with the neckless *Gunda's* outline seen in the flickering orange flames. Ed recognised a couple of the workers from his factory. One of them called out.

'Come out *sahib*, we want the women.'

There was a voice shouting out '*Nahi, Nahi* burn them all down these *shaitan ke bacché.*' It was the Swami's chief fundraiser, the Gonda *Gunda*, emerging from the rear of the small crowd.

'Why are you here?' called back Joan. She stood on the veranda in her cotton nightdress.

'Because you're a *churail*, a reincarnation of evil and you must die before you kill any more people,' he said. They advanced further and one of the torch carriers threw his flaming stick at the bungalow which also landed on the veranda. Joan again moved to kick it off the platform successfully. There was another which set light to the cushion on the cane chair and immediately flames a few feet high had engulfed the entire chair. Joan pulled a *duree* from the floor and with Ed's help used it to cover as much of the burning chair as she could. This calmed the flames for a moment, but the crowd were now shouting louder and another flaming torch landed on the roof of the bungalow. Joan could not see what happened to this one but could smell the kerosene burning above her and see it light up the ground around the bungalow.

Then Ed swore and tied a red *loonghi* around his waist, emerging to face the mob with his gun. 'No Ed, no more violence, please!' yelled Joan holding the barrel of his gun downwards.

'You *behan chodes* will have to die before you get me or these women,' he said throatily.

'Don't be silly, we're not scared of that bird gun. *Chullo*,' said a voice from the mob.

But Storey's gun had served its purpose for the moment. The crowd had at least stopped advancing on the bungalow. Guns, even the old disabled variety that hadn't been fired in decades, seemed to possess a menacing quality about them which deterred most people and Ed's shotgun was about as threatening as any weapon could get. He stood in front of the house, his half naked silhouette quivering as the flames began to die down on the roof of the bungalow, his gun pointed into the darkness.

'*Bastards, bastards,*' he shouted with a hoarse rage which bordered on desperation as he knew that the gun had only won him and Joan temporary protection. Soon, one of the members of the mob would be overcome with enough bravado to prove that he could take on the *sahib* and make himself a hero dead or alive. The glow from the flaming torch on the roof died down and darkness descended again.

'Ed come back in here please, come back,' shouted Joan, but her voice was swallowed up by the darkness.

There was what sounded like a hoot and a war cry in the blackness from behind the line of Swami's men accompanied by more commotion and more men's voices shouting. In a couple of minutes a pitched battle had ensued.

Ed moved closer to see what was going on, while Joan shone the torch in the direction of the noise. To their disbelief they saw a group of women kicking and *lathi* charging the men with the worst swearing and cursing they'd heard.

'It's the *hijiras*,' Ed shouted back at Joan.

Suddenly this cavalry of *hijiras* appearing out of the darkness brought some hope for Joan. They were clearly a match for the men, swinging out with whatever weapons they had in their possession. It was hard to tell in the dark who was winning the battle and Ed was not going to be a bystander so he ran into the crowd swinging the butt of his gun. Joan had lost sight of him now as she screamed, 'Ed no, don't, don't!'

Her cries of restraint fell on deaf ears as Ed lunged out at anyone who looked like a man in the battling throng.

Lakshmi had rallied *hijiras* from far and wide to take on the Gonda *Gunda*. This would be one of the last opportunities to finally see him off. For the would-be MLA, this was a chance to get rid of the pregnant *ferrengi* who could destroy his whole campaign, along with the hated *hijiras*. There was so much at stake.

The fighting continued to rage, men were lying on the ground knocked unconscious, some were bleeding and crying out in pain for help. For ten minutes the fighting continued at its most ferocious until the numbers of *hijiras* vastly outnumbered the Swami's men. The *hijiras* had suffered so much at the hands of the Swami's men and this was their opportunity for revenge. Now they were here fighting for their lives.

Joan caught sight of the gruesome figure of a man who had been set on fire, running to and fro for his life as the flames created a trail behind him. She watched in disbelieving horror at the brutality of what she was seeing. The flames went out and then there was complete darkness again.

There was the sound of a trumpet blowing a discordant series of notes which pierced through the dark. It was like a battle cry coming from the *hijiras*. There was more shouting and then another series of blasts from the trumpet and then there were cries of a man in excruciating pain.

Joan heard a truck and saw its blinding lights piercing through the darkness. Khaki clad policeman were emerging from it also carrying *lathis*, brought in by Mallothra's lookout who had fallen asleep, only to be woken up with the noise of the pitched battle. The warring factions began to flee, dropping their flaming torches which had by now reached the end of their light-giving life.

Finally Joan left the safety of her veranda with her electric torch in hand to survey the scene where bedlam had reigned only minutes earlier. With the lynch mob, the *hijiras* and the vanload of policeman, there was a huge crowd of people somewhere out there, mostly in the dark. Many of the combatants who were able to walk or run had fled when the police van turned up. Some of the injured could not escape the police and were rounded up. Those who had fallen in battle still lay on the ground groaning for help.

Joan caught the arm of the first policeman she saw.

'Sergeant, have you seen Storey *sahib*?' No he hadn't, and neither had any of the other constables who were all walking around rather dazed by seeing women and men casualties in this pitched battle. The truck was brought closer to the scene of the affray and additional lights deployed to search the area. There were two men handcuffed and led to the van, a couple still lay on the ground groaning in pain. Joan saw one of them was Shivaji himself. His *dhoti* was soaked in blood and he rolled about the ground shouting, 'Save me, save me.' Joan thought he recognised her in the dark as he turned away to face a policeman who was standing over him.

'I can identify this person, sergeant,' said Joan. 'This is Sri Shivaji, one of Swami Naik's fundraisers and I believe he organised the lynch mob. He appears to have sustained some injury to his groin. But I still haven't seen Mr Storey?'

'There's a man badly burned in the ambulance *memsahib*. We couldn't identify him as his face was black, covered in burns. He could be the Apna factory manager.'

Joan ran to the ambulance and shone her torch into the dark vehicle. She just glimpsed a man lying on the floor before Inspector Mallothra jumped out of the vehicle and shut the door.

'Mrs D'Silva, I cannot let you into the vehicle at this moment. This area is sealed off for the detection of crime. I'm sorry.'

'Good God Inspector, I was just with him minutes ago,' she protested.

'No madam I cannot allow it. This is a crime scene.'

'What, is he dead?'

'I cannot make any comment madam, please,' he insisted.

She banged on the door of the van.

'Oh Ed, please Ed, please don't leave me,' she cried helplessly. She thought she heard him call out to her from inside the vehicle. Just an hour earlier he was proposing to whisk her away from the horror of this night. Now he lay motionless incapable of lifting a finger; how sudden, cruel and unpredictable was fate?

A radio crackled into life, more ambulances were on their way. She remembered the infirmary where Matron kept the bandages. That was not far. Joan fled the van into the dark towards the infirmary to see if she could find anything to help others who still lay on the grass. She smashed through a glass cabinet to get at the rolls of bandages. There were medicines there too, but Joan had no idea which ones might help. It was bandages she needed. She ran the couple of hundred yards back to the police vans like a crazed woman still in her cotton nightdress.

By now the ambulances had arrived and the doctors were examining the Gonda *Gunda* to see if there was anything they could do to help him.

'This is just unbelievably brutal,' he said. 'He's been castrated.' The man still continued to writhe in pain until the doctor administered a shot of morphine to sedate him.

Joan didn't really hear what the doctor said as her mind was more on Ed. A doctor and an orderly went around the field at

Joan's insistence, as there were at least a few people still on the grass, crying out in pain.

'Please make space for us madam,' said the doctor in an attempt to get Joan out of the way and allow him to get on with his job. The medics looked very grave and proceeded to attend to the men lying on the grass.

'More saline bag,' one shouted out to the orderly, 'this one is nearly dead. He also needs a lot of blood quickly. Get him into the ambulance as soon as you can.'

Joan went over to a doctor again to ask for information about Ed's condition.

'I'm sorry madam, I cannot divulge any information at this stage; we have to go now. Please come to the General Hospital in the morning and you will be provided with everything,' said the doctor.

'But I can't wait till the morning, doctor. I need to know if he needs me by his bedside.'

'Sorry, it's strict policy. I cannot bend the rules madam.'

The ambulances drove off into the night, lighting up the banyan trees in a series of blue flashes. Joan watched the strobe lights pulse out of sight until they were no more.

The authorities had taken away the man who had put his life on the line to protect her and now all she wanted was to be with him. She walked back to her bungalow trembling, crying and just coming to terms with what the last hour might mean to her life.

'Oh God please save him, forgive me for whatever wrong I've done. I'll make it up to you I promise but please save him! Save him! Save my man!' she yelled into the dark night. She saw his gun covered in mud and blood on the grass and held it close to her. Any part of Storey or his close possessions would be a comforting substitute for the real man.

By now most of the teaching staff living in the school grounds had been woken by the noise. None had ventured out during the fighting for fear of having got caught up in the violence. Even the *chowkidar* who had hidden out of sight in case he became the victim of a *lathi* or machete emerged. Matron, in her nightgown, was the first to reach Joan still in a daze clutching Ed's gun.

'Are you alright my dear?' she said holding Joan's arm. 'You're shivering. Let's go in and I'll make you a cup of *cha*.'

Despite the warm night Joan was in a cold sweat quivering with the shock of the harrowing ordeal. Her legs, from the knees down, didn't seem to want to hold her up anymore.

'*Accha*, *hah* thanks,' she said as Matron led her back to her bungalow. Her veranda smelled of a sickly combination of kerosene and charred wood. The cane chairs stood half burned and still smouldering with broken glass strewn all over the wooden floor.

'You're in a state of shock my dear and I'm not surprised. Not after those *Gundas* tried to burn you down in your own place. I've never seen anything like this, here in our own school grounds. Will we not be safe anywhere? I'm going to give you a strong sedative to put you to sleep or else you'll be a wreck in the morning.'

Jai had continued to sleep through the turmoil outside. Joan knew that the Swami's men had really come for her in an attempt to silence the person that could destroy his chances of ever getting elected. Jai would never be safe here. She would have to get away like Bahadur once she was strong enough to travel.

Matron's sedative was strong and Joan fell into a deep sleep minutes after taking her cup of tea. In her sleep she dreamt of Ashok and her son Errol both dressed smartly as page boys walking in solemn step behind her and her late husband who held her hand. Together they walked down the aisle of the church where they had been married. The church was filled with a strange assortment of people from the *hijiras* all dressed in their ornate finery, Bahadur, the teachers from the school and dozens of the children from her class. The man in the front pew who stood tall and erect with his back to her would soon be joined with her in matrimony.

When she got to the end of the aisle, the tall man who would soon be her husband turned around to take her hand. To her horror she saw the Gonda *Gunda's* face, his smile now a demonic red-toothed grin which dripped betel nut juice from his lips. She screamed and awoke in a cold sweat as the sun rose above the banyan trees.

Unconditional love

No one called on Joan to tell her about Storey's condition. She showered and dressed in the full hope that at some stage that day she would be reunited with the man she loved. She remembered his stories of how he had been inches away from death in dismantling the most treacherous, unpredictable land mines in the Egyptian desert and how he seemed to have been gifted at birth with a succession of lives which he drew on endlessly. Surely this time would be no exception.

Jai was awake, with colour back in her cheeks. The sunken eyes had disappeared and she seemed cheerful, oblivious to the danger she had been in a few hours earlier. Joan made her some sweet tea and a boiled egg with toast, her hands trembling as she spread mango jam on the bread.

She called at the refectory to ask to see her son Errol who was finishing off breakfast.

'Darling *beta*!' I just wanted to hug you today and make sure you were okay. Are you?' she said holding him to her chest, much to his embarrassment as the other boys looked on.

'I'm fine mum, are you?'

'Well I'm fine too my son,' she said. 'I just wanted to be reminded of what a nice *buccha* I have.'

Errol hoped she would soon recover and be her old self again. His mother was the rock from which he gained his confidence. She was the solid, reliable, unshakeable one; always there when he needed her.

'Ma shall we spend the day together?'

'No *beta* you've got so much to do in school, maybe another time, *hah*?' she said hugging him again and waving goodbye.

The General Hospital was a twenty-minute bicycle ride away. When she arrived, there was some hesitancy about who she was; a close relative, friend or well-wisher.

'Madam, I'm not being allowed to give any information on this person Mr Storey, unless it is a close relative or official of Carver Brothers,' said the clerk at the administration desk by the entrance. 'But I will consult with the Matron.'

The hospital nursing staff was made up almost entirely of Anglo-Indian women who had taken up caring for the sick as a career. Since Independence, there were more real options for women than men from the community, in teaching, nursing and secretarial work. Men having lost their privileged position in the Railways had fewer employment options to pursue.

Matron Thomas of Lucknow General was a formidable woman without whose stewardship the hospital would have been incapable of dealing with the thousands of people that passed through its doors every day. Her instructions were never disobeyed by anyone and she made her Amazonian-like presence felt when she arrived at the Reception in a white uniform, stiffly starched square headscarf and a broad blue belt.

'My dear, how can I help?'

'And are you a relative?'

'Well no, a friend.'

As she spoke she thought they must formalise their relationship as soon as he was able to leave hospital. She could see herself married to Ed, she thought. There was the problem with him wanting to emigrate but she felt she could persuade him that he had a future where he was. Getting married would immediately legitimise their union and she remembered how nice it felt in her dream, walking up the aisle to what she thought was Storey, her husband to be.

'My dear, you know we don't give away any details to non-relatives. Anyway how do you know Mr Storey?'

'Well we developed a little more than a friendship Matron. In fact he was living with me after the Apna factory sacked him.'

'Ah yes, I've heard about you, the teacher from Calcutta. Storey and I went to the same church in Alambagh for a while and you're related to Gerry and Irene.'

'Yes, Irene is my sister-in-law.'

'Ah well in that case I'll let you know unofficially my dear. Do sit down and let me get you a cup of tea.' A hospital orderly handed Joan a cup of tea as she sat down on one of the cane-covered *morahs*.

The Matron sat next to her and gently touched her arm. 'I've got bad news about Mr Storey. He has been in our special burns unit, suffering from blood loss and multiple first and second degree burns.'

'First and second degree burns?' asked Joan.

'He's in a very bad way my dear, I'm really sorry. We're doing everything we can to pull him through.'

Joan gasped putting her hands to her mouth.

The rest of what Matron said was a blur. The sight of a person in flames running for his life drove through her like a red-hot poker. The slow motion film reel played over in her mind as Matron appeared to keep talking about next of kin and the state of his injuries. She retched and the orderly gave her a paper napkin.

Were men she loved really fated to die premature and horrific deaths? Was she really a witch? These questions plagued her mind. She sobbed uncontrollably and the Matron kept supplying her with paper napkins.

'Could we offer you another cup of tea my dear? You need to sit down in the Outpatients area until you're stronger. I know how hard this must be for you,' said the Matron. 'Inspector Mallothra has been and wants to conduct a full investigation with all witnesses but I believe none have come forward and no arrests have been made. I'll inform Father at the Catholic Church in Alambagh, but we don't have any record of any relatives dear. Do you know who we should call?'

Joan shook her head. There was very little she knew about his past, other than when he was in the Indian Army serving in Egypt or his work at the Apna factory. They had talked little about his family, where he was born, his parents and all the little things that someone you love shares with you. But then, Joan thought, they had just met and people who have just fallen in love only want to talk about the present rather than the past.

'I believe I was his nearest before the attack, in fact he risked his life trying to protect me. I'll be here when he recovers,' she said to the Matron.

'That may not be for a while. We need to get someone to get you back home now. There is no way you can go back on your own. I'm also going to give you something to help with the shock of what you have just been through. Pray my dear, that his recovery is swift and equally that our dear God takes him speedily if that is his will. You won't want him lingering on forever if his body can't take it.'

Joan got back to her bungalow and saw that Jai was gone. She knew that Matron, the school's sentry, would know her whereabouts. And indeed she did. Mallothra had come for her accompanied by an American man in a new white Ambassador car. He had been sent by the embassy in Delhi to take her to a place of safety and Jai had asked Matron to tell Joan that she was okay and would be in touch as soon as she was settled.

Now she was alone, subdued, her head was heavy and her eyes puffed out as if she had been stung in the eyes by a swarm of wasps. She washed her face in cold water and showered to wash away the horrid events of the last twelve hours. There was a note from Kellor on her dining table saying that he had heard the sad news about Storey and wished to offer his sympathies and that he had arranged for someone to look after her class for the rest of the week. He had left a covered fruit bowl on the table and some *samosas* in a plate, but food was the last thing on her mind.

She went in search of Ed's personal effects, those few items which constituted the entire stock of his material possessions. Joan thought that now in what could be his last hours, she should try to find out more about the man she loved. How was it she knew nothing about his relatives, his parents or where he was born? How could they have been so intimate without her knowing the most rudimentary things in everyday relationships?

233

His suitcase opened with a simple click. He had not bothered to lock it. There was an assortment of documents, certificates and authorisation papers to gain access to places of government significance. There was an album of photographs and a pile of letters held with a large rusty bull-dog clip.

Joan chose to look at the pictures; because she believed they told a bigger story about the person than words could ever describe and as if to prove her point the first page of the black leather-bound album opened up to reveal a square sepia picture of two people on their wedding day. She turned over the protective tissue paper to examine the couple who were both stood outside a church with palm trees. These must be Ed's parents. The bridegroom was a tall moustachioed European man in military uniform, the bride a much shorter South East Asian looking woman.

There were more pictures of his parents in sunny places, mostly by the sea and one with them in a foursome of badminton players. Later Ed was pictured with his fellow sapper friend somewhere in Egypt by the pyramids, with his hockey team with Ed leaning in a confident nonchalant pose on a hockey stick. There was one taken quite recently of the senior staff at the Apna Factory with Mathur stood by his side and a selection of more intimate pictures with women, a different one every time; there was one with what was clearly his belly dancing friend, done up in her dancing regalia. There was another with an oriental-looking woman sat in his lap and a third colour portrait picture of someone who had written: 'To my darling Ed, Missing you terribly, Nel'.

She turned her attention to the small pile of letters. Top of the little pile was one from the British Army with a Rangoon address telling him with deep regret that his parents had perished in the Japanese bombing of Singapore. There was a letter of appointment from his company informing him of appointment to managing director. But it was the last of the little pile, a thick envelope that immediately aroused her curiosity. It had money in it, a pile of hundred-rupee notes of which there were at least fifty. That would easily take care of Ed's hospital expenses.

'Mrs D'Silva, I'm sorry to say that I had no advance information of the attack on your residence last night, my lookout fell asleep at the time. Please accept my sympathy for the condition of your friend Mr Storey. Such a terrible fate to befall a man of such bravery taking on that mob. Please be assured I will find the perpetrators with the best efforts of my men,' said Inspector Mallothra when he visited Joan the evening she returned from the hospital.

'I heard you came for Jai this morning. Is she safe Inspector?'

'Yes, now under the control of the American Embassy security apparatus and out of my jurisdiction. It appears another friend of hers who also ran away from the Swami's den of depravity has sought sanctuary in the Embassy and recommended that this girl Jai be given protection. Now the Ambassador is asking top people a lot of questions about the activities of the Swami.'

'Inspector, you probably don't stand a cat in hell's chance of arresting anyone do you?'

'We're making enquiries, please be assured.'

'You must have had a busy day interviewing all the wounded. Surely there was someone who saw something?'

'They are all very silent. No one will talk about how they were there or what actually happened. Even the Swami's fundraiser, the Gonda *Gunda,* despite his injuries, will not press any charges against anyone. There is so much fear about what might happen to them. This was the most horrific thing I have experienced.'

'Was it the *hijiras* who castrated him?'

'Yes, almost certainly. Just between you and me, I think some justice has been done in a way that neither our own forces nor the Americans could achieve. Although I could not approve, you understand. "Rough justice", Mickey Spillane might say.'

'You mean you do approve but could not say so openly?'

'Ah yes, Mrs D'Silva divine retribution I think. I know God was doing his work. It would not be right for me to intervene in God's work.'

'And what of Mr Storey? What about his attackers, do they get away with it?'

'The way he appeared to throw himself into that battle was almost as if he had a death wish. Some of the seriously wounded are still in Lucknow General under guard; perhaps they may talk later. I will keep you informed.'

Mathur called on Joan the next day turning up in a cycle rickshaw by her bungalow.

'*Namaste* Mrs D'Silva,' he said with a gentle smile. 'I was going to the hospital to see Mr Storey and came to ask if you would like to attend with me.'

'Good morning Mr Mathur. That is so kind of you but they are not allowing visitors.'

'Well actually I phoned them this morning and apparently he is now awake and responding very well to the treatment.'

'Oh well in that case I will accompany you. Please come in while I change into something a bit more suitable for a hospital visit.'

Mathur sat on the veranda while Joan went inside to put on a dress. She inserted the wad of notes into her handbag with the intention of paying the hospital to ensure Storey received the best care. Mathur and Joan rode in the cycle rickshaw together into town. To protect themselves from the biting heat of the midday sun they sheltered deep under the tarpaulin hood of the three-wheeled vehicle and Joan's liberal application of lavender water, to cool her neck and face, wafted pleasantly in the direction of her travel companion.

'Mr Mathur, how do you believe in a God at times like this; when a loved one is hurt by such treachery?' she asked as the rickshaw puller gradually inched his way up a steep incline.

'The thing is I don't have a God as such Mrs D'Silva, more a way of dealing with life. In the *Bhagavad Gita*, which is very good to read in times of loss, it says that *"you are what you think; hence thought is action, being and becoming; what one thinks one becomes"*. I don't hold a God responsible for what has happened.'

'That's funny Mr Mathur, it is exactly how I handle loss in my life. I intend to get on with teaching just as it is and damn the Swami and his men,' said Joan with a smile, patting him on the knee as they went past the hospital gates. Mathur flinched a little but quite enjoyed the gesture coming from the lavender-infused young lady sat by him.

The duty nurse advised them not to stay too long and that Storey needed the minimum of disruption. He was sitting up in bed heavily bandaged, covering burns on most of his torso, his left leg, hands and the side of his face. He looked at Joan through his right eye and attempted a smile. She held back a tear and held his unbandaged hand. Mathur signalled a *namaste*.

'Ed, I'm so thrilled to see you sitting up. How are you feeling?'

'Bit drugged up so no complaints. But I'm not going to be looking too good when they take this lot off. How are things at the works Mathur?'

'Oh, getting acclimatised with the new man Mr Storey and it's very good to hear the production line rolling again.'

'Oh good. Well I'll be out of here very soon. I can feel myself getting better by the minute since you walked in Joan.'

Joan fussed around the bed for a while making sure he had a full glass of water and ensured that the bed covering was neatly tucked in the sides. They engaged in small talk about the school but no one mentioned the Swami or the *hijiras* and Joan mindful of the nurse's warning steered clear of those subjects. It was the nurse who signalled to them to end the visit and Joan kissed Ed's hand as they left.

Joan paid four thousand rupees at the hospital administration desk. She hoped Storey would come back to her soon. She'd have to clear it with Kellor if he moved in for a long-term period of convalescence. Despite several requests from her sister-in-law, Joan did not move back in with them. She was more resolved than ever to take Mathur's advice and use the power of thought to get Ed's killers put away and if they came looking for her again then she would be there for them. Gerry reluctantly gave her a few more cartridges for the gun that Ed had left behind; the one that he had used to try and defend her. She was more determined than ever to protect herself.

Convalescence

When Joan went to visit Storey towards the end of the week, some of his bandages had been taken off his left foot and arm and he was limping around his hospital bed with the help of a stick.

'Ed, you're up. Are you sure its okay to walk around in your state?'

'Absolutely, exercise is good for recovery. First lesson they teach you in the army hospital is to get moving as soon as you can.'

'Are you in pain?'

'Oh, nothing that a *sher* like me can't cope with. Look Joan, I'm getting out of here in a couple of days; I can't stand hospitals. I've arranged to go and convalesce in a place where I'll be looked after very well.'

'But Ed, the Principal says it's okay for you to come back to my bungalow for a while.'

'That's very nice of you, but you're away in class all day and I don't want that Matron breathing down my neck all the time and all those people gossiping about me being a kept man and all.'

'Oh Ed, where will you go?'

'I've got a little place in mind where I spent many happy

239

days as a child. The people who run it are very kind and it's just what I need. And you need to get some space from me too to think about our own lives, you know my proposal before I got burned up like this.'

'This is a little sudden for me. Where is it exactly that you plan to go?'

'It's a bit of a trek from here by train. Do you know Juhu, near Bombay?'

'That's a day and a half by train!'

'Yes, but you could come with me and settle me in. I'll be fine to travel in a week's time. I've asked the orderly here to get me two first class tickets.'

'Ed, I've got my classes.'

'You could take a bit of *chutti*. For me! Eh!'

'And Errol, what about him?'

'Well he has his studies.'

'I'd like him to come too. He loves trains. I'll have to clear it with Kellor.'

And so a few days later Joan was taking her first short holiday for many years. She packed two large tin cases as if they were going for months.

'We don't need quilts Joan, it's actually quite warm there and everything comes with the guest house you know; linen, towels etc.'

'Not sure you can trust other people's towels Ed, I know of someone who caught an awful *dhobi* rash by using towels in a guest house, but I'll agree to leaving the sheets behind.'

Kellor was uncomfortable about agreeing to Joan being away for a week's leave in the middle of term but the attack had earned Storey a considerable amount of sympathy in the Anglo-Indian community for his bravery at taking on Joan's attackers. Errol seemed delighted at a long train journey ahead of him and he collected a bundle of comics from one of his friends at school.

Juhu was an old-fashioned seaside resort with a large expanse of sand, breathtaking sunsets over the Arabian sea and a sprinkling of guest houses and hotels with an airport nearby. Storey had telegrammed ahead to the Holiday Inn, a small establishment run by a family of Armenians who had settled in India for several generations. He booked two rooms, one for Joan and Errol to share and one for himself.

They alighted at Santa Cruz station and caught a taxi to the guest house. On the way Storey kept pointing out landmarks that he remembered as a young boy on holiday in the area.

Errol was bleary-eyed after having stayed up all night with the excitement of the journey by train but the arrival at the seaside had him jumping with the delight of a two-year-old.

'Ma, it's so big and scary,' he said as they stood on the sand dunes which went on for miles as far as the eye could see. The waves off the Arabian Sea, several feet high, came crashing down to the shore creating a cascade of white froth and spume, which Errol thought looked like cream. Fisherman were casting off their sleek home-built fishing boats into the waves in an exhibition of man's collective power against the almighty force of the sea. They heaved and pushed their boats against the relentless force of the waves into the roaring water. And in the middle of all this people were galloping horses across the flat sand. Every now and then a plane came over on its approach to the nearby aerodrome which added to Errol's excitement as he had never seen aircraft fly so low.

Joan explained to Errol how far the horizon was and how the earth's curvature made it look like the end of the water and how people once believed the earth was flat. That evening they feasted on the best prawn curry Joan said that she had ever tasted, made by the owner's wife. They sat on the porch of the guest house sipping cold beer and later Joan's favourite, rum and cola.

Errol was despatched to bed to catch up on a night's lost sleep while Ed and Joan went to sit on the sand dunes and watched the phosphorescence of the waves in the moonlight. Since Ed's recovery the two had grown closer and Joan gave him all her attention. Joan held his good hand under the yellow glow of the moon and said, 'Ed, this is wonderful, just what we needed after what you've been through. Now I need to stop feeling guilty about leaving my pupils and running away with you.'

'People do things because they like to and you must have secretly wanted to run away with me. I'm immensely grateful.'

They talked about how Storey spent his early days at this guest house as a child and how there used to be so many Anglo-Indian families from the Railway Colonies of Jamshedpur and Vizag holidaying at the resort and how he had kissed his first girlfriend when he was seventeen, just by the sand dunes where they sat.

'Her father was furious when he found out as she was only fourteen and I was forbidden to go anywhere near her after that. But she kept stealing away in the night to meet me and we conducted an illicit affair till the end of the holiday.'

'And I'm no substitute for a fourteen-year-old girl, am I?'

'Oh no madam, my intentions are strictly honourable.'

Over the next couple of days Errol swam his first few lengths with the help of one of the fishermen who taught him how to duck under the waves as they leapt over him. He went to sea most days in a boat and caught small silvery fish in nets, which they eat fried in mustard oil. At night Joan and Ed would go out walking on the sand dunes by moonlight and tell each other stories about their past. Gradually the full picture of Joan's life fell into place for Ed but Joan continued to feel she knew very little about him.

On their penultimate day they visited the Catholic Church in Santa Cruz and the school of St Aloysius, run by Jesuits. They met the principal, Brother Abraham, who proudly showed them around the school and was delighted to be talking to a teacher who loved her profession.

'Have you ever considered coming to work here in Santa Cruz?' he asked Joan. 'The life is wonderful and I can offer you a position with a nice bungalow for all three of you thrown in. We need people like you.'

'Thank you brother, it's very nice of you to offer but we're not married and I'm quite happy where we are at The Martinere,' said Joan very quickly as if to dispel the idea instantly.

'Ah well, if ever you do get married and want a nice rewarding job, get in touch.'

Later that evening when they were walking in the moonlight for the last time before their journey back home, Joan asked Storey, 'And now where to for you Ed? Are you coming back with us or going somewhere else?'

'I don't know Joan, I'm a bit lost really.'

'Surely you have all the choices in the world. They'd even have you here in Santa Cruz if you asked the Principal.'

'Joan the truth is I want to be near you. I just can't get you out of my system. This holiday has made me want to be even closer to you. I've never met anyone like you; beautiful, sensitive, strong; I could go on.'

'Please do go on.'

'I'm probably going to completely blot my copybook with you now. I'm sure I'm in love with you but I know I need to do much more to convince you that it is worth you spending the rest of your life with a fellow like me.'

'Oh Ed, you show such generosity. You have given me such a lovely time and looked after me so well, it's all a simple girl like me really wants at the end of the day. I'd love to be saying "yes" right now. You nearly gave up your life for me and now here's me dithering. It's hard for me to explain.'

'Don't explain, I accept the way you feel. You did ask me where I was headed next and I tried to express my confusion.'

'And I'm confused too Ed, darling Ed. I'm so confused.' It was the first time she had called him 'darling' and he noticed, and responded by putting his arm around her. They sat and gazed at the waves in silence.

When Joan returned to her room, she showered to wash away the sand from her feet, put on her nightdress and lay on her bed replaying the events of the evening, Ed's proposition and his reaction to Joan's disclosure.

'Ma, are you happy?' said a soft voice from the other bed.

'*Beta*, are you awake, so late? You'll be tired in the morning and we've got a long journey ahead of us. Yes of course darling I'm happy. Haven't you had a lovely time?'

'Yes Ma, I liked being in the sea and being near the aerodrome seeing those planes.'

'Oh good, now get some sleep.'

'Ma, will you marry Uncle Ed?'

The directness of the question made Joan pause for a second. She was not used to answering questions about her personal life with her son who she had so far assumed was not of an age to understand the complexities of the attraction between a man and a woman. But Errol had grown up so much in the short time he had been a boarder, cutting the umbilical cord of childhood dependence on his mother. She'd never have dared ask her mother a similar question at the age of eleven.

'I haven't decided darling. Do you like him?'

'He's okay Ma but he did cheat at hockey and I don't think he likes me a lot.'

'Oh, now that can't be true. He's very concerned about your schooling and your future and wants you to do really well.'

'Ma, will Uncle be coming back to live with you?'

'I don't know *beta* he hasn't decided yet, he needs to be here to get much better.'

'Do people have to be married before they live together?'

'Yes of course but there may be exceptions where someone is looking after the other who may be injured or ill. Now you should really be going to sleep.'

Errol was quiet for a minute or two then he piped up again.

'Ma, if you marry Uncle will we still be in Lucknow?'

'Darling you're too young to understand. I'm not marrying anyone at the moment. Now go back to sleep.'

Joan could see that Errol did not share her feelings for Ed who may have been in the process of sweeping her off her feet but had never expressed the desire to get to know Errol. Joan made a mental note of the extra care that she had to take to bring them closer together.

That night she dreamt the same dream she had several weeks earlier of walking down the aisle to get married, but now the face was Ed's from the beginning. And instead of turning into the hideous *betel*-chewing *Gunda*, the face remained his until they were about to recite their vows but then somehow Errol was in between them and they could no longer see each other.

The next day the three had breakfast together. Errol looked glum at the prospect of going back to school and Joan tried to encourage conversation at the breakfast table without much success.

'I hope we see you again soon,' said Kristina, the co-owner of the guest house.

'That depends on my work,' Joan said. 'But I certainly had a lovely time.'

'You know I really thought you two were married. You make such a perfect family and I do love young Errol's enthusiasm for everything.'

Her husband overheard the comment and came over.

'Kris, you're embarrassing these people. Probably the last thing you want to hear eh Ed?'

'Well no, I actually proposed to Joan last night.'

'You see George, I was right. There is love in the air,' squealed Kristina and began to sing a popular song.

> *'Take one soft and tender kiss,*
> *Mix it with a night of bliss,*
> *Garnish it with love…'*

'That is so romantic,' she shouted. 'George, do you even remember the first time you proposed to me?'

'Yes and you kept turning me down.'

'It was the flowers that finally did it, the white lilies, a big bunch of them. I just love lilies, Joan.' Kristina's passion for the flowers was evident from the way the guest house was decorated with pictures of lilies in paintings and drawings on every wall. There was even a vase of purple plastic flowers on the dining room table.

Ed called for two rickshaws to take them to the station.

'I've decided to stay here for a while longer Joan, until I'm strong,' said Ed.

'Oh!' she said, not fully prepared to be leaving him behind.

'I'll drop you off at the station and put you on the Lucknow train.'

'Thank you Ed, that's very sweet of you.'

On the journey to the station Errol and Ed chatted away to each other about the sea and boats which were the young boy's new addiction. He said how he would want to go away and be a sailor when he grew up so that he could see the world for free. Ed thought that was a good idea and wished he had done that when he was young. He told him an abridged version of the coming of age story of Treasure Island and Errol wished he could find a map of buried treasure like the young Jim Hawkins.

At the station the train to Lucknow was late coming in and Storey excused himself for a few minutes. By the time he returned the train was pulling into the platform ready for boarding and Ed pulled out a bunch of white lilies from behind his back and handed them to Joan.

'Marry me when I return fully recovered Joan, please,' he said kissing Joan on the platform, much to the embarrassment of Errol and the surprise of the other passengers.

Trouble at school

The Martinere schools celebrated their Founder's Day once a year and it was the only day of the year when young members of the opposite sex were allowed into the boys' school to mark the social occasion. For the teenagers the weeks prior to the event had been marked by a heightening of smutty jokes and sexual innuendo about the opposite sex. Boys earmarked the girls they were going to try to talk to, and girls sniggered and giggled their way through their imagined selection of boys to know and those to avoid.

For some reason they had decided to rag Errol about Anita, a very tall lanky girl with long black plaited hair and glasses, who had visibly grown by inches in the last year. He detested this behaviour with a vengeance and vowed not to be seen anywhere near her to prove to his peers that he was not in the least bit interested in her. For now there was not much he could do but deny that he had never laid eyes on the girl, or cared much for any of them, and each denial brought a fresh slew of insinuations that the two of them were planning some tryst behind the bicycle shed at some time during the day of celebrations.

Notes, purporting to be in Anita's hand, asking Errol to meet her at some point or another, were openly passed between the boys and he began to get quite gloomy about the prospect of Founder's Day wishing that it would soon pass and that he might be able to get back to his normal days of cricket and class and evening study.

Of course the real chances of any secret meeting between the sexes would have been about as possible as taking *Laika,* the Soviet cosmonaut dog, for a walk on the moon. The teachers of both boys' and girls' schools supervised the day with the greatest attention, ensuring that any interaction between the sexes took place right under their noses.

First, there were the sporting activities which involved several races where the girls and boys took it in turns to run, jump or hurdle their way between two points while the vast majority shrieked their support from the sidelines. The frisson of excitement increased the noise and fervour with which the young people engaged in their enthusiastic support of their colleagues.

Horace, Errol's house prefect, was the sort of older boy that teachers loved to have around, but the boys hated. He was everything that Errol didn't want to be when he grew up and yet Horace was the authority that everyone obeyed and you ignored his bidding at your peril. He oiled his hair, something that Errol and his friends thought only one's father did and they called him *taylie,* the oil man, behind his back. He wore a clean singlet at all times and a white handkerchief tucked into the lapel of his blazer which no one ever saw him use.

Horace barked instructions to his house in the dormitory on the Saturday morning when the boys were assembled.

'Okay now you've heard Sir talk about the importance of Founder's Day to our school and we expect the best behaviour from everyone. All make sure you've cleaned your boots, nice and shiny, ironed your shirt collars and especially cleaned your nails. Matron will be doing an inspection just after breakfast and anyone not up to our standards will be sent back to dorm and kept there until they're considered fit to be seen outside. Deepak, that hair will not do the way it is and you Errol come and see me after this, you hear.'

Much as Errol tried to keep out of harm's way, Horace, who managed to exploit the vulnerable as much as he could, found him ripe for extracting all the humiliating value he could. Errol stayed behind as the other boys went off to the refectory for breakfast.

'I need a job doing Titch,' said Horace giving Errol his current school name which was by no means original as Horace called anyone he thought inferior to him by the same name.

Errol didn't say a word, just staying where he was and waiting for instructions.

'Titch, they say that Anita girl has got eyes for you. Why is that Titch?'

'I don't know Prefect. It's a made up story. I've never spoken to her. They're just teasing me Prefect.'

'Well whether it's made up or not Titch, just know that she's mine, so don't get any ideas. Right?'

'Definitely, Prefect,' said Errol relieved that someone else was ready to take responsibility for this girl that he had absolutely no time for.

'But I need a job doing Titch. Now listen. I want you to get her down to the crypt this afternoon to visit the Claude Martin sepulchre.'

'Me, Prefect? But…'

'No buts boy, just a "yes OK" will do.'

With that Horace was off having delivered his instructions to execute a task that Errol had no idea how he might complete.

'Looking worried?' said Ashok. But Errol was not prepared to disclose the challenge of his impossible task lest his tormenters ruin any chance of him getting to even speak to Anita.

Not having ever spoken to a girl, Errol was filled with the sort of dread that someone might experience when about to encounter a demon or spirit with unknown powers. So when he first cast his eyes on Anita in church, she was not quite what he was expecting. Yes, she was tall, much taller than him, but had quite a cheerful face enhanced further by the long plaits she wore with two blue ribbons tied to them at each end.

They sat on opposite pews in the nave of the church holding cyclostyled sheets of paper giving the hymns and the order of the ceremony. The girls all wore blue gabardine pinafore dresses and white blouses, the boys dark blue blazers. The principal Kellor introduced the ceremony welcoming the school congregation and did a short reading. Then he asked everyone to stand and sing the hymn 'Lead kindly light'.

That was when Errol caught her looking at him, and she waved. Errol was stunned that she had picked him out and was actually communicating with him, or was it Ashok next to him?

'Hey *yar*, look she's waving at you. I knew you were a bit of a *bagheera hah*?' whispered his friend.

Errol ignored the wave and looked at his hymn sheet mouthing the words to the hymn but then there again, when he stole another sideways glance at her, she waved again and she appeared to be pointing towards the exit with her eyes and left finger as if to indicate that she wanted to see him outside afterwards.

Horrorstruck, Errol was now swallowing hard. His mouth

was dry and he couldn't finish the hymn with the unwelcome anticipation of having to meet and talk to a girl he had never met before. The ceremony ended and the boys and girls began to file outside onto the wide open space overlooking the *bund* and the *Gomti*. Teachers milled around everywhere shaking hands, wishing the pupils and their peers a happy Founder's Day.

Errol followed the crowd outside slowly, as though he was walking to a certain death, a condemned man. He had lost sight of Anita now as he came out into the blazing sunshine, the brilliant white of his shirt blinding him momentarily. Then someone tapped him on the shoulder and he heard a voice above his head talking down at him, 'Happy Founder's Day, Errol.'

At first he was stunned into silence seeing it was Anita herself.

'Oh, Happy Founder's Day,' he responded finally.

'You look just like your picture,' said Anita.

'You have a picture of me?'

'Yes, it's been passed around all the girls. You're cute. I won you in the lottery last night in our dorm. Look, let's go and have a *nimbu pani* and watch the next race.'

'I was wondering if I might show you the sepulchre, you know where Claude Martin is.'

'*Arey* you're a fast mover for your age. No let's do that later.'

'*Hah*, I'll tell you what...' and she held the palm of her hand up to his ear and whispered in it so no one could hear. Errol didn't catch what she was saying in her muffled whisper. The feel of her warm breath in his ear and the smell of what was probably her hairspray suddenly triggered sensations in the young teenager that he had not experienced before and his fear of Anita gave way to an enjoyment beyond anything he could wish for.

Ashok and the other clique of younger boys had by now noticed a dialogue developing between the two and were beside themselves with nudges and winks and generally raucous playground behaviour, enough to attract the notice of one of the male teachers who went over to warn them about their antics. Errol ignored them. Even Horace the bully seemed to disappear in the background assuming that his campaign for Anita had been thwarted by some inexplicable attraction she had for Errol.

'Seems like the older girls wait all year for this. I can't see why,' Anita said.

'Look there is a bigger boy that I want you to…' Errol was cut off mid sentence.

The PE teacher had begun to blow his whistle signalling the beginning of the sports activities for the day and those who had entered for the various races had begun to take their positions.

There had been a shortage of entrants for the relay race in the 'lower teens' category and Errol was enlisted as one of the runners. Anita held his glass of lemonade. Errol ran as fast as his legs could carry him in lane two, but despite the best of his efforts ended up towards the end of his group as they finished the circuit.

The screams of the girls competed with the boys reaching an excruciating crescendo of noise in the last lap. The winning relay team stood on a raised platform and received their purple ribbons commemorating their victorious sporting achievement. Boys and girls applauded and Baby Brownie cameras clicked to capture the occasion. Sadly, Errol was not in the photos still recovering from the effects of his exhaustion.

'Come on Errol drink your *nimbu pani* and let's go and sit on the grass and talk.'

Errol downed the glass of the bitter lime drink that despite copious amounts of sugar had not managed to soften its harsh acidic texture.

'Is your mum here today?'

'Er no I think she's gone out somewhere else. And your mum and dad?'

'Well my mum doesn't come to these things. I don't have a dad.'

'I'm sorry. I don't have a dad either, he was killed in a train crash.'

'Oh, that's sad. My dad left my mum. I never met him.'

Errol smiled shyly at Anita and she smiled back.

Return to Lucknow

My darling,
Not a minute of the day goes by without me thinking of you.

My wounds have healed well and the local quack gave me the all-clear yesterday saying that I could begin to think about cosmetic surgery to get the disfigured side of my face corrected. The sea air seems to do me good but I can't say the same about being apart from you. Kristina and George have been spoiling me terribly here at the guest house and I must have put on several pounds with their stuffed parathas and Khir since you were here last.

I've also had some wonderful news in the last day. I went to the bank yesterday to draw some money which I inherited from my father's small pension and heard that his mother died last month and left me a comfortable endowment which has been deposited with National Grindlays in Bombay.

To the serious business of my letter. Now I'm solvent again and free from being a wage slave for those ingrates at Carver Brothers I can afford to keep you in a most comfortable lifestyle. We could move into a lovely seaside bungalow here at Juhu and you'd be free from the terrible memories of Lucknow.

Joan, I'm on my knees as I write this letter. Please marry me and I'll be the best husband to you in the whole world. I'm

*catching the Delhi Mail train next week and I should be with
you just after this letter arrives. Please consider this proposal
seriously.*

Ed

Joan read the Airmail letter filled with confusion. She cycled
over to her sister-in-law who read the letter and let out a little
squeal of delight when she got to the proposal paragraph.

'Joanie, this is so exciting. Become a kept woman. Why not?
I must tell Gerry the news; oh, what fun!'

'But Irene, I can't bring myself to be beholden to another
man, not any more. I've enjoyed my independence these last
few years. I know I have to pay dearly for it by not having
enough for a new dress or constantly watching the cowries.
But at least I can do what I like.'

'You've got to think about that boy my love. Errol will soon
need money for college and books and that sort of thing. He
can't get a cushy job on the Railways any more. Anyway he's
bright and he'll go to an Indian Institute of Technology no
doubt.'

'Oh Irene, I'm so confused. I really am.'

Two days later early in the morning Ed got off the Delhi Mail
train and arrived on Joan's doorstep. They hugged and kissed.
He had left his luggage at the Cantonment Guest House where
he had arranged to stay. He looked as if his time by the sea
had agreed with him. There was little sign of any
disfigurement to his face although a large scar ran the length
of his left hand and up to his neck. Ed wore a long sleeved
khaki shirt which covered most of the affected area. Joan
looked at him and remembered why she had been attracted
to him at Sunday Mass, the first time they met.

'Joan, what do you say? I've come all prepared.'

'Ed, I've been thinking a lot about this. Do you think we can talk to Errol first? I'd like you to be the one who asks him. He's my only real flesh and blood now and what he thinks will be important.'

'But Joan he's still only a child, how could he possibly know how much I love you and how important your happiness is for him?'

'Please Ed. This will make me happy.'

'Okay, well let's get him now. You know I believe in striking while the iron's hot.'

They walked holding hands through the school grounds and into the refectory where the smell of breakfast wafted through the entrance and the clatter of spoons on the white enamel plates rose above the sound of boys. The duty master signalled to Errol to come over and meet Joan. Errol didn't see Storey until he was outside.

'Errol *beta*, look it's Uncle Ed. He got back from Juhu this morning and we wanted to talk to you about something really important.'

'Good morning Uncle.'

'Hello Errol, how are you? Could we sit down outside for a few minutes under that peepal tree while I ask you something?'

Errol squinted in the early morning sunlight looking slightly confused as he followed Ed to the peepal tree while Joan looked on, full of a mother's pride that her boy was just about to be asked for her hand in marriage. There was he, no longer her baccha that she had suckled, cradled and sung to sleep every night. Now he was standing up looking very grown up alongside a fully grown man ready to listen and make judgement on whether Storey deserved to marry his mother.

The peepal tree in all its magnificence stood steadily by to witness the consultation and Ed with a look of sincerity about him bent over at eye level with the boy, his hands expressing that something quite large and expansive was about to happen in their lives. He laughed, probably at one of his jokes but Errol appeared motionless throughout this interchange. Joan began to think the suddenness of this proposal might have caught her son unawares. Perhaps they should have waited till the evening when they were at her bungalow.

And then they were walking back towards her. Ed nodding seemed to indicate that he was pleased with the outcome but Errol looked expressionless.

'Well that's all settled then Joan. Errol agrees and he'll be chief usher.'

'Darling that's wonderful. Oh you don't know how happy I am to hear that.'

The new parish priest greeted the news with enthusiasm and told Joan that he would be pleased to marry the couple in the cathedral. This would be the first wedding he would be officiating over since his appointment and he was keen to sweep away any of the ill feeling created by his predecessor as he needed all the new support he could get. There was still a hardcore of parishioners who preferred the old traditional ways of Father Rosario and had not taken too well to the progressive 'happy clappy' new priest. Wedding banns were published on the parish notice board declaring that:

Joan D'Silva and Edward Christopher Storey wish it to be known that they would be joined in holy matrimony at the cathedral church on 1st May.

Irene was very excited by the prospect of a wedding.

'So what do you call me after you're married, an "ex-sister-in-law"? I'm so pleased for you Joan, you can call me anything.

I never thought you'd end up with him but now that you have we're very happy. He'll make such a good father for Errol.'

'Renee, I hope that he and the boy get on well. My *beta* means so much to me.'

'So tell me how did you change your mind? What, did he do go down on his knees and offer you the Kohinoor?'

'Persistence pays off I think Irene. He has been very persistent. But I'm getting to the point where the balance between independence and companionship has shifted to the latter. I love men Irene, I'll tell you that. And Ed is a very manly man!'

'So, on a scale of nought to ten where ten is being in love with the man with a vengeance, where are you?'

'Oh Irene, I can't put numbers on things like that.'

'Go on tell me; six, eight, nine...'

'No Irene, I'm not falling for that game, no,' she said.

'Is he going to move into the bungalow with you after you're married?'

'I'm not sure we'll stay in Lucknow at all, Irene,' said Joan. 'Ed and the Principal don't get on, as you know, and Ed would prefer to move away to Bombay and leave some of the horror we have known behind us. We have another option too, this school in Santa Cruz has offered me a position on much better pay and in some ways I'm minded to take that and get away from Lucknow and the painful memories I have. Irene, I still have nightmares about that night when Ed was burned.'

'Well, hope you can put all that behind you now. Gerry has insisted that we have your reception at the Institute and that he pays for it. He's going to give you away so it's the least he could do. And is Errol looking forward to being chief usher?'

'I don't know what's going on in that boy's head you know. He's gone all quiet on me.'

'He probably wants to keep his mum all to himself, like it used to be. Children always have a problem adapting to their new stepfather. I wouldn't be too worried about that my dear.'

With only three weeks to go till their wedding, Joan and Ed had much to do in the way of preparation for their big day. Their guest list was limited to a few teachers and well-wishers from the school. Ed wrote out a few invitations to people he knew at the club but thought it unlikely that any of them would attend. The Anglo-Indian community in Lucknow, with their numbers dwindling, loved a wedding which was now getting rarer by the year. But there were few people he knew to invite. Gerry decided to invite a few people from his circle of friends to make up the numbers.

'We've had two hundred acceptances to the church and to the reception,' said Ed, when they had a week to go before their wedding day.

'I hardly know any of them,' said Joan. 'It's one big show really for Gerry and Irene. They have no children so we're being treated like their own.'

'How is the *durjee* getting on with your wedding dress?'

'I went for a fitting today and it looked lovely. Irene said I looked very nice in that peach coloured satin.'

Irene had chosen the pattern and material for her outfit. The tailor had taken much care to ensure that Joan was pleased with the cut and finish of the bodice and both women approved with a little hand clapping, which pleased the old man enormously. He longed for another Anglo-Indian bride with a figure as appealing as Joan's where he could put his many years of skill at cutting to the test.

Wedding day

Gerry had asked Mallothra to post a jeep with a few constables on duty outside the cathedral on the day of the wedding to ward off any potential trouble.

'Better to be safe than sorry eh *Inspectorjee*, we don't want another repeat of the horror at The Martinere.'

On the afternoon of the wedding, a Saturday, Ed travelled to the cathedral on his own from the guest house. He had worn a beige gabardine suit with purple silk lining, which Gerry's tailor had made for him, and at his full height of six-foot-three, he looked every part the handsome groom.

Joan was to travel to the cathedral in a *tonga* that had been decorated with white ribbons and marigolds. The single horse had a garland around its neck and a string of tinkling bells hung from the carriage. The decorated *tonga* was Ed's idea as he wished Joan to arrive at the church 'like a princess' and Irene had helped decorate the ribbons and the bells the night before.

'Now Joan do you really wish to dress yourself at your bungalow tomorrow? We don't want you being late for your wedding and leaving that poor Ed biting his nails at the steps of the altar, dear,' said Irene.

'No Renee, I'd prefer to dress myself. That way I can take

all the time I want. Don't worry I won't keep anyone waiting; I'll be bang on time.'

On Saturday morning, Kellor sent her a bouquet of lilies which was a gift from the school. He had granted her permission to let Ed stay at the bungalow as her husband until such time she could make up her mind about their future employment. Joan had told Kellor of her probable intentions of moving to Bombay but had asked if Errol could continue to stay as a boarder. The idea of leaving him broke her heart but she didn't want to drag him away from his friends and make him start another new life again.

Joan washed her hair and dried it on the veranda in the bright sunlight, giving her jet black mane a healthy shine which accentuated the special gleam in her eyes. She took her wedding gown, which hung resplendent from the door of her *almirah,* and slipped it over her body, zipping up the bodice on the back and turning around to look at herself in the mirror for the first time since her fitting. She looked a picture-book bride, straight out of a magazine cover and even her own image sent a shiver down her spine. She thought of her first husband, George, and their very simple wedding in 1950, with a small lump in her throat. She would never forget him, but she was ready to move on. She did a little twirl in the privacy of her own space.

There was spontaneous applause as the organist opened with the first few bars of 'Here Comes the Bride' and Joan strode out down the aisle with Gerry by her side. He glowed with pride as if he was the luckiest man on earth to be marrying off such a beautiful bride. Joan glided down the aisle with the dignity and poise of a swan. No one could take their eyes off Joan as a couple of hundred heads turned in the direction of her travel. Errol stood at the back of the church watching as his mother receded away from him. He clutched the sheet giving the order of the ceremony a little tighter.

Ed had no best man and stood alone waiting, head bowed.

'You look wonderful,' he whispered when she joined him.

The priest spoke of the commitment that two people make in taking their vows and how pleased he was to be marrying two newcomers to the parish. Joan and Ed exchanged looks and smiled as he spoke. And then came the declaration.

'Now Dearly Beloved, I am required to ask anyone present who may know of any reason why these persons may not be joined in lawful matrimony, to declare it now.'

There was a brief pause as the priest cast his eyes about the congregation in the customary way.

'*Jee haan*, I am objecting,' a man called out from the back row and although Joan could not see the person, she thought she recognised the voice. The congregation were all now turning around straining to see who the person was. Errol was at the back of the church and could see a man in a long *kurta*, dressed unlike all the other guests, walk down the aisle towards the altar.

"This man is already being married."

Joan blinked. She couldn't believe that her marriage to Ed was being disrupted in this way. But somehow, rather than feel anger or fear suddenly she felt a deep inward relief as if a burden of responsibility had been taken away from her.

The face of the stranger was now visible. It was Shivaji, The Gonda *Gunda*. But he looked like a broken man, back bent, as he limped into full view of the congregation. He turned around and faced the wedding guests.

'*Namaste*, ladies and gentleman, my name is Shivaji and I

was your independent candidate for MLA. Until my life was destroyed by the friends of this lady here.' He leered at Joan. 'She is about to marry a man who has already abandoned his wife with child and has refused to acknowledge her for the last twelve years. I respectfully appeal to the priest not to complete this marriage.'

'You bastard!' shouted Ed and rushed towards him. 'I'll kill you!'

In immediate response the *Gunda* drew a revolver from inside his *kurta*. The long barrel Smith and Wesson looked ancient but menacing.

'*Bus,* I think you should stop there,' he said with a toothless smile and Ed froze. There was a gasp that ran through the congregation. '*Accha,* now listen everybody. This is also the man who blackmailed his own factory and caused the death of innocent people.'

Picking up the pieces

'Ed, is this true?' Joan asked. Storey's ashen face said it all. She knew the Gonda *Gunda* was telling the truth.

Shivaji aimed the gun squarely at Ed.

'You and I are finished in Lucknow, Mr Storey. It is time for us both to leave,' he said, his hollow mouth widening into a treacherous smile and his finger moved to the trigger.

'Shivaji, don't kill a man in cold blood. Do you want God to punish you in your next life?' said Joan, holding out her right hand, as she moved towards the *Gunda*.

'I will be rewarded by punishing a bad man and you too for your seductions,' he said moving the barrel of the revolver towards her. But Joan continued her approach, her face expressionless.

'*Bus*! Stop there.'

Gerry had throughout this time been focused on the revolver. He had an identical one in his collection of guns, used by the Indian Army in the latter part of the eighteenth century, notoriously unreliable with a heavy recoil. It was worth the risk. The *Gunda* now had his back to the front row and completely missed Gerry's lunge from behind which brought the two of them down. There was a bang, the revolver fired but the recoiling weapon gave too much of a jolt for

Shivaji to hold on to it. Gerry held him down while a few of the other men and young Errol who ran up the aisle managed to overpower the frail man.

Joan stood outside the church as Storey and the Gonda *Gunda* were marched away in handcuffs. Errol stood beside her with his arm around her shoulders.

The next day Mallothra came to visit Joan.

'We had our eyes on him already. When we were investigating the fight at your bungalow we found a child's typewriter and this book buried beneath the verandah.'

Mallothra showed Joan a small book called *The Guide to the Identification of Himalayan Fungi*. She picked it up and it fell open to the page on *Aminita Phalloides* circled in black ink with the words *Amatotoxin poison* heavily underlined.

'We found his fingerprints all over the typewriter,' said Mallothra. 'It is unlikely that he intended to kill people with this poison. Braithwaite's death was probably a result of a heart attack brought on by the presence of Amatoxin. We are going to charge him with manslaughter and blackmail. And of course the embezzlement of 20 Lakhs from Carver Brothers.'

'Inspector, how did he get his hands on the money?' said Joan.

'We found one of the old bearers at the club who believed that there may have been a tunnel connecting the labyrinth with the Cantonment Club. We discovered a door in one of the outbuildings that had been locked for many years with a new padlock fitted to it. This led to the *Imambara* labyrinth from which he retrieved the cash.'

'That explains why he had five thousand rupees in cash in his wallet and why he was suddenly able to take us on holiday. Has he confessed to all of this? Do you know where the rest of the money is now?'

'Some of it is in National Grindlays Bank but the rest we don't know. However justice will be done in the end India style, I'm sure. The sooner he tells us where it is the better for his health. You know how ruthless these *Gundas* in jail can be if they find out that he is hiding twenty Lakhs somewhere.'

'Now, Mickey Spillane would have had an intuition at some stage who the real blackmailer was. Did you?'

'*Hah*, *hah*, but that was much later on. Unfortunately my own prejudice against the *hijiras* put me on a false trail. When I thought that he would die in hospital, I was looking for next of kin, traced Storey's army record and found that he was discharged suspected of black-marketeering in army rations. Now Mrs D'Silva, he has made one request which I would ask you to consider as it may help us build our prosecution case.'

'And that is?'

'He wants to see you.'

'Completely out of the question Inspector. I want nothing from that man. I just wish he would go away, out of my life completely.'

'Please be considering it more closely madam.'

There was a pleading in Mallothra's eyes. His whiskers were less upright today, perhaps he hadn't time to wax them in the usual way and the effect made him look much less severe.

'I'm not going to your horrible jail to see him.'

'No, we will bring him to my office near the *thana*.'

'Did he ask for this or is it your suggestion?'

'No, the request is one hundred and ten percent his own.'

Joan went for the appointed meeting the next evening at Mallothra's office. It smelled of stale Capstan cigarettes with dusty files piled high on his desk leaving very little room for the blotting pad which was covered in blotches of a deep blue hue of Indian ink. The air was hot and humid and the only relief was a table fan that squeaked noisily as it moved from side to side blowing a puff of air each time it passed in Joan's direction.

Mallothra appeared at the glass door with a constable attached to Storey handcuffed and chained at the feet, a privilege reserved for high risk prisoners. He was wearing a blue shirt that looked like it hadn't been changed for days, his face was dark with stubble and his eyes sunken deep into two dark cavities. The noise of the heavy chains accompanied their entry and neither Joan nor Storey made eye contact. They sat him down on a wooden bench in the corner of the room several feet away from Joan. Mallothra announced that he would be outside the room if she needed him and walked out leaving the constable to ensure the conversation was carried out safely.

No one said a word for the first few seconds.

'I'm sorry Joan,' were the first words from Storey. There was no response from her. She had set out to make him feel as uncomfortable as possible. 'I know I have caused you a lot of pain and humiliation and I wanted to apologise to you personally.'

'Hardly necessary. The damage is done, now let's get on with our lives.'

'This isn't easy for me Joan.'

'I didn't ask for the meeting.'

'I wanted to clarify my feelings for you. I really did fall very much in love with you. I'd never met anyone so special. I just had a series of failed relationships and then you came into my life.'

'You mean, you barged into mine with all that showy stuff with your servants, company car, shooting rifles and stories of belly dancers.'

'That's me Joan. Call me insecure or whatever, but I worked bloody hard to crawl out of the drudgery of a railway colony and the possibility of being an unemployed Anglo-Indian man for life. I had to lie a little to get ahead in life. I was just a cook in the army but I told Carver I was an engineer and they sent me for special training in London. But I was frightened I'd be found out sooner or later as I climbed up the ranks and then that Gonda *Gunda* fellow found out the truth about me and my previous life. He wanted money, lots of it to fund his nasty political campaign and I was stupid enough to fall prey to his blackmail. The stupid idea came into my head that I could fabricate a ransom, pay off the bastard and have some left over for a comfortable retirement.'

'And you didn't once stop to think about poisoning and killing people?'

'No Joan, I'd never intended to do that and anyway the poison was not known to be lethal to man. I didn't think that stupid old Mathur's wife would use test samples for cooking her goat curry. No, I just wanted the lab to find the poison so they'd pay the blackmailers, but my plan backfired. Twenty Lakhs, just think of it, would set me up for life in a nice house in London. And I thought nothing could be nicer than taking you there with me.'

'And now you're going to jail, where you'll have plenty of time to repent. There is a way that you could get out quicker Ed.'

'Yes, escape.'

'You could tell them where the money is. And if you're really sorry and you want my forgiveness then that would be a precondition.'

'No way, Joan. That money goes with me to my grave. I've already given Mathur two Lakhs to help him out and I had to put up bail for that *hijira* who was beaten up at the factory.'

'Mallothra tells me that you might get there quicker than you think when the *Gunda's* friends in prison find out you're hiding a big tin of Apna with a Rajah's ransom in it.'

Epilogue

Ed Storey's revelations about the Gonda *Gunda* being the hidden hand behind the extortion had helped to lighten the heavy load of disappointment of falling for a man who had misled her. However his refusal to disclose the whereabouts of the rest of the money prolonged Joan's mistrust of her own judgement. In none of their moments of intimacy would she have guessed that Ed was contemplating a blackmail on such a large scale.

Returning from the *thuna*, Joan decided she wanted to take Errol out of school for the rest of the day. Her son was the only one in this world she knew she could trust unconditionally. She went to ask permission from the principal.

'*Pukka shaitan* that fellow, I always knew he was a slippery bounder. Pity you had to fall prey to his tricks Joan,' said Kellor.

'Did you know anything about this affair, Dougie?'

'I'd heard that he'd fathered a child who was in our girls' school but didn't know for sure. Then I found out who she was. Her name is Anita and she's been here since she was four. We've got a fund at the school for poor children of Anglo-

Indian families. I understand that her mother is one of the Swami's harem.'

'That must be how the Gonda *Gunda* knew about it,' Joan mused.

'I should've warned you,' said Kellor. 'But I don't think any advice I'd have given after the *tamasha* at the dance would've been credible.'

'Maybe not,' Joan admitted.

'You go and get your son, you've both earned the afternoon off I think,' Kellor told her.

'Darling I'm going to show you how to make *parathas*, they are your favourite aren't they?'

She poured warm water into a bowl of *atta* flour and asked Errol to wash his hands and continue the process of kneading the dough, something he very much enjoyed, squeezing the moist flour through the gaps between his fingers and watching tentacles of yellow dough curl out of his hands, finally ending up with a cohesive ball. Joan covered the dough for ten minutes with a kitchen towel before they were ready to continue.

'Now the fun bit, we're going to roll these into *parathas*,' said Joan as she created small balls of dough. Soon Errol was working the rolling pin to flatten one of the balls into a plate-sized disc.

'Darling, you're going to have to do better than that, it's all lopsided.'

'But it will taste the same Ma.'

'If a thing is worth doing then you must do it well, *beta*.'

Soon Errol was effortlessly producing perfectly round, thin plate-sized sheets of dough and Joan gave him a '*Shabash* darling' clap every time he completed one. Next she showed him how to layer each sheet of dough with ghee and roll them out again ready to be cooked on a hot *tawa*.

'You're going to make someone a very nice husband one day my love!'

Joan burst out laughing at the sight of her son with a piece of dough stuck at the end of his nose and reached out to him with a cloth to wipe it away.

'Mum do you think you'll ever try to get married again?'

'You know what they say *beta*, never say never.'

'Ma, I'm really glad you didn't marry Ed Storey.'

'Do you know Errol, I'm really glad too.'

She gave her son a long hug as the first *paratha* began to burn on the sizzling hot *tawa* emitting a wonderful aroma of pure *ghee*.

Glen Peters'
Fowl Curry

Fowl Curry is served after a shoot and this is the recipe that I've perfected. You would probably want to use a bird like guinea fowl that has been cleaned and feathered by your butcher. Even better if he has chopped it up into chunks; that will make it easier for you in the kitchen.

Chop up together a thumb of ginger, three cloves of fresh garlic and two large onions. These days you have those wonderful blenders which make life easy. Next, fry three large dessert spoonfuls of curry powder and mix in a generous dollop of butter (or ghee if it is available). When the curry powder spices have turned dark brown, add the ginger and garlic mixture to it and watch it sizzle, stirring all the time.

Next, pop in the chunks of fowl and stir until the meat turns brown. Keep the heat at medium. Throw in three large fresh chopped tomatoes and add salt to suit your taste. Cover the meat with water and simmer for ninety minutes.

Then decant off any liquid and reduce it to a thick sauce by stirring in a separate pan. Add the reduction to the meat along with a tablespoon of vinegar and a dollop of mango chutney.

Serve it in a bowl topped with fresh chopped coriander and basmati rice as an accompaniment.

Enjoy!!!

Image from Francis Ceramics

Glossary

Accha	Good or okay
Angrezee	English
Are	Exclamation
Aré yar	Term of friendship
Babu	A Bengali gentleman or a clerk
Badmash	Naughty person. Used often as a term of affection
Badmash	Crook
Baksheesh	A tip or bribe
Behanchod	Swear word roughly translated as 'sisterfucker'
Beta	Term of endearment for a son
Bhageera	Wild cat
Bhanghi	Lowest caste, usually reserved for sweepers and cleaners
Chat	Street food in India
Choli	Blouse worn with the sari
Chowk	Market
Chowkeedar	Watchman or guard
Chukkah	Slang for gay person
Chullo	Come on / Let's go
Chutti	Leave, time off
Coolie	Porter, usually at stations

Crore	Ten million
Dacoits	Criminals in the countryside that rob and often murder
Dharshan	Blessing from a saintly person
Dhobi	Washerman
Fakir	Sage or holy man
Garbar	Trouble
Goonks	Fools
Gunda	Generic term for crooks or criminals
Hah	A response that usually means 'yes'
Hijira	A transsexual or transvestite
Hookah	A variant of the smoking hubble-bubble
Jalabees	Sugar and flour swirls, fried and soaked in syrup
Jaldi	Quickly
Jao	Go
Jheal	Lake usually in a forest setting
Jujups	Soft-centred boiled sweets
Khana	Food or meal
Khanna	Food
Khansama	Male servant that cooks and cleans
Khansamin	Female servant that cooks and cleans
Khatam	Finished
Khutta	Sharpness or acidity in fruit that adds flavour and interest
Kundalini	Libidinal force lying at the base of the spine
Kurta	Long loose shirt or blouse
Kutta	Dog
Lakhs	One hundred thousand
Lathi	A sturdy stick for defence or attack. Usually a police weapon
Maidan	Playing field

Memsahib	Lady, usually European or Anglo-Indian
Morah	Cane chair
Nai	No
Pahailwans	Wrestlers or strong men
Parathas	Unleavened bread made with clarified butter
Pillau	Spiced rice in the Persian or Mughal style
Pugree	Turban
Puja	Worship
Punka	Fan
Purdah	Literally means curtain behind which women were hidden from men
Puris	Deep-fried unleavened bread
Putaka	Firecracker
Samosas	Pastry stuffed with savoury filling and fried
Shaitan	Satan
Shamina	Marquee
Tamasha	Happening
Thana	Prison or police station
Tonga	Pony trap or two-wheeled horse-drawn carriage
Wallah	Used as a word ending to an occupation e.g. Rickshaw wallah

PARTHIAN

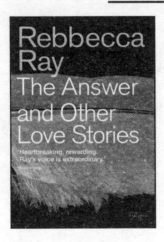

www.parthianbooks.com